AN AMERICAN MAIL-ORDER BRIDE CHRISTMAS COLLECTION

E.E. BURKE

An American Mail-Order Bride Christmas Collection (Victoria, Bride of Kansas, Santa's Mail-Order Bride) is a work of fiction. Names, characters, places and incidents, other than those clearly in the public domain, are the product of the author's imagination or are used fictitiously.

Cover Design by Erin Dameron-Hill
Train photography by Matthew Malkiewicz

Published by E.E. Burke
ebook ISBN: 978-0-9980712-0-6
Paperback ISBN 978-0-9980712-2-0
www.eeburke.com

VICTORIA: BRIDE OF KANSAS

E.E. BURKE

CHAPTER 1

December 1, 1890, Fort Scott, Kansas

anted, woman of good standing, possessing homemaking skills, willing to care for and educate a motherless child.

David O'Brien laid the pencil on the desk. That might work if he was advertising for a housekeeper or governess, but what young lady seeking a husband would respond? Ordering a bride ought to be simple. Like requisitioning inventory. Why then, was it so difficult to come up with a forty-word personal advertisement?

He scrubbed his fingers through his hair. Saints above, he didn't have to do this. He wasn't a farmer who lived in some remote area; he had choices. He could woo one of the ladies in town. His selection would be limited to those willing to marry a divorced man with a six-year-old, which reduced the list of candidates considerably. Besides, he didn't have time to go courting. He had a store to run.

David dug for his timepiece, popped the catch with his thumbnail. Almost eight. The walk needed to be swept and the store prepared for opening. Ordering a bride would have to wait.

As he stood, he took a moment to rub at a dull pain radiating down his right leg. The old injury ached like the very devil when the weather turned cold. Moving around the desk, he squeezed past filing drawers crammed into the small office. The storage area presented another obstacle. Crates, barrels and sacks of dry goods and groceries filled the limited space. If he scrimped, he might have enough to rent the building next door.

His folks had talked of expanding. Irish immigrants with big dreams they hadn't lived long enough to fulfill. *O'Brien's* stood as a tribute to them, his legacy.

Inside the quiet store, mellow scents of tobacco, leather and coffee mingled with the sharper odors of cheese and dried meat. Even fresh fabric had a unique fragrance. He loved the smell of a general store. Far back as he could remember, he'd been surrounded by these familiar scents and found them comforting. He stopped to put another log into the pot-bellied stove, and upon opening the grate released smoke into the air—one smell he did not find comforting.

He grabbed a broom by the door and went outside. Keeping the sidewalk swept meant less dirt tracked into the store. If those clouds were any indication, he'd soon be shoveling snow.

Why, he ought to put snow shovels in the front window. That upstart New Yorker who'd opened the Five Cent Store across the street might not carry them, seeing as shovels cost more than a nickel.

"David?" Maggie peered out the front window and

4

waved for him to come inside. His sister usually got Fannie her breakfast before they ventured downstairs. Had his daughter wandered off again?

With a sigh, he returned inside. He'd never be able to keep up with a curious six-year-old and run the store without his sister's help. If he put off expanding, he might be able to hire someone. But Fannie needed more than a caretaker. She needed a mother.

Fannie stood by the counter wrapped in her heaviest coat. Being bundled up to her eyeballs should make it more difficult for her to slip away. Her aunt had secured a woolen scarf around her head and face, not even a strand of hair remained visible, only a pair of inquisitive eyes.

Maggie laid her hands on Fannie's padded shoulders. "Sweetie, why don't you go out back and check on the kittens. Have you named them yet? What about that orange tabby?"

David waited, sent up a silent prayer. *Dear God, please.* How long could his daughter remain silent? The doctors' advice had proved useless. Bribes hadn't worked. He didn't have the heart to follow through with threats. His poor child had suffered enough. Having a new mother might help. He'd run out of other ideas.

"No names yet? All right, well, go on with you, then," Maggie said with a cheerful smile.

He released dismay in a heavy breath. He no longer shared Maggie's optimism, and he had long since stopped being cheerful.

Dutifully, Fannie turned and disappeared into the back room, sent on the errand, no doubt, so Maggie could speak with him privately. Otherwise, his sister would've gone along. She loved playing with the kittens as much as Fannie did.

Maggie waited a moment and then checked the back room. Perhaps to make sure Fannie was out of earshot. There was nothing wrong with the child's hearing. Satisfied, his sister moved quickly in his direction.

She wore the light blue suit with velvet trim he'd purchased as a gift after she'd graduated from that teaching school in Emporia. Her dark hair was styled on top of her head in a loose arrangement she called "careless." Maggie was never careless with anything, save her hair.

"You look very nice this morning. What's the special occasion?"

"That's what I wanted to talk to you about." She fingered a small gold watch she wore pinned to her bodice, a sure indication she was nervous about something. Her hand went into a deep pocket sewn into the side of her skirt. She often kept hard candies hidden away for herself or Fannie, candy she swiped from the jar on the counter while he pretended not to look. "I have a confession to make."

"Candy thievery? I already know about that. We'll negotiate jail time."

"No, it's something worse, or better, depending on how you look at it."

David tightened his hold on the broom. A part of him wished to sweep her away before she could tell him what he already knew; she had accepted a teaching job near Kansas City, three hours away by train. "You're leaving after Christmas. You already told me."

"Don't look so worried." She went up on her toes and dropped a kiss on his cheek. "I won't leave you without help."

He released a pent-up breath. Thank God, she'd changed her mind. The thought of marrying again put him in a sweat. "I knew you'd reconsider."

Maggie responded with a look of sad reproach. It went without saying that he was being selfish. He couldn't expect his sister to put her life on hold indefinitely. She deserved to pursue her dreams, which was why he had to go through with his plan.

A year ago, he'd told her he intended to send off for a mail-order bride. She'd declared it *romantic*. Ordering a bride was the least romantic thing he could imagine. Besides, he wasn't looking to find love and didn't want love to find him. He'd had enough of that unreliable emotion, thank you. He would take a more reasonable approach to marriage this time.

"I'm about finished with the advertisement." He reached into his coat pocket and pulled out the notice, which had been tinkered with and folded so many times it was smudged and dog-eared.

Maggie averted her gaze. The natural pinkness in her cheeks darkened, or was he seeing things? The day was early and the interior of the store remained dim. He would turn up the lights if gas weren't so expensive.

Overcoming his reluctance, he held out the paper. "Do you have any suggestions for wording?" He took pride in his sister's education, and she had a gift for writing. He barely got by. "I promise I'll post it tomorrow."

"You don't have to post the ad."

His spirits lifted, despite his best intentions to be selfless. "You'll stay?"

"No." Her tone had a sharp edge. He met a pair of eyes so dark it was difficult to tell where the irises ended and the pupils began, eyes the same color as those he saw in the mirror each morning. His father had told him their "black eyes" were handed down from some long-ago Celtic warrior. He and Maggie had also inherited that ancestor's fighting spirit. Generally, they didn't face off against each other, so her irritation with him made no sense.

"What is it you're saying?"

She pulled something out of her pocket that looked like several envelopes tied with twine. "These are letters from Miss Victoria Lowell. Letters she wrote to you."

He set the broom against a table. Surely, he hadn't heard what he thought she'd said. "Letters to me? Who's Vic—?"

"I suspect Miss Lowell will have your letters when she arrives."

He'd heard that clearly enough. "I haven't written any letters, and I don't know any Victoria whatever her name is."

David frowned at the letters in Maggie's hand. He jerked his attention to his sister's face—guilty as hell. Alarmed, he reached out for the packet of letters in her hand. "Give me those."

She took a step backwards. "I will. But let me explain first. I posted an advertisement with the *Grooms' Gazette*—"

Panic tightened the vise pinching his chest. "What the devil?"

"I had to do something, David. You weren't going to. All you do is talk about it. You know I can't leave without making sure you and Fannie will be all right."

By God, she'd ordered him a bride, like she would order a pair of shoes for his birthday.

"I even took care of the correspondence, because I know how much you hate writing, and I've arranged everything." She babbled on, undaunted by his growing fury. "Miss Lowell will be perfect. You'll see."

"*Arranged* everything? You mean, you've already sent for her?" David's temperature soared a hundred degrees. He took a threatening step, contemplated turning Maggie over his knee. Never had he laid a hand on his baby sister, not even when she put salt in the sugar barrel and he got the whipping. He had protected Maggie and taken care of her, ever since the day they'd been left homeless...and this was how she repaid him. "What the hell have you done?"

Maggie met his furious glare with an unrepentant one. "I've done you a favor, that's what I've done. Mark my word, Davy, one day you'll thank me."

She shoved the packet of letters into his hand. "Miss Lowell arrives at the station today at noon. You have a few hours to acquaint yourself with your new bride by reading her letters, so I suggest you get started."

DEAD LEAVES STUMBLED across the tracks and somersaulted over the boarding platform, swirling around the hem of Victoria's traveling suit before dancing off to tumble down a set of stairs. She dropped her satchel next to the large case she'd hauled off the train.

After three exhausting days and sleepless nights, she had arrived in Fort Scott, near the southeastern Kansas border. Beyond the brick and stone depot topped with an impressive clock tower lay the bustling railroad town that would be her new home. The past, with all its unhappiness, was behind her. Soon, her life would change. Things would be different. Better. She would no longer suffer false friends and unsympathetic family. She would no longer be lonely and unloved. Today, she would meet her romantic suitor, a man she had traveled over a thousand miles to marry.

"David Patrick O'Brien," she spoke his name under her breath, loving the way it tripped off her tongue. "Where are you?"

Other passengers streamed past as she bounced on her

toes and craned her neck to see over their heads. She'd never actually met Mr. O'Brien, but she would recognize him from the cabinet card he'd sent with his first letter. With a shiver, she drew her fur-lined cape close to block the cold wind while she searched the faces of strangers in the thinning crowd

A whistle sounded. The locomotive gave an impatient huff.

Those departing were leaving, and passengers going on had boarded. Ten-minute stops didn't allow for the luxury of loitering.

Her anxious gaze swept the platform. Where could he be?

She fumbled with her satchel and retrieved the cabinet card. Unnecessary, considering she'd studied it enough to memorize every feature. The photograph showed a darkly handsome, if somewhat serious, young gentleman wearing an old-fashioned suit with a starched collar. Possibly, he'd had his picture taken a few years back and he might look different now, or perhaps he hadn't seen her. That seemed unlikely. She was the only passenger remaining beside the train.

One of the porters handling luggage approached. "Miss? You waitin' for somebody?"

How nice someone had noticed her. She was beginning to think she was invisible.

"Yes, my fiancé is meeting me."

"Gettin' hitched?" The porter grinned, his teeth very white against his ebony skin. "Ain't he the lucky one."

She hoped Mr. O'Brien agreed. He had replied to her inquiry within two short weeks, had proposed in the second letter and with the third had sent her fare and urged her to *come to me with all haste.* A man that eager to be wed wouldn't abandon her at the train station.

"Perhaps you've seen him?" She held out the cabinet card.

The porter took a good look at the photograph and then returned it. "No ma'am. Ain't seen anyone around looks like him."

"Oh…" Victoria's hopefulness deflated. "Well, thank you."

Black smoke from the retreating train blew across the platform and into her face. The stinging smoke made her eyes water. She blinked.

"You all right, miss? Here, take my handkerchief."

"Thank you, but no, I don't need it. I'm not crying. It's just the smoke." The tendency to weep at misfortune had been drummed out of her at a very early age.

"Course not. Pretty lady like you got nothin' to worry about." The porter eyed her large suitcase. "Want me to take that for you? You might want to wait inside."

The depot would be a warmer place to linger, but Mr. O'Brien had specifically told her to remain on the platform and he would find her. Didn't seem wise to leave just yet. "Please put it by the door until my fiancé arrives."

Victoria withdrew a gold eagle from a change purse and handed it to the porter, relieved when he carted the heavy suitcase away. He would get another tip when he took it to Mr. O'Brien's carriage. Or was that too generous? A frugal seamstress named Poppy had warned her to be prudent with her money. She'd used most of her available cash to set up a fund for women left jobless after a garment factory burned down. Philanthropy aside, she felt responsible because her family had benefited from the income the factory had produced.

She tucked her change purse back into her bag. If she contacted anyone back home, including the banker, her father would send someone after her. Not because he wanted her—he'd never made a secret of his disappointment—he simply disliked losing anything that belonged to him. A thousand miles ought to be far enough away to escape from beneath his heavy thumb, and being wed to an Irish Catholic shopkeeper would virtually ensure being disinherited.

David O'Brien wasn't rich, but he'd assured her he could support a family comfortably. At any rate, she wasn't marrying him for his money. She wanted something that couldn't be bought, something she hadn't been able to find in her wealthy, influential social circle. Something she would travel to the ends of the earth to find. True love.

So, where was he, the man who had swept her off her feet with his romantic prose?

She took another look at the end of the platform where several people who'd exited the depot were milling about. One man had his shoulders hunched against the wind and a woolen scarf wrapped around his face, so she couldn't make out his features. However, he seemed too short and rather rotund. Her fiancé stood five feet ten inches in his stockings, and had described his build as lean. Honestly, she wouldn't care if he was short, round and bald-headed as long as he treated her with the same kindness and respect he'd shown in his letters.

Victoria hugged her arms and began to hum, *A Kiss in the Morning Early*, an Irish love song he'd shared in his second letter. She'd asked around among the factory workers and had found an Irish girl, Sarah Fitzgerald, who taught her the song. Victoria imagined her love singing it to her, and kissing her each morning. Sarah had declared Irish men to be very romantic.

Her Mr. O'Brien wouldn't disappoint. No, indeed, he would not. He had promised he would be here, and he would keep his word. The man who'd penned poetry and sent her love songs wouldn't jilt her, as Bertram had done.

MUTTERING EXPLETIVES, David leapt off the seat of the wagon, holding onto his hat so the wind wouldn't blow it away. He hitched the horse and loped across the street in the direction of the depot as fast as he could go, given his uneven gait.

He had a good excuse for being late and it wasn't due to misjudging the time. Not that he expected the unwanted bride his sister had ordered to understand. By her own admission, Miss Lowell had never worked in a mercantile. Why Maggie thought she would make him a *perfect* wife was beyond him.

Still, he felt bad about leaving her out in the cold. If she was as smart as she sounded in those letters, she ought to have the good sense to go inside the ladies' waiting room where a stove would be lit. The Gulf depot had a very fine diner. In fact, she could have dinner before the next train arrived. He'd give her money for food and a return ticket. That was the least he could do, considering none of this was her fault.

Smoke lingered above empty tracks. The train had departed. Damn railroad, never ran on time unless he was late.

He started up the steps to the platform.

There stood a small woman in a long, dark cloak with a

hood pulled over her head; beside her sagged a tapestry satchel. He couldn't see her face because she was peering off in the opposite direction, as if searching for someone.

Him?

David's scalp tingled. The odd sensation raced down his arms, beneath his skin. Not anticipation. Anxiety, more like. He didn't look forward to meeting Miss Lowell and delivering the bad news about his sister's inexcusable deception. Maggie had thrust a handful of letters at him and then taken Fannie and vanished, leaving him holding the bag—or letters in this case. Furious or not, he would shoulder the responsibility, as he always had.

He silently willed the woman on the platform to turn so he could see her.

She twisted around, grabbing at her hood as the wind tore it off. Loosened hair whipped across her face. With gloved fingers, she brushed at the errant strands.

Some call it flaxen. I'd say it's more the color of honey.

She'd given an apt description. His fingers itched to touch her hair and find out if it was as warm as it looked.

Her eyes widened as he approached. She'd been honest in describing them, too.

Not blue or green, but a blending of both, constantly shifting, like the color of the sea. Being prone to fanciful imagery, you might call them mermaid eyes.

He wasn't the least bit fanciful, but he could see how one might mistake her for a mythical beauty. As legend had it, mermaids lured sailors to their death. This one didn't appear dangerous, only cold. Her cheeks and the tip of her nose had turned red. Why hadn't she gone inside? Maybe book learning didn't equate to common sense.

David snatched off his hat and attempted to smooth his hair—a mess made worse by the wind. "Miss Lowell?"

She gazed up at him with something akin to awe. "Mr. O'Brien." The odd way she said his name, turning the *O* into an *Ah*, sent a tickle up his spine. "I'm very pleased to meet you, at last."

What could he say? He hadn't known she was arriving until this morning. He'd admit his sister set up this arranged marriage, and neither of them had to honor their commitment because it was a farce. That's what he'd say, if he could peel his tongue off the roof of his mouth.

Saints, she was even lovelier up close. Petite to the point of being fragile, like fine china he refused to carry in the store because it broke too easily.

At last, he found his voice. "A pleasure to meet you as well."

"You look exactly as I expected," she murmured.

"Ah, well..." He felt foolishly awkward and unsure. "You aren't at all what I expected."

Her look of wounded confusion put in a kink in his insides.

"What I mean is, your photograph is nice, but you're prettier in person."

"Oh..." She put her hand to her chest as if relieved. "Thank goodness. I thought you meant you were disappointed."

She couldn't be serious.

"Not with you."

A shy glimpse through her lashes turned his insides to mush.

Careful. The warning from some still-functioning part of his mind jerked him away from the dangerous edge of infatuation. Beauty aside, he knew nothing about her. Well, except for what she'd put in those letters. In between waiting on customers, he'd read them. Well educated, from

15

a family of good standing, she had been through a rough time, which she said gave her an *especial sympathy* for his situation. Left to his own devices, he wouldn't find a better bride, and certainly not before Christmas.

David's nerves twanged like an out-of-tune fiddle. Blasted cold had stolen his reason. Accepting her under false pretenses was as bad as Maggie deceiving her. He could not lead this woman on and let her believe he'd written those letters.

She drew up the hood of her cloak. "Is it always this windy?"

Good, she might decide for herself she didn't like it here. He made another pass with his fingers through his hair before he secured his hat. "If you don't like the wind, you won't like Kansas."

Alarm flashed across her face. Then she squared her shoulders, standing erect as a toy soldier. "I can manage the wind."

She declared it with such confidence he almost believed her, notwithstanding one good gust would blow her away. *Brave lass.* She'd come so far, all the way across the country, and she carried herself with dignity and grace.

David couldn't bring himself to destroy her dreams, not out here on the railroad platform, buffeted by a cold, cruel wind. He'd take her back to the store. Let Maggie explain, considering she had created this mess in the first place.

Decision made, his tension eased. He reached for her satchel. "Let's go somewhere warm."

"Warm sounds wonderful." She motioned in the direction of the depot door. "There's the rest of my luggage."

A porter stood guard near a large case closed with straps. Of course Miss Lowell would have more than one small bag. She'd come out here believing she was getting married.

With a sigh, he headed for the suitcase. He would address Miss Lowell's misconceptions later, after she had some food in her belly to soften the blow. After she'd rested, his sister could bring her back to catch a train.

The porter smiled at Victoria as if he knew her. "Glad to see you found your groom, miss. The conductor and station manager was arguin' 'bout which one could talk you into takin' his place."

Already hopeful replacements were lining up.

David didn't care. He wasn't keeping her. Still, he didn't appreciate having his tardiness pointed out. He gave the porter two bits. "For watching her bag."

The old fellow shook his head and tried to return the money. "You don't need to—"

"Keep it." He wasn't in the mood to hear more about Victoria's admirers. "I'll take her luggage."

Ignoring her surprised expression, he hefted the heavy case with his right hand and took the smaller bag in his left. The uneven weight caused him to favor his bad leg. Not a great deal. She might not even notice.

Miss Lowell glided beside him as they crossed the platform. When they reached the stairs, she touched his arm. "I could carry the satchel, if it would help."

She'd noticed—and considered him too infirm to make it down a few steps. If there was one thing he couldn't abide, it was pity.

"No, I don't need help," he said flatly, and then added, "Thank you."

Hurt flashed in her gaze a second before she lowered her head and the hood concealed her expression.

For Pete's sake, she was being polite and he was acting

17

like an ass. He'd shown up late, had been tongue-tied and inconsiderate. Then again, he hadn't anticipated having to leave his business in the middle of the day to fetch a bride he didn't want.

He tromped down the steps and set the large case on the ground in order to assist her. She lifted her skirts and descended without waiting for his hand. Growing frustrated, he tossed her bags into the back of the wagon. He knew proper manners, but she wasn't giving him a chance to display them.

"Allow me." He grasped her around the middle and his fingers circled an unbelievably tiny waist. Desire, longing, possessiveness, or some potent combination of all three, slammed into him. He thrust her upward with such force she nearly fell over the buckboard.

He mumbled an apology, should've known better than to put his hands on her. When he swung up to the seat, she shifted her skirts to make room, or she was trying to get away.

"I hope you didn't run into any trouble on the way to the station." Her concerned tone just made him feel worse.

Miss Lowell wasn't to blame for any of this. She'd come out here in good faith and deserved patience and kindness, even if he couldn't give her what she wanted.

Gathering the reins, he turned the horse onto the road leading away from the station. "No, there's no trouble. One of my customers had a large order that required my assistance. In my business, I can't afford to be rude."

"Of course not, I understand."

He doubted she had any first-hand knowledge of the effort it took to earn money. The fur trim on her fine wool cloak, her decorum, even her manner of speaking, gave her away. Which begged the question, why had she left behind her comfortable life?

She'd mentioned a scandal created when her betrothed broke off their engagement. Unbearable shame, David understood. The ceaseless gossip and ugly rumors, the pitying glances; he couldn't walk into church without feeling judged. If Miss Lowell had suffered half of what he'd put up with, he couldn't blame her for leaving, and even admired her spunk in setting out alone to start over. It wouldn't hurt to get to know her better and find out if there might be a way he could help her.

The horse bobbed its head and leaned into the traces as it pulled the wagon onto the bricked road leading through the center of town. Clopping hooves, jangling harnesses and a distant train whistle filled the tense silence.

David had no problem creating conversation with customers, but for some reason, his tongue remained tied around this woman. Courting made him nervous, but he wasn't wooing Miss Lowell. He would admit to a strong attraction.

The voluminous cape enveloped her dainty but well-proportioned form. He'd encircled a trim waist and detected the slight flare of her hips. A familiar ache speared through him. It had been a long time since he'd been with a woman, and he had never been with one this beautiful. The idea of keeping her appealed to him more than it should.

"Look out, you idiot!"

The shout jerked David's attention to a red trolley car rumbling down the middle of the street. He hauled on the reins, just managing to turn the horse and veer from disaster. He ignored the blustering driver, who shook a fist at him.

Miss Lowell clung to the seat. "Your horse appears to be dozing."

A nicer way of saying he wasn't paying attention. He was tempted to point out that he wasn't careless, but then decided to let the matter pass. No need to make excuses to a woman who'd be leaving.

She stared straight ahead, gripping her cloak at the neck to keep the wind from blowing her hood back. Had he been prepared for her arrival, he would've hired a carriage. As it was, he left in such a hurry he'd forgotten to bring a lap rug or blanket.

"Here, take this..." He slowed long enough to shrug out of his overcoat. "The wind makes the air feel colder."

"Are you sure you don't need your coat?"

"I'm not cold." Not unless cold feet counted.

She pulled his coat around her with a grateful smile. "Thank you. I shouldn't be so chilled with this heavy cloak."

"Hard to stay warm when you don't have extra padding." The quip was out before he could stop it. He would've slapped his forehead if both hands weren't on the reins. *Extra padding* might keep her warmer, but she didn't need to put on weight, as he'd implied.

"Sorry, what I meant to say is, you aren't..." The correct description escaped him.

"Fat?"

"Large."

"No, I have never been large."

"Nor have my feet. They fit quite well into my mouth." He cringed, again. His reaction to being nervous, crack another bad joke.

She gripped the lapels of his coat, appearing unfazed. "You'd think I would be used to the cold, being from Massachusetts."

Bless her. She'd rescued him from further embarrassment by introducing a non-offensive subject. "You're from Boston, or thereabouts."

"Thereabouts."

He had heard all sorts of accents, but hers wasn't familiar, almost British, but not quite. Upper crust was the term that came to mind. How had Maggie managed to snare a beautiful, highborn lady with nothing more than a few letters? In Miss Lowell's responses, she'd called him *entertaining* and *witty*. Obviously, Maggie had lied.

"Will the ceremony be tomorrow?"

Her question pulled him out of his musings. "The ceremony?"

The look she cast said he was in danger of dropping from the rank of rude hayseed to drooling halfwit. "Our wedding ceremony."

"The wedding, of course..." What other ceremony would she mean?

Dread spiraled to pit of his stomach. There would be no ceremony. He had to tell her. Except, he wasn't prepared to crush her hopes while avoiding traffic. In fact, it felt wrong to send her away without at least giving her a chance.

A crazy idea, but it had merit. Miss Lowell possessed extraordinary beauty, fine manners and a quick wit. That she hadn't asked him to turn around by now spoke well of her patience—or sense of humor. Things might work out, once he got around to explaining he hadn't written those letters. If he told her that, after offending her repeatedly, she would leave and then he'd have to start the grueling process of finding a willing bride, and he was running out of time.

"Do you have a day in mind?" She sounded less confident. More worried.

He wouldn't be rushed into marriage, as he had been

before, but he couldn't drag his heels, either. Maggie would be gone after Christmas.

Miss Lowell could stay with them until then. That would give Fannie time to get to know her, and he could judge how the two of them would get along. Three weeks ought to be enough time to decide whether the Boston miss would suit.

"How about Christmas Eve?"

CHAPTER 2

"Christmas Eve?" Victoria laced her fingers tight to keep her hands from trembling. First, her betrothed had been late, and now he wanted to delay the wedding by three weeks. His suggestion wouldn't be so alarming if he hadn't told her how eager he was to marry. She could think of no reason he'd want to delay, unless she'd somehow displeased him.

Prettier than her photograph, that's what he'd said. He might like her face, but be less interested in her form. Men preferred lush bodies, so she used bustles and specially designed corsets to create the illusion of fuller curves. Mr. O'Brien must've realized this when he put his hands around her waist. She'd experienced a tingle of pleasure at his touch, but then he'd teased her about her lack of padding. Perhaps the remark hadn't been in jest. After all, he kept looking at her strangely.

Victoria straightened her spine. Slumping wouldn't make her more attractive. "Where will I stay until then?"

His forehead scrunched as if he hadn't thought about such a small thing as her reputation. "You can room with my sister, Maggie. Fannie sleeps next door. That'll give you and her a chance to get to know each other better. Make the transition easier."

"I suppose that does make sense." It would make more sense if he'd brought it up in his last letter instead of now, as if he'd just come up with an excuse for delay.

She pulled the hood lower, as the wind kept catching it, trying to rip it off. Being nervous, she hadn't conversed much. Perhaps he thought she wasn't bright. Bertram had dubbed her "Miss Goldfinch." She hadn't appreciated being compared to a flighty little bird. Granted she was small, but she wasn't a birdbrain.

Even if Mr. O'Brien wasn't impressed by her appearance or wittiness, that still didn't explain his tardy arrival or his odd behavior. He'd gawked at her, stammered, spoke in short, curt sentences when he spoke at all, and had heaved her into the wagon as if he were handling a sack of grain. Where was the sweet, sensitive man who'd penned such heart-stopping prose?

Nerves could explain it. Bashful men communicated better in writing than speaking, and he might be one of them. She would try to put him at ease and look for the opportunity to make a good impression.

She straightened with fresh resolve and took in her surroundings. A busy railroad town, he'd called it. The congested traffic would support this observation. However, she hadn't expected her new home to look so...well, civilized. "Fort Scott looks different than I pictured."

"How so?"

"There are more buildings, and a great many are made of brick and stone. Even your streets are paved."

"Locally made brick, the stone is quarried nearby. We

have a lumber mill, so you'll see plenty of frame buildings, as well."

Oh good, she'd managed to get him to converse. About construction. Still, it was an improvement over awkward silence.

The cold air smelled faintly of wood smoke. To the east, skies remained clear, but the wind was blowing in heavy, dark clouds from the west.

She sighed with disappointment. "I was hoping to see those endless blue skies you wrote about. We don't have many clear days in Boston. There's always a haze from the factories."

"There are few factories out here. We have a large foundry and a sugar processing plant, but the wind blows away the smoke." As if to make his point, a gust lifted his hat. He grabbed the brim and tugged it down.

"We have to wait until there's an ocean breeze for the skies to clear."

It struck her, again, how far she'd traveled. There was no ocean for over a thousand miles in any direction. She was in the middle of the country, on the edge of what had been the frontier not so long ago.

"Wasn't Fort Scott originally the site of an army fort? Where is it?"

"There haven't been soldiers here since the railroads got built." Mr. O'Brien pointed at a crowded street. "You can't see it from here, but just down there is what used to be the center of the old fort. We turned the parade grounds into a city park."

"Amazing how quickly things change..." The wagon's wheels bumped over iron rails. "And now you have street lights and trolley cars."

"You were expecting dirt roads and covered wagons?"

Her lips curved at her fanciful notion of what a Kansas town would be like. "Yes, I suppose I was...and buffalo."

"You won't see any buffalo wandering the streets of Fort Scott. The herds in Kansas were killed off more than twenty years ago. During the summer, you'll see—and smell—the cattle when they bring the trains up from Texas.

He guided the wagon around a corner and came to a stop at a hitching rail. The streets here were also bricked. As elsewhere, a wide boardwalk ran the length of the block, which in this case housed mostly frame structures.

She peered up at a sign hanging from the edge of a porch roof that extended out over the sidewalk from the second floor. For some reason, he'd brought her to his place of business. Exhaustion had set in, and she was more than a little hungry. Still, she should be pleased he wanted to share his life's work.

"O'Brien's Dry Goods, Fine Groceries and Family Provisions," she read. "That sounds very impressive."

"It'll be even more impressive when we take over that empty building next door. I'm planning to expand. Might even carry bicycles." Her betrothed stepped down, and after a moment appeared at her side.

She placed her hands on his shoulders as he grasped her waist and lifted her to the ground and discovered that touching him also produced a thrill. This time, he didn't throw her, but carefully set her on the ground. She gazed into eyes so dark they appeared fathomless.

He glanced away, as if uncomfortable with their sudden closeness. She had to get him talking again. He'd written about reopening the store his father founded, which had been destroyed in an awful fire that killed his parents. She'd grieved for his loss and admired his resilience.

"When did *O'Brien's* reopen?"

"Eight years ago, after most of this area was rebuilt."

"There's another mercantile right across the street," she pointed out. That store had an attractive red and white striped canopy. "Is that usual?"

"Only if you're a thieving blue jay and think nothing of moving in on someone else's territory."

She filed away her betrothed's sentiments about his neighbor, who sounded like someone she should avoid.

He tucked her hand into the crook of his arm and escorted her inside.

Victoria blinked to adjust her vision to the dim interior. For some reason, the ceiling lamp wasn't lit. Perhaps it didn't work. Something smelled like vinegar. She spied the source near the front, a barrel of pickles. Further back, a potbellied stove occupied the center of the store. Around it, tables overflowed with household items, shelves held shoes and clothing. Behind glass, groceries as well as guns were displayed. Hanging from the beams were more items: pots and pans, farm tools, and, heavens, even a slab of smoked meat. She wasn't sure what she'd expected Mr. O'Brien's store to look like, but her imagination hadn't formed this cramped, chaotic environment.

He seemed to be waiting for her to remark. She had to say something nice. Honest, but complimentary.

"You have a great deal of merchandise."

His mouth curled up on one side. "Everything a body could want is what I tell people."

"Yes, I can see that."

"You're back!" The hail came from an attractive, dark-haired woman behind the counter who looked to be about Victoria's age. She said something to the customer she'd been waiting on, an older gentleman in farmer's denims, and then hurried over with a broad smile.

Classic features, dark, luminous eyes and black hair...his sister?

"You must be Victoria. I'm Maggie O'Brien. David's sister." Her future sister-in-law hugged her neck.

Victoria lifted her arms, not sure whether it was polite to return a hug. This was something they didn't do in Boston. "It's my pleasure to meet you, Miss O'Brien."

"Please, call me Maggie." She darted a look at her brother that could only be interpreted as worried. "Has David told you—?"

"That you're eager to meet her, yes. Miss Lowell will be sharing the room with you, so you'll have ample opportunity to get to know her." He arched an eyebrow—caution, or a warning—which was met with an expression of surprise.

Something strange was going on. What was he supposed to tell her? He'd interrupted his sister before she could say.

Two well-dressed women standing by a display of dishes and kitchenware craned their necks to observe the exchange. Victoria couldn't make out their expressions, but there was no mistaking their curiosity.

The awkwardness of the moment made her stomach knot. She cast about for an opportunity to comment and break the tense silence. Her upbringing hadn't prepared her for conversation about general stores. She didn't purchase household items. Their housekeeper, Mrs. Kilburn, did that. Beside the stove, a barrel had been turned upside down and someone had put a checkerboard on it. The pieces looked as if the players had walked away in the middle of a game.

"My father plays chess. When he was in one of his more generous moods, he taught me. I don't know how to play checkers. Perhaps you could show me."

Mr. O'Brien gave her a distracted look. "I don't have time for games."

The way he said it made the activity sound frivolous. Her father took his chess very seriously. "Do you have other hobbies?"

"Hobbies?" He said the word as if he'd never heard it before. "If you consider balancing the accounts a hobby."

Did he realize he was beginning to sound boring?

She quickly reminded herself that her husband was a man of business. Her father kept very involved with his investments, too. She hadn't thought a shopkeeper would be so consumed by his work. Perhaps he was just teasing. She'd picked up on his dry sense of humor.

"Where's Fannie?" Mr. O'Brien asked his sister.

"She's...." Maggie gestured to where she'd come from. Only the farmer remained. "Where did she go?"

Victoria turned at a shuffling sound.

A little girl peeked around the glassed display at the front end of the counter on the other side of the store. She'd apparently crept to a new location without being seen. Not too difficult with so many places to hide.

"Come out, dear," Maggie urged. "We want you to meet Miss Lowell."

The child shook her head, making her dark curls dance. She was the very image of her father, with the exception of her chin. Mr. O'Brien had a square chin. His daughter's face called to mind a mischievous pixie.

"Mind your aunt, Fannie." His tone warned against disobedience.

Fannie stepped out from behind the counter, but ventured no further. She had to be nervous, poor thing. Given the tragic circumstances her father had been honest enough to share, Fannie would need a great deal of patience and understanding. The last thing she needed was to be dealt with harshly.

To prevent a showdown, Victoria hurried over to introduce herself. She bent her knees, squatting as low as the bustle would allow, and offered a friendly smile. "Hello, Fannie. I'm very pleased to meet you."

Suspicion reflected in eyes the color of strong coffee.

Victoria was prepared for resistance. Mr. O'Brien had reported that Fannie was shy and withdrawn. A present would help break the ice. "I've brought you a gift. If your father can collect my small bag, I'll give it to you."

Interest flickered in Fannie's dark gaze. Her lips remained sealed.

Victoria's palms grew damp. She could hardly make a good impression if Fannie wouldn't speak to her. This first meeting had to go well or he wouldn't believe she was as good with children as she'd claimed. She liked children. Therefore, she had assumed they would like her. Fannie might prove her assumption wrong.

Her confidence wavered. Nevertheless, she glanced over her shoulder at her future husband. "Would you mind retrieving my tapestry satchel?"

He gave a nod. Did he seem reluctant? She couldn't imagine why he objected to her giving her future stepdaughter a gift.

"Outside," he said to Maggie under his breath, and turned on his heel.

His sister followed with a knitted brow.

Victoria gave up trying to guess what trouble brewed between them. She was too tired and heart sore. Nothing had gone as she'd imagined. Her intended hadn't welcomed her, made her feel wanted, or even seen to her comfort. Her patience would have to extend to Fannie's father.

After a moment, her legs began to twitch. She stood to relieve the pressure. Bustles weren't designed for squatting.

The three customers remained motionless, like well-placed statues. The two women had on long coats trimmed with braided piping. Their hats looked more festive than practical. They appeared to be related, and from a family of some means. The farmer's grizzled beard reached the bib of his dungarees. His coat, which hung open, had the appearance of being homespun. Differences aside, they were all in *O'Brien's* for one reason—to purchase goods. If the customers became impatient they might leave, and then she would be held responsible, having sent Mr. O'Brien on a personal errand. His explanation for being tardy made it clear her arrival had disrupted his business.

It stung to realize where she came on his list of priorities, yet she might've expected it. The men she knew were more concerned with their affairs than they were with their wives. Her husband-to-be appeared no different in this regard, although that aspect of his nature hadn't come through in his letters.

"Is there anything I can assist you with?" she asked the older lady, determined to do what she could to help. Her betrothed would appreciate the effort.

"We're just looking," replied the matron.

"Yes, just looking," echoed the younger woman.

The farmer tugged down the brim of a shapeless hat. He appeared to be smiling, but it was hard to tell through that bushy beard. "Did O'Brien hire you? Didn't think he had a clerk."

It would be impolite to announce her engagement without her betrothed present and a proper introduction.

Victoria hesitated, hoping her future husband would return. When he didn't make a convenient appearance, she decided she didn't have a choice. His customers might draw the wrong conclusion and *that* certainly wouldn't help his business. "I'm Miss Lowell, from Boston. Mr. O'Brien has asked me to marry him."

Fannie's response was instantaneous. Looking horrified, she whirled around and darted past the two women, running through a doorway at the rear of the store.

Victoria blushed, feeling foolish. The child's reaction made it clear she knew nothing about her father's engagement.

The older lady smiled. "Welcome, Miss Lowell. I'm Mrs. Robinson and this is my daughter, Nancy. We'd love to get acquainted when you have more time. We'll run along now, and let you tend to Fannie."

The two women started for the door.

"Ma'am..." After giving his hat brim another tug, the farmer left, fast on their heels.

Despair dragged on what was left of Victoria's confidence. Her lack of knowledge in childrearing was exceeded only by her ignorance about the mercantile business. There was nothing she could do now about losing those customers, but if she thought to impress Mr. O'Brien with her skills at mothering, she had better find his daughter before he returned.

*A*s soon as David walked out the door, he took his sister's arm and hauled her around to the back of the wagon. The cold hadn't kept people inside. Shoppers thronged the sidewalks and the street. He kept his voice low to avoid being overheard by passersby, or Victoria if she had good ears. "She doesn't know you wrote those letters."

Maggie pulled back, eyes wide with amazement. "You didn't tell her? Why not?"

"Because... It seemed like the wrong time."

He tugged at his collar. His nerves jumped and he couldn't think straight, all from the short time he'd spent in Miss Lowell's company. Had he been less enamored, he would've taken her to one of the hotels, except that meant more expense he couldn't afford. "I decided to let her stay for a few weeks, to see if she can manage Fannie. She can room with you."

Maggie's jaw came unhinged. Something akin to delight lit her eyes, and her smile said *I-told-you-so*. "You like her."

Oh no, he wasn't letting his sister take the bit into her mouth and run off with this idea that he'd somehow fall in love and live in blissful union with a mail-order bride he hadn't even ordered. "No more interfering," he warned. "You've done enough."

Maggie folded her hands behind her back. "I wouldn't dream of interfering."

He leaned to one side, peering behind her. "Do you have your fingers crossed?"

She held out her hands, looking innocent. "Why would you think that?"

"Because you seem to have developed a hankering for matchmaking. Don't get it into your head I'll marry that woman just because you brought her here."

"She has a name, David. Victoria. Can you say it?"

"Yes, I can say it, but it's not proper to call her by her given name."

"It is if she's your fiancée."

"She's *not* my fiancée."

Maggie frowned, disapprovingly. "She accepted a proposal, not an offer for an evaluation."

David gripped the back of the wagon, struggling to keep his temper under control. "I'm not the one who proposed."

His sister's arms fell to her sides. "If you aren't sure, even after meeting her, then I think we ought to tell her you didn't write those letters."

"Good grief, Maggie." David plowed his fingers through his hair. Dealing with his younger sister for all these years, it was a wonder he hadn't pulled it out. "First you tell me you've arranged a marriage, now that I've agreed to give it a shot, you want to pull the rug out from under me."

"But if you don't intend to marry her, it's not right to keep her here and give her hope."

A dull throbbing started behind his eyes. He rubbed his forehead. He had known from the moment he'd met his unintended intended that he couldn't walk away and wash his hands of her. That's not what an honorable man would do. "I'll do the right thing. If Miss Lowell proves she can be a good mother, I'll..." He swallowed the resistance clogging his throat. "Marry her."

Maggie glanced at the store with a look of uncertainty. "You shouldn't marry her solely out of obligation."

A muscle jumped in his clamped jaw. "You have your head in the clouds if you think a mail-order marriage can be based on anything *but* obligation. Isn't this what you wanted? To put me in an impossible position to force me to marry, so you could leave."

Hurt welled in Maggie's eyes. "No, that's not what I wanted, not at all. Fannie needs a good mother, and you need a good wife. That's why I read every response and spent hours considering them, selecting the person I knew would be the right one. I want you to be happy, David. I want Fannie to be loved. That's what I want."

Maggie whirled away, but not before he saw tears spill down her cheeks. She didn't weep and carry on, as Rachel had done at times to bend him to her will. His sister was the least manipulative woman he knew, which was why he couldn't fathom why she'd been so deceitful. She risked his anger, risked alienating him.

She'd done it because she cared.

Guilt tightened his throat. He shouldn't have accused her of being selfish. He was the one who had held on for too long. She'd been forced to pry his fingers open to get him to let go of her, and it wasn't just because of Fannie. He feared losing his sister. With the exception of his daughter, he'd lost everyone else.

Despite her interference, Maggie hadn't really hurt him. She had put him in an awkward spot, as well as Miss Lowell, even if the spunky woman didn't yet realize it. She still had hope, the kind that died as easily as flowers after the first snowfall.

David put his hand on Maggie's shoulder and spoke in a low tone. There was no way to prevent people from noticing they were in deep conversation, but he didn't want to give the eavesdroppers any fodder. "When the time is right and she won't be so hurt, I'll tell her about the letters."

Maggie twisted around. Blotches marred her creamy skin, and her eyes were red-rimmed, but there were no more tears. She searched his face with an anxious gaze, and then threw her arms around him. "I'm sorry, Davy" she murmured against his chest. "I meant well."

Her apology drained what was left of his anger. He rubbed her back. "You've got a big heart, Maggie. That's not a bad trait."

After a moment, she drew away and her sweet smile was back. "Victoria does seem nice, and she brought Fannie a gift."

"Ah, almost forgot..." David hauled the heavy case out of the wagon and set it on the sidewalk. What had she packed, bricks?

"She said it was in the tapestry bag." Maggie dabbed at her eyes with a handkerchief.

He took hold of the carpetbag. Nice of her to bring a gift, although he worried she might be offended if Fannie didn't thank her properly. "Did you tell her about Fannie not speaking?"

Maggie looked chagrined. "I didn't come right out and say that because Fannie can speak, she just chooses not to. I said she became withdrawn after her mother ran off."

A chill passed through David that had nothing to do with the frigid wind. "You told her about Rachel?"

"I told the truth—that your wife ran off with another man and then divorced you. It was bound to come out. Better for her to hear it from you."

Yes, Miss Lowell would hear the gossip. There was no preventing it. Knowing that still didn't help. She would poke and prod and ask questions, like most women.

David's insides twisted into a painful knot. He hated talking about Rachel's betrayal. Just made him feel worse. He shifted the tapestry bag to his left hand.

Maggie grasped his right. "David, she shared painful things, too. Didn't you read her letters? What she wrote about that awful man who jilted her only a few days before her wedding?"

"Yes, I read them." That was another reason he couldn't just tell her she'd been duped and send her on her way. Rejection left soul-deep wounds, regardless of the reason.

Mrs. Robinson and her daughter exited the store, throwing surreptitious glances at the bags he held. They started up the sidewalk toward their waiting carriage.

"I should've introduced them," he murmured under his breath.

Maggie nodded.

Phineas Gregg strolled outside. He touched the brim of his hat in greeting. "My woman went into that Five Cent Store to look around. Got to find her afore she spends ever' nickel we got." He winked at his own joke, and then eyed the large suitcase. "Met that nice young lady you brung home. Fannie's new ma."

What could he say? He hadn't instructed her not to tell anyone. She didn't know she was on trial, and he couldn't refute her claim without damaging her reputation and looking like a fool.

David pasted on a smile and hefted the heavy suitcase.

"Feels like she packed a load of bricks. Maybe she thinks we need them to build a house."

The long beard lifted as a broad grin spread across the old man's face. "Good luck to you two. I'll be sure an' tell the missus. She'll want to come by and visit."

David waited until Phineas crossed the street and entered Sumner's Five Cent Store before he heaved a frustrated sigh. "He tells his wife, and the whole town will know by suppertime."

Maggie gave him a look of sympathy. "You can't blame Victoria for telling them about the engagement. It was only a matter of time before the news got out."

"I'm not angry with her." He didn't look forward to her reaction when he got around to telling her he wasn't the one who'd extended the proposal. With any luck, he would be prepared to ask her to marry him immediately afterwards. That would save them both a great deal of embarrassment.

"You needn't worry, either," he assured Maggie. "My anger's spent."

Relief flooded her face. "I'm glad you're not mad at me anymore. And, like you said earlier, this may work out for the best."

"For the best. Did I say that?"

She shrugged. "Something close to it."

Maggie, the perpetual optimist; life had forced him to be more realistic. If things worked out, fine. If not, he would help Miss Lowell get a fresh start in Fort Scott, or somewhere of her own choosing.

"FANNIE? ARE YOU BACK HERE?" Victoria felt her way around a barrel. She paused by sacks of flour piled as high as the top of her head. Navigating the storeroom proved more difficult than making her way through a winding cave, and if the child kept silent, she might never find her.

Her hand encountered a stair rail. Had Fannie gone up to the second floor? Oh, why was it so dark in here? Mr. O'Brien really ought to purchase some working lamps.

Victoria unbuttoned the fastening at her neck and draped her heavy cloak over the rail. The garment was bulky and getting in the way. "Fannie? Please answer me. I don't know my way around."

She knew the child had to be back here, waiting, perhaps hoping she would give up. Not after assuring Mr. O'Brien she would be a good mother. She would not be outwitted—Victoria groped past a stack of slatted crates—not unless she fell and broke her neck, and then it wouldn't matter.

She squinted at a weak light coming from what appeared to be the back wall. Drawing closer, she saw a door ajar. Fannie had escaped out the back, it seemed. What if she had run away? Even if she hadn't gone far, she could take ill in this cold, windy weather.

Oh dear, oh dear, oh dear...

Victoria peeked out at a narrow alley. Along the back of the buildings beneath stairways leading to top floors, bins were filled with trash. Empty boxes and crates were stacked one on top of the other. A movement caught her eye.

Fannie crouched in the dirt beside a vegetable crate pushed up against the back wall of the store. The frightened child reminded Victoria of a stray pup she'd found once, which had taken refuge behind the stables. The poor creature had regarded her with that same look of wounded wariness. When she'd tried to pet it, the dog bit her.

Since that time, Victoria had learned a few things about

frightened creatures. One had to move slowly and be patient. No petting until trust was established. Treats helped, but Mr. O'Brien hadn't yet returned with her bag and she didn't want to spare the time to find it, or to explain why Fannie had bolted.

The child's resistance was to be expected. Fannie must know her aunt planned to leave, another abandonment in her mind. Mr. O'Brien might be strict and become harsh when angered. Victoria had experienced both. Her mother had died when she was young. Her stern father hadn't known how to show affection, and when he remarried her stepmother had wanted nothing to do with her. She, like Fannie, had felt lost, confused. She might not possess many mothering skills, but she understood the child's pain.

Moving slowly, Victoria squatted down next to the little girl. "I used to have a secret place when I was your age. Is this where you come when you want to be alone?"

Fannie pulled her coat around her and wrapped her arm wrapped protectively around the crate. She narrowed her eyes at Victoria, conveying her distrust.

Mew. The tiny cry confirmed what had brought her out here.

"Oh, you have a kitten." Victoria got down on her knees and peered inside the crate.

A tiny orange tabby, mewing its distress, walked on wobbly legs atop a ratty pink blanket. The kitten looked very young—too young to be taken from its mother.

"Is this your pet?" Victoria reached in to comfort it, but when Fannie grabbed her arm she immediately withdrew. "I won't touch it, if you don't want me to. But I promise, I would never hurt it. I love kittens, too. I wasn't allowed to have one, but the stable boy owned a cat and he let me play with it."

Fannie pushed part of the blanket that had fallen out of the crate back inside. Her anxious expression made her distress clear, but she still didn't speak.

Victoria rubbed at her arms to generate warmth. She should've worn wool instead of silk, but she'd wanted to look nice, fashionable. Who knew she would be kneeling in the dirt? "It's very cold out here. Why don't we go inside where it's warm?"

Fannie hugged the crate protectively. Perhaps she was worried about the kitten with the weather taking a turn for the worse.

Victoria remained on her knees. Her stepmother had scoffed at her childish concerns. She wouldn't make that mistake with Fannie. This presented a golden opportunity to forge a bond. "What if I take the crate and blanket, and you get the kitten? We'll go inside together and find a warm spot."

The girl scooped the kitten into her arms, guarding it with her hand so the little creature wouldn't leap away and fall to the ground.

Getting to her feet, Victoria picked up the crate. She followed Fannie inside the darkened building. With the sun hidden behind a mass of clouds, less light came inside through the door and small windows. That, combined with the clutter, made it difficult to see which way to go, although Fannie seemed to have no problem. She moved catlike through the maze.

"Fannie! Miss Lowell!" Mr. O'Brien's calls reached the rear of the building.

"We're back here—" Victoria stumbled over something on the floor. "It would help if you would put on a light."

A moment later, light flooded the storage area.

So, the building did have gas lighting. Mr. O'Brien just

didn't see the need to turn it on. He and his progeny must have the same ability to see in the dark.

Fannie sat down at the base of the stairs and settled the kitten in her lap.

Victoria lowered the crate to the plank floor in front of several large burlap sacks, and slid it through a fine dusting of what appeared to be flour. "Underneath the stairs, that's a good place to put the crate. Have you named it yet? Is it a girl kitten, or a boy kitten?"

Two successive thuds came from behind her. Victoria whirled around, seeing her large case next to the stairs and beside it, her tapestry bag.

Mr. O'Brien wore the same frown he'd left with. He hadn't taken his hat outside and his hair had a tendency to go wild at the slightest provocation. The wind must've been very provoking; that, or he'd been running his fingers through it because he was frustrated with someone. Her perhaps?

"What are you doing back here?"

Her spine stiffened at his churlish tone. She was fed up with his uneven moods and secretiveness. "Thank you for retrieving my bag. Did you return to the train station to find it?"

"We weren't gone that long."

"You were gone long enough to have an extended chat."

When he spied the kitten in his daughter's arms, Fannie tucked it behind her. The poor thing began to yowl. Mr. O'Brien must not allow pets and his daughter had been hiding the kitten. That would explain the baby blanket in the crate.

Rather than let Fannie be the recipient of her father's ire, Victoria squared her shoulders and took the blame. "We found a kitten outside. I told Fannie to bring it in. It's getting colder. An animal that young won't survive if temperatures drop below freezing."

His gaze turned speculative. "Where are the others?"

"Others?"

"There were five kittens and a mother cat."

Victoria turned to Fannie, who was back to hugging the frightened kitten. "That's why you're distressed. They're missing."

Fannie remained silent. She might be afraid her father would get angry because she'd brought the kitten inside. Victoria tensed, ready to leap to the child's defense.

Mr. O'Brien knelt next to the step where his daughter sat, huddled over the remaining kitten. He began to rub the tiny creature's head with his forefinger. "Mama cat moved her litter somewhere, I'll bet. Cats are smart like that. They know when bad weather's coming and make sure their babies are safe."

His low, resonant voice swept over Victoria. Each time he ran his finger over the kitten's head, she could feel it, almost as if he was stroking her. Shivers danced across her skin that had nothing to do with the cold. She stared at his hand, mesmerized.

"The kitten's mother will come back for it. We'll leave the door cracked open and put the crate under the steps so she can find it." Mr. O'Brien had become very gentle with his daughter. He attempted to alleviate her fears, not scold her for them.

Victoria breathed a sigh of relief. She didn't understand why he'd been so grouchy earlier, but she was glad to finally see this side of him. This was the man who had wooed her with tenderness. "Your father is right, Fannie. Mothers are very protective."

He lifted his head. His dark eyes, so like his daughter's, reflected deep distrust. "Not all mothers."

Given his wife's desertion, David O'Brien's lack of faith in motherhood didn't surprise her, but she didn't expect his doubt to be directed at her.

Deep wounds didn't heal overnight, she reminded herself. Given time, he would see and believe in her faithfulness. His proposal proved he was willing to take the chance, a huge step for a man in his situation.

Victoria sat down next to Fannie. The poor child had to be wondering why her mother hadn't stayed, or whether any mother would. "Mothers *should* protect their babies. That's what God intended. But some mothers are selfish, uncaring. I've even heard of mother cats that will reject and abandon a kitten. When that happens, another cat will accept it, unless it only cares for itself, or its own kitten..." as Victoria was painfully aware. "But the cat that wants the abandoned baby will love it like its own."

Fannie raised her head, her mouth drawn in a solemn line.

"Do you understand what I'm saying, about mothers?"

"What Miss Lowell means is, most mothers are good mothers, and stepmothers can be good mothers, too, but it isn't the kitten's fault if they aren't."

Victoria turned an astonished gaze on Mr. O'Brien. She hadn't said that, exactly, but he'd provided a perceptive interpretation. Part of her still ached for approval and acceptance, two things she would never get from her stepmother or her father, no matter what she did or didn't do. As her betrothed had so astutely pointed out, it wasn't *the kitten's fault* they couldn't love her. "You're a wise man, Mr. O'Brien."

"Only when it comes to kittens." He sat on the step on

the other side of Fannie and circled his arm around his daughter. Her shoulders lowered, along with her defenses, and she leaned into him, trustingly.

Victoria longed to embrace them both, only she hadn't been raised in a family that showed affection and wasn't confident enough. Even if a hug would be premature, there was no reason she couldn't affirm him. A compliment might be just what he needed. "I admire a man who is wise in the way of cats. That proves you're intelligent. But I could tell that from reading your letters."

*D*avid reached for the kitten, rather than look Miss Lowell in the eye and admit he was not the author of those letters. It went without saying she wouldn't praise his intelligence if she ever did read anything he wrote.

For her part, she had shown remarkable insight and sensitivity when dealing with a touchy subject: a mother's love. He agreed that giving birth didn't guarantee proper nurturing, his wife being a perfect example of a bad mother. Miss Lowell had strongly implied she would be a good mother. He would withhold judgment until he knew her better.

Fannie twisted away and hugged the mewling kitten to her chest.

"Careful now," he warned. "It's little. You don't want to hurt him. We need to put the kitten back into the crate, so the mama cat can find it."

His daughter shook her head. Curls swung into her face and tears swam in her eyes. She feared losing something she loved. That kind of loss scared him, too.

However, admitting as much would make him appear weak.

Hunched over, Fannie guarded the kitten in her lap. The tiny thing was too small to leave its mother, so he couldn't let her keep it. At the same time, he couldn't bear to see her cry when he removed it. Maybe the gift would distract her.

"Let's see what Miss Lowell has brought you." He leaned forward and met her gaze, his stomach knotting at the admiration shining in those remarkable eyes. She wouldn't look at him like that after he told her the truth. "What's in that bag of yours?"

She looked at the satchel as if she forgot she sent him after it. Her reflective mood persisted as she stood and brushed dirt and grass off her skirt. Perhaps she'd been forced to chase after Fannie on her hands and knees. It wouldn't be the first time someone had done that.

"I wish I'd known you liked kittens," she murmured.

Good grief, she didn't have a dog in that carpetbag, did she?

She bent to open it, and reaching in, withdrew a large object wrapped in what looked like a cashmere shawl. An expensive item of clothing, and she'd used it for packing, more evidence she didn't know the value of a dollar. If she became his wife, she would have to learn to be more frugal.

Fannie's head remained down, but he could see her looking up through her lashes.

David had to admit to curiosity, as well. He rested his wrists on his knees and waited. He should've anticipated Fannie's reaction to a new mother and prepared her. Victoria was smart to bring a peace offering.

She unwound the soft fabric to reveal an exquisite childlike doll. Its pale hair looked real, as did its aqua glass eyes. The head, formed from bisque porcelain, had hand-painted eyebrows and lips. Even the cheeks had a faint pink tinge. The doll looked like a younger version of Victoria, right down to its fashionable clothing.

Fannie gave up being coy. She still held the kitten, but her attention was riveted on the doll.

David recognized it as one of the popular, expensive types made by a French company. Those dolls were luxury items, status symbols purchased by the wealthy. "That's a *Jumeau*," he pointed out.

Miss Lowell gave him a pleased smile. "Yes, you know of them?"

"It's my business to know merchandise. I own a general store."

"Oh, of course, I should've thought before I said something so foolish. You sell dolls."

"Not that kind. My customers can't afford them."

Her smile faltered. She'd interpreted his statement of fact as criticism.

"Very generous of you to give her one." More than generous, giving a six-year-old a costly, fragile doll seemed extravagant, even wasteful. Come to think of it, why would a woman rich enough to purchase an expensive doll as a gift answer a personal ad from a lowly shopkeeper? That was a question he would ask when Fannie wasn't squirming with impatience.

"Would you like to hold her?" Miss Lowell asked.

Fannie's eager expression said she would. She wouldn't ask for it, though. She'd sit there longing to hold it without saying a word.

David gave in and made it easier on her. "Let me hold the kitten while you look at the doll."

Fannie scooped up the kitten and nestled it into David's

cupped hands. He stroked the whiskered cheek with this thumb while she eagerly reached for her gift.

She cradled the doll, fingering the shiny curls and silk ribbons dangling from the bonnet. With the tip of her finger, she traced a bowed mouth. Her lips lifted in response.

If David hadn't been holding the kitten, he would've kissed Miss Victoria Lowell. She'd made Fannie smile. That was something he hadn't been able to do since his wife left.

A loud meow echoed in the storeroom. The kitten in his hand stirred, started crying.

"The mother cat. She's in here somewhere." Victoria started for the rear of the store. She peered around a pickle barrel, providing a nice view of her bustled backside. "Kitty, kitty? Where are you?"

David dragged his attention away from the lovely scenery and stood. "It's coming from over there." He indicated the far wall where canned goods lined multiple shelves. Handing Victoria the kitten, he made his way past barrels and crates, following the cries. He pushed aside a stack of boxes. The mother cat emerged from behind them, winding her lithe body around his leg.

The gray and white tabby had shown up on the doorstep one day and Fannie had wanted to make it a pet. As a boy, he'd been scratched by a cat and had gotten deathly ill. He told her to leave it outside. Undaunted, Fannie continued to open the back door and let the cat in. He would find it and put it out. When it became apparent the cat would birth a litter, he'd provided an empty crate and put it outside, with a stern warning to Fannie that he would take the cat somewhere far away if she left the door open again.

The cat gave another plaintive meow.

Much as he didn't like cats, David was relieved this one had made an appearance. In spite of his reassurances to Fannie, he hadn't been certain some hungry coyote hadn't gotten to the stray. "Looking for something?" he asked the meowing cat.

Victoria lowered the kitten to the floor. "Here you go, safe and sound."

The tabby and her orange kitten touched noses. The kitten began to mew, and the mother immediately started licking it.

Victoria laughed. The sound of spontaneous joy was something David hadn't heard in a long time, something he'd like to hear more often. She leaned over, addressing the cat. "Don't worry, your baby is fine. Fannie took good care of him."

Faint meows came from beneath the lowest shelf mounted on the brick wall. David bent to take a look. The four other kittens crawled across a pile of rags, tumbling over each other in their haste to find their mother. The resourceful cat had gotten inside again—no doubt after Fannie left the door open—and relocated her litter to a warmer spot.

David came to his feet. He couldn't fault the cat's determination to protect her brood, nor did he have the heart to scold Fannie for her dogged disobedience on their behalf. He lifted his hands. "I give up. You may stay inside."

The cat meowed and led her kitten away with her nose in the air, showing David what she thought of his decision to throw her out in the first place.

A sound came from behind him, a giggle. Startled, he twisted around.

Fannie had the doll folded against her chest and a big smile on her face.

Saints be praised, that giggle had come from her!

His lips lifted with no effort as he turned with gratitude

to Victoria. He felt a bit ashamed for his judgmental thoughts concerning her extravagance. Had he realized what a special gift might mean to his daughter, he would've gladly spent whatever it cost. "Thank you for giving Fannie the doll. You've made her very happy."

"Oh, I hope so. I thought long and hard about what I should give her. I'm glad you're pleased." Victoria's eyes shone with relief and, heaven help him, sweet affection.

She might wish to please him now, but what about later, when he didn't meet her expectations. It had taken him too long to realize Rachel had only married him to escape poverty. Then she'd left when she found someone who promised an easier life. Victoria came from wealth and was used to ease. She had all the more reason to resent hard work and sacrifice. He'd been blind to Rachel's faithlessness, and he might be equally blind to Victoria's faults if he allowed himself to care too much. He couldn't take that risk. If he married her, he would have to guard against the temptation to fall in love.

"LET ME TAKE YOUR BAGS UPSTAIRS." David reached for her suitcase, the heart-stopping smile vanishing as if it had never been there. "I'll show you to your room. Then we'll get you something to eat. I'm sure you're famished."

Her stomach rumbled. Famished, yes, and tired. She wasn't sure which she wanted more, food or sleep. He'd said her room was upstairs. The implications took a moment to reassemble inside her tired brain. They lived above the store?

Victoria turned to ask Fannie, but the girl had already run off, perhaps to show her aunt the new doll. Fannie's delight with the gift went a long way toward easing Victoria's fears. The doll had been a gift from her mother and was her favorite. The look of wonder on Fannie's face made giving away the precious *Bébé* worth it.

Hiking her skirts, Victoria followed her future husband up the steep stairs. Fatigue had set in and she could hardly lift her feet. She longed to have a nice dinner, take a bath and curl up on an actual mattress stuffed with cotton. Even sharing a bed with one person would an improvement over jostling with dozens of passengers for berths provided in the rail cars.

Mr. O'Brien's slight limp was more noticeable when he had to negotiate steps, especially while carrying heavy items. He hadn't mentioned the disfigurement in his letter. It made no difference. Everyone had imperfections. Some just showed more than others. However, she wouldn't repeat the mistake of offering to help him carry her bags. He might snap at her again.

In some ways, he reminded her of an old turtle she'd discovered at a pond near her home. The grumpy tortoise would poke his head out every so often, sometimes let her touch him, but the slightest perceived danger would send him back inside his shell.

Mr. O'Brien reached a narrow landing. He unlocked a door, swung it open, and then waited.

She preceded him into an apartment. The central room was furnished with a sofa, stuffed chairs, scattered tables and a set of shelves stuffed with books. Nothing fancy, but comfortable, the kind of place where a family might gather.

A pleasant chime sounded from a glass-domed clock on the mantle. Its pendulum—four chrome balls on ornate spokes hanging from a thin wire—gleamed as it spun clockwise then counterclockwise. Her father had purchased one of the anniversary clocks when they first appeared, saying the miraculous new devices would run for more than a year without intervention. He collected clocks, automatons, wind up toys; he was far more interested in mechanical marvels than he was in human beings. David hadn't seemed like that in his letters. He'd come across as interested in her thoughts, as well as respectful and understanding of her feelings. She'd seen glimmers of that man since arriving, infrequent, but enough to know he existed.

"Follow me." Mr. O'Brien moved past her with the suitcases. He went down a short hall and into a bedroom.

The furnishings were simple, almost sparse: a four-poster bed with a cheerful blue and white coverlet, a tall wardrobe, dresser and dressing table complete with pitcher and basin. Over the window, a heavy drape was drawn back to reveal sheer lace curtains. The view was the wall of the adjacent building.

The bedroom reminded Victoria of the upstairs rooms her family provided for servants. This might be an apartment Mr. O'Brien rented out, and he decided it would be more appropriate to put her here instead of taking her into his home before they were married. Or he might not have room in his house, as his sister wasn't leaving until after Christmas.

He set the tapestry satchel on the table and lifted the large case onto a chair. "Fannie's room is across the hall."

With that, he snuffed out Victoria's vision of a nice house and a green lawn.

She straightened with determination. What did she care where they lived, so long as they loved each other. David O'Brien wouldn't have written those letters, or asked her be his wife, if he didn't long for love. She simply had to find the right key to unlock his heart.

"You'll room with Maggie—until she leaves." The hooded look he gave Victoria set off a tingling sensation beneath her skin.

Not knowing how to respond, she hugged her arms. She'd never had these physical reactions with Bertram, not even when he'd pressed her for a kiss. He'd told her men viewed sexual relations as the primary advantage of marriage, outside of procreation. Proper women weren't supposed to know about such things, much less dwell on them. She must not be proper, because seeing her future husband standing in the bedroom where they would consummate their marriage set off all sorts of improper thoughts.

He returned to where she remained glued to the threshold and stood close enough she could make out fine lines beside his eyes. Laugh lines. She hadn't seen him laugh, yet there was the evidence he had smiled and laughed a great deal at one time. Whether she could find a way to bring laughter back into his life remained to be seen. He'd smiled when Fannie giggled, a relieved, grateful smile. She would think of ways to coax other smiles out of him.

His well-shaped lips captured her attention, and a slight cleft beneath his lower lip where he had missed shaving a spot of dark bristle. She couldn't recall noticing Bertram's facial hair, if he had any. The dark shadow on Mr. O'Brien's face looked very manly. She suspected he shaved daily, even down his neck. Did the same dark hair grow on his chest? Would it feel rough, or smooth?

"Miss Lowell?" One of his dark eyebrows arched in a query. "Is this arrangement agreeable?"

She jerked her gaze from his chest to his eyes. Thank

heavens he couldn't read her mind. "Yes. Thank you. It's fine."

A worrisome thought struck. Were the facilities inside, or out? She'd read that many families out west still used outhouses. That must be what they meant by the term *roughing it*.

"Where...where are the...where do we...?"

"There's a bathtub and toilet at the end of the hall."

Indoors, thank God.

The corner of his mouth curled up in a half-smile. "We're almost civilized."

Her nerves jumped. He *could* read her thoughts. No, he couldn't. He was just teasing her again. "I'm so glad to hear it. I was afraid I might have to live in a tepee."

His smile broadened.

Oh heavens. Dimples.

Her insides melted faster than butter on hot toast. Quite possibly, he had this effect on all women, if he smiled at them like that. He had better not. From now on, she wanted those smiles directed only at her.

As she stared at him, smitten, his expression underwent a transformation. First, the smile fell away. Then the amused light in his eyes became a blaze, which drew her like a moth, helpless to resist. The attraction grew stronger as he stepped closer. Exciting, but also a bit frightening.

"Mr. O'Brien." She managed his name, in a hushed whisper.

"David," he corrected. Even his voice set off vibrations.

He cradled her face in his hands with the same gentleness he'd shown the kitten. "Victoria."

"Hmm?" If she rubbed her cheek against his palm, he might stroke her. That would be nice.

"Your eyes are very expressive."

"Are they?"

"Aye, and right now, they're begging me to kiss you." Before she could reply, he dipped his head and brought his lips to hers. A soft touch at first, and then with firmer pressure; warm and lush and so...

Her eyelids fluttered shut. *Oh my.* He did the most amazing things with his lips...delightful things...electrifying and soothing at the same time. That didn't seem possible, but she was too muddled to analyze it. Lured by the exotic sensations, she didn't think it strange when he put his tongue inside her mouth and teased hers into a seductive dance.

This was how he kissed? Bertram's dry pecks didn't compare with David's sumptuous mouth-to-mouth exploration.

As he deepened the kiss, her head grew light. She teetered at the edge of a cliff; something wild and wicked urged her to step off. His fingers tightened around her upper arms. She was glad he had a firm enough grip to uphold her else she might hurtle into the unknown.

Trusting him to protect her, Victoria lost herself in the glorious kiss. She had no idea how long she stood there, allowing David to ravish her mouth.

Slowly, he ended it, their lips clinging until the last moment. Still holding her arms, he gazed at her with a smoldering look that made her insides quiver.

"Kiss me again," she whispered.

"Victoria." Her name rumbled up from his chest, sounding rough, as though it hurt him to say it. For once, his eyes spoke for him. His hungry gaze, as well as his heated kisses, made it clear he yearned to possess her, but something held him back. She wished she believed it was chivalry, but that wasn't what she saw. He distrusted her, even after she'd let him kiss her until her toes curled.

She ought to push him away. Only that wouldn't work in her favor. He would withdraw into his shell and the frustrating cycle would start again. She had to break through his resistance, but how? The answer came with surprising clarity. Reluctant lovers needed to be wooed.

Generally, men did the wooing and women responded. She wasn't sure how it was done or if she had the courage, but she had to try. This might be the key to winning his heart. If she could convince him to lower his barriers, he would learn to love her.

Take the risk, her heart urged.

She reached up and cupped his jaw in her palm, as he'd done to her. His lower lip, so inviting, she couldn't resist running her thumb over the smooth flesh. Taking another bold step, she drew his head down and pressed her mouth to his. She wasn't certain she was doing this properly, but he'd given her excellent instruction, so she applied what she'd learned.

He groaned—a sound that could mean pain or pleasure. Grasping her shoulders, he brought her closer, taking her mouth with greater mastery than before. Pleasure, she decided.

A moment later, he propelled her backwards into the bedroom.

Her legs struck the bed. She fell while still holding onto him, dragging him down with her. He caught himself on his arms, perhaps to avoid crushing her, but he didn't even try to prevent pressing his hips intimately against hers.

He ground himself against her, all the while kissing her with wild abandon.

The barriers had certainly come down, and in the

process her defenses were laid to waste. Any thoughts of resisting were swept away in wave after wave of sensation.

Passion surged like the ocean in the midst of a raging storm. In this instance, she wasn't observing the tempest from the safety of a high point. She'd jumped with both feet into the churning sea. Fierce currents pulled her under, but instead of drowning, she sank into a pleasurable realm where her entire world narrowed to one man.

She plunged her fingers into her betrothed's thick hair, fondling feather-soft curls, dragging her nails over his scalp until he moaned along with her. Heaven help her, she wanted nothing more than to have him initiate her into lovemaking. In fact, she just might insist on it.

The snick of a door and a patter of footsteps penetrated her sensual stupor.

Her mind lurched back to reality. Frantic, she shoved at his shoulders. "David, someone's here," she cried against his mouth.

As he drew back he looked dazed and then alarmed as the sound drew closer. He twisted around at the same time she stretched her neck to look over his shoulder.

Fannie stood in the doorway, wide-eyed, clutching her doll.

Victoria gasped. Horrified, she pushed at David's chest. "Get off!"

He scrambled to free her, but in his haste, slipped and tumbled over the side of the bed. When he came up off the floor, his face had darkened to deep red. His brows knitted into a heavy scowl and his hair stuck out every which way from having her fingers buried in it. He looked fierce, frightening.

Fannie reacted with the quick instincts of a doe. She whirled and dashed away.

"Stop, Fannie, wait," he bellowed.

"No, don't—" Victoria grabbed for David's arm, and missed. He had a right to be furious, she'd all but invited him to ravish her, but it wasn't Fannie's fault, and the child shouldn't be chastised for a foolish woman's mistake. "Don't go after her angry, please. She doesn't understand."

David paused at the door and stood there a moment. He didn't turn around, as if he couldn't bear to look at her. "That makes two of us."

CHAPTER 5

*D*avid found Fannie in the far corner of the storeroom, huddled near the kittens. She held tight to the doll Victoria had given her. Not surprisingly, she said nothing. He didn't have much to say either, couldn't begin to explain his inexcusable behavior to a six-year-old. Instead, he sat on his heels next to her and petted the cat.

"Didn't mean to frighten you. I was...helping Miss Lowell get settled. We fell." His neck grew warm at the lie. They wouldn't have fallen if he hadn't pushed Victoria into bed. What had possessed him to do such a thing?

Fannie's expressionless mask didn't tell him what was going through her head, so he had to guess. His daughter must be confused. Hell, *he* was confused.

Victoria blushed like an innocent, but kissed like a hoyden. Surprise was too mild a word for what had jolted through him when she'd kissed him. The combination of sweetness and fervor had the same effect as a strong opiate. Had they been able to finish what they'd started, he felt certain he would've gone to seventh heaven. Thankfully, he hadn't ascended that far before Fannie showed up. But he'd gone far enough.

Fannie had appeared surprised, maybe even a little curious. She was too young to understand what went on between men and women, and he didn't intend to enlighten her anytime soon. Maybe never.

He hadn't told her of his plan to marry again because he hadn't done anything about it and saw no reason to upset her. Now, Victoria was here, he'd admitted publicly she would be his wife, so that's what they needed to talk about.

"You like Miss Lowell, don't you?"

Fannie shook her head, but at the same time hugged the doll tight.

So, she wasn't sure how she felt about Victoria. He wasn't sure how he felt either, not entirely. Except for lust, that feeling he knew for a fact, as it still pulsed through him. But that wasn't something he'd be discussing with his daughter.

"If you want to like her, that's all right. I like her—" David caught himself, not quick enough. Granted, he did like Victoria, but he didn't want to give Fannie the idea that liking was related to what he and Victoria were doing on the bed.

He propped his hands on his knees. Get to the subject. He and Victoria would soon share a bed. Maybe sooner than he'd planned, considering. He had better prepare Fannie. "Miss Lowell and I plan to be married."

Fannie acted like she wasn't listening. She scooped up the orange tabby. Startled, it swiped at her and caught the doll's hair in its claws. With a shocked gasp, she yanked the doll away. The kitten hung on for dear life.

"Here, stop pulling. It's just scared of falling." David gently removed the kitten's claws and set it down. The little fur ball dashed off in search of its mother. That kitten wasn't the only one afraid of a hard fall.

David scrubbed his fingers through his hair. How the devil had he become infatuated with Victoria when she hadn't even been here a full day? Admittedly, she was beautiful, and she'd been kind to Fannie. Other pretty women had been kind, and he hadn't wanted to kiss any of them.

Fannie stood, clutching her dolly, and took off back inside the store, running to her aunt. She rarely ran to him when she was scared, maybe because he wasn't very good at offering comfort. She needed a woman's touch. All the more reason he had to work things out with Victoria. For the time being, though, there was no point in pushing Fannie to accept a new mother. She liked the doll. After she got used to Victoria, she would like her, too.

A creak came from the staircase.

He stiffened.

"David?" Hearing Victoria call his name released a tendril of excitement. She'd said it so sweetly when she'd begged him to kiss her.

Upstairs, he'd noticed her eyeing him with interest. He had to admit that felt good, especially after Rachel had damn near emasculated him when she left him for another man. He'd only intended to give Victoria a chaste kiss. That intention had flown right out the window the moment she let him taste her. When she'd begged him for more, he'd stopped thinking.

"I'm over here." He had to make his way around boxes to get to the stairs, and by the time he reached her, she had made it to the bottom step.

Standing on a six-inch riser, she still wasn't at eye level.

So dainty. He should've considered that before he shoved her into the bedroom and climbed on top of her.

She peered anxiously in the direction of the door leading into the store. "Did you find Fannie? Is she all right?"

"Everything's fine. I explained." At Victoria's look of horror, he quickly amended just what he'd *explained*. "Only that we'll soon be married. About the other, like you said, she doesn't understand."

"Thank goodness." Victoria kept her gaze averted. Embarrassment? She hadn't seemed to have that problem earlier. She tucked back a golden strand, one of several loosened from the heavy knot atop her head. "Do you suppose she might've thought we were wrestling?"

At least one of them could joke about it.

"I should've let you do the explaining, that makes more sense than what I said—that I was helping you and we fell.

She cast her eyes downward. "I'm so ashamed. The way I behaved..."

"Don't be." He didn't want her to regret her attraction to him. She'd given him back his confidence. He'd been sleepwalking through life until she came along. "I'm the one who should apologize."

She finally raised her eyes and looked very relieved. "You won't think poorly of me for—"

"Letting me kiss you? No. I enjoyed it. Very much."

"So did I." Her lips curved upward. His body throbbed with painful readiness.

Without thinking, he took her arms and drew her closer for another kiss. There was no reason they had to wait until Christmas, considering he'd compromised her.

Or had he?

He stopped, inches from her lips, as his brain fought to

regain control. The scandal she'd mentioned, somewhat vaguely. Quite possibly, she was already compromised. That would explain her desire for a hurried wedding and why she'd thrown herself at him.

His chest tightened until breathing became difficult. He released her and took a step back, frantically calculating how long it had been since she'd responded to the advertisement. Six months? She'd be too far along to hide a pregnancy, and her stomach looked flat. Not to mention, he'd been sprawled on top of her. He would've noticed a bump.

"David?"

He jerked his gaze to her face, and her blush deepened. From innocence, or guilt?

"Come with me." He would take her to his office. Everyone within earshot didn't need to hear them when he demanded she explain what she'd meant by *scandal*.

"What's wrong?" Victoria easily slid through the narrow space between the file drawers and his desk. A pregnant woman wouldn't fit. So, she might not be carrying an illegitimate child, but it was possible she'd engaged in an affair and that's why she'd been jilted.

"There's something I need to ask you...have a seat." He offered her the only chair, and then leaned back against the edge of the desk.

"What is it?" She curled her hands in her lap, gazing up at him, heartbreakingly anxious.

His determination wavered. Oddly enough, he wasn't angry as much as disappointed. He understood why she wouldn't want anyone to know about her dalliance. It was possible she had simply trusted the wrong man. Confronting her about the loss of her innocence would be hurtful. If he'd guessed wrong, she would be so offended she would never forgive him, and he would've thrown away a golden opportunity.

VICTORIA'S TEETH chattered on account of the cold office, or a bad case of nerves. David was staring at her hands, or looking at her lap. While she stood on the stairs, he'd been ogling her midsection, possibly her breasts. Embarrassment drove away the remaining chill.

"You never told me why you answered a matrimonial advertisement." His question came out of the blue, and had no bearing on what had just happened.

Nevertheless, she would answer, and hopefully address whatever it was that had caused him to stop. She yearned for another kiss, but he was obviously in no mood for kissing, so she rested her hands on her knees and sat up straight, as she'd been taught.

"My father has investments in a number of factories. One of them, a shirt factory, burned down in August...or was it September?" She couldn't think clearly with David frowning at her.

"I went to see if I could help the seamstresses who were put out of work. All of them are young women, many are single, and some are supporting children. One poor young woman—Gabrielle—had been abused by her stepfather, so she'd left home and gone to work at the factory. She had nowhere to turn if she couldn't support herself. She was desperate."

"The owner was unwilling to assist them, even though he told my father they'd be taken care of, so I made a donation out of my own funds. I didn't realize at the time how much cash I might need later. But that's not the point. I befriended the manager, Roberta McDaniel…"

Victoria gazed at one of the filing drawers, trying to sort through a jumble of memories on top of worries. "Dear Roberta, she's very dedicated to the workers, and concerned about her friends. She recommended that the ladies consider answering advertisements from men looking to marry, become mail-order brides. I should write to her, find out how she's fared with her groom in Wisconsin. A dairy farmer, I believe. I told her I'd selected a shopkeeper. I don't think I could bring myself to milk cows…"

"What are you talking about?" David's gruff voice snapped her attention to his dark, suspicious gaze.

She didn't like the way he'd directed her to the chair and then leaned against the desk, which made it seem like he was looking down at her. "I am answering your question. How I obtained a copy of the *Grooms' Gazette*. It came from Miss McDaniel, only she would be a Mrs. now."

How bravely that young woman had faced her unknown fate.

"Miss McDaniel's courage convinced me to take my destiny into my own hands. She even allowed me to use her apartment address, so my family wouldn't find your letters. I thought starting over as a mail-order bride would be good for me."

Actually, she imagined it would be romantic, and it had been, when she received David's first letter. She waited, hoping he might respond by affirming his affections.

Instead, he folded his arms across his chest. If only he'd put them around her as he had before, so she wouldn't think he despised her. "You left a fortune behind to answer an ad from a divorced shopkeeper."

No, she'd left a fortune behind for a man she thought might love her.

She looked down, feeling foolish and discouraged. He had revived her hopes and dreams through his letters. Just moments ago, they'd shared the most magical kiss. Now he acted like she'd done something wrong. She didn't understand the reason for his ire, and his distrust was breaking her heart. "I left because of the scandal I told you about. My former fiancé jilted me, and then he married my sister. He shamed and humiliated me. How could I stay after that?"

When David didn't answer, she lifted her head to look at him.

His scowl had softened. "Why didn't your father defend your honor?"

She wrung her hands in her lap. Her father's indifference had always hurt her, but it was his betrayal she would never get over. "My father wanted his first-born to be a son. He told my mother as much, said he had no use for a female heir. She took me away and they were estranged until she died. Less than a year later, he remarried a woman who had a son and a daughter. He adopted them and gave his full attention to grooming Charles. My stepmother doted on Louisa. She virtually ignored me—until Bertram paid me suit. Then she turned positively mean. I realized later it was because she wanted Bertram to marry Louisa. I'm sure she had a hand in getting them together. They had an *affaire de coeur*. When they were caught, they had to marry."

The surprise on David's face drove a nail through Victoria's heart. Now she understood why he acted as if she'd wronged him.

"Did you presume I was the one at fault? Why? Because I kissed you?" She swallowed the urge to cry. No, she would not break down. She should never have tried to woo David. Despite his reassurances, it was obvious he believed the worst about her. Well, if he wanted the whole ugly truth, he would have it.

"My father didn't believe me either, and I gave him less reason to doubt me. He accepted my stepmother's story when she told him I'd driven Bertram away, and he threatened to marry me off to one of his business associates. That's why I had to get away from him. But I wouldn't have agreed to this marriage if I hadn't thought you..."

No, she refused to humiliate herself further by admitting to her romantic notions, or making excuses for her foolish behavior.

"Victoria, I..." David shook his head.

He still didn't believe her. The crack in her heart widened.

"Bertram pressed me for more than I was willing to give. Then he told all his friends I was the one who broke off the engagement because I disliked the prospect of marital relations." She met David's horrified gaze. What a disaster she'd brought about by kissing him. Really, she should've known better. "Ironic, isn't it? With you, I behaved like a wanton, and Bertram thinks I'm a cold fish."

DAVID KNELT at Victoria's side. He laid his hand on the arm of the chair, didn't dare touch her after what he'd put her through. Her shoulders were slumped. She looked beaten. Defeated. No wonder she hadn't shared these things in a letter. She'd been abused and shamed by the very people who should have loved and protected her. Hot rage coursed through him at the thought of Victoria's father forcing her to wed some lecher twice her age.

"Your father is an ass."

She slid a wounded glance in his direction. "I won't argue that."

"And Bertram ought to be horsewhipped."

"Are you volunteering to do the honors?"

"Gladly."

The half-smile melted away as her expression slid back into sadness. "I fear I've given you the wrong impression. There's nothing I can do to prove my innocence."

Guilt gnawed at his gut. Victoria had come out here thinking he believed in her. He could tell her he hadn't written those letters, but what good would that do? It would only make her feel worse, and more alone than ever.

"You don't have to prove anything." He shifted to one knee. "I don't think you're wanton." He couldn't leave it at that. "You aren't cold, either. Far from it."

She stared off at some far point, at a place in her memory. "Everyone believed Bertram, not me. I was so humiliated. There was no one I could turn to. At one point, I considered ending my life."

Her life must've been hell if she'd been willing to languish in purgatory. The thought of it sent an awful chill through him. He grasped the chair arm with both hands. "Don't even consider doing something like that."

She straightened into the prim posture she'd adopted earlier. "Lowells don't commit suicide. It just isn't done."

A regretful smile tugged at his lips. She had faced rejection and humiliation, and still she kept her chin up along with a sense of humor. "Forgive me for doubting you. I understand now why you did what you did. You must've been desperate."

Her brow furrowed and the hurt returned to her eyes. "Do you really think so little of me?"

"No, no, of course not. I meant..." He'd done it again, insulted her without meaning to, and she wasn't the desperate one, anyway. He had to find a good mother for Fannie. That was the most important thing, and he couldn't lose sight of it. If Victoria's success thus far with the doll was any indication, his sister's mail-order bride could be exactly what he was looking for—if he didn't drive her away first.

"Victoria, I don't think poorly of you." He wasn't gifted with words, but he could come up with something better than that. "On the contrary, I think you're brave and beautiful, and...you've already made Fannie happy."

She searched his eyes with frank appraisal. "I'm glad I've contributed to Fannie's happiness. But I can assure you, Mr. O'Brien, I am not so desperate I'd marry a man who distrusts me."

CHAPTER 6

*E*arly the next morning, David left the apartment. Victoria hadn't stirred. He didn't knock to let her know he was leaving, telling himself she needed her sleep after a long, exhausting day. Not only that, he wasn't sure how to undo the damage he'd done.

He had given into his suspicions rather than trusting his deeper instincts. There was a reason he'd been drawn to her. She had an innate kindness and sensitivity, something he lacked. He had sensed she would be good with Fannie, and he wouldn't easily find another woman like her.

Now, he might lose her.

He'd insulted her by doubting her innocence. She would lose what little faith remained when he told her he wasn't the one who had won her trust to begin with. He wasn't sure what he should do. Tell her the truth and hope for the best, or let her get over this latest offense before he broke her heart again.

He took his usual route down Wall Street, an ambitious nod to the better-known financial district in New York. The heels of his shoes rapped against the brick pavement as he crossed the street and passed the railroad land office, located next door to his landlord.

Yesterday had been the first of the month; the day David paid his rent. In all the commotion, he'd forgotten about it. He'd never been late on a payment before, and he vowed he never would be again. Promptness demonstrated respect, and he owed Mr. O'Connor both.

Eight years ago, when he'd approached the wealthy businessman about renting the property where his parents' store had sat, O'Connor had given him generous terms, and offered to advise him. David valued their friendship, and he considered Buck O'Connor the closest thing he had to a father.

As usual, Mr. O'Connor invited him in, offered coffee and launched into conversation. Their meetings generally ran an hour or more, and not just because his landlord had a gregarious nature. He always took time to inquire about how David's business was going and provide helpful suggestions.

Today, David didn't have time for an extended visit. He had to get back to the store, and to Victoria. He hadn't mentioned his upcoming nuptials, not wanting to get into an even longer discussion. After the pleasantries, he stood to take his leave.

He laid an envelope on the desk. "Here's the rent for this month. I apologize it's a day late. I'll have the money for the building next door by the first of the year."

"See that you do, and don't be using a bride as your excuse for being late next month." O'Connor's craggy face didn't crack. Not even a hint of a smile. His pale eyes, however, gleamed with amusement.

"I take it you've been talking to Phineas Gregg."

"His wife posted a public notice in the Gulf depot."

O'Connor said with a deadpan expression.

He stood, a towering figure at well over six feet, and came around the desk. The man had to be over fifty, but he still moved with youthful energy. His fair hair, mostly white now, was as thick and unruly as David's, and also brushed his collar. He frequently went around with his shirtsleeves rolled up over ropy forearms, and he preferred leather vests to three-piece suits. He also wore a gun.

David had never seen him use the firearm, but he'd heard talk of a checkered past. Confederate guerilla, outlaw, spy for the Settlers' Land League—those were only a few of Mr. O'Connor's previous *occupations*. He'd settled down twenty years ago with a wealthy widow, who was a fascinating character in her own right, having lost and made several fortunes. The couple lived in a grand manor on the rich side of town.

"Congratulations." The taller man gripped David's shoulder and put out his hand.

David grasped the calloused palm in a firm shake. "Thank you, sir."

"When's the big day?"

"Christmas Eve."

O'Connor stepped back and arched a sandy eyebrow. "You don't look too happy."

David didn't quite know how to respond. He'd been very content for a short time yesterday, when he'd kissed Victoria. Before everything went to hell.

"It's complicated."

His mentor gave a sharp laugh. "Don't know of a marriage that isn't. Mine didn't start out simple. Would've been a sight easier if we both weren't so bull headed. I wouldn't have it any other way, though. Amy, she's my..." He seemed to search for the right word.

David offered a favorite maxim. "Your better half?"

The older man's attention sharpened. "Better than what? She sure as hell didn't have much to work with, but she took me on anyway. Amy gave me a heart. She gave me back my life. There's no half to it. Without her, I wouldn't be whole." His lips twisted in wry smile. "That doesn't mean it can't get complicated from time to time."

The poignant tribute from a rough-around-the-edges wisecracker came as a surprise.

"I never took you for a poet."

"Poet?" O'Connor chuckled. "I can't rub two words together that rhyme."

"That may be, but if I'd come up with something as inspiring as that little speech, Victoria might not be on the fence."

"She's having second thoughts?"

"Second, third, maybe more…" David wandered over to the bookcase, not really looking for anything. He wasn't sure how much he wanted to share, even with his mentor. "I haven't handled things well. But in my defense, I didn't even know there was a bride on the way until yesterday morning when she arrived."

"Boyo, that does sound complicated." O'Connor settled his hip on the corner of the desk and crossed his arms. "Think you better have a seat and let's talk."

David trusted Mr. O'Connor, but he wasn't comfortable going into the details of his personal life, or Victoria's. "Can't today. I have to get back to the store."

"Fair enough." O'Connor came to his feet. He handed David the envelope with the rent money. "Here, take this, consider it a wedding gift, and I'll throw in the first month's rent on the adjoining building."

"That's not necessary." David didn't want charity and

tried to return the money.

His landlord wouldn't take it. "Be sure and tell me if there's anything else you need."

The man's generosity was too much, and yet he wouldn't be refused. David returned the envelope to his pocket. "Thank you, sir. I can never repay you for all you've done for me."

"Don't expect you to." O'Connor picked up a framed photograph off the desk, a picture of his wife. As he gazed at it, his rugged face softened. "Over the years, people have done things for me that I couldn't repay, not if I had all the money in the world. Consider it a gift...sort of like having the love of a good woman."

David nodded, not wanting to say that for him love hadn't been a gift, but a curse. He sensed things could be different with Victoria, if she was willing to take him as he was and not as she expected him to be. That could only happen if he told her the truth.

He stopped on his way to the door and retrieved his bowler. "You said things started off rocky with Mrs. O'Connor."

His mentor grinned. "Sure, if you call a canyon rocky."

"What kept you apart?"

"Secrets."

Of all the coincidences... David threaded his fingers through his hair and secured his hat. Maybe it wasn't coincidence he'd ended up here today. "That's my problem, too. There's something important I need to tell Victoria. I fear when she finds out, she'll cry off."

O'Connor's expression turned solemn. "Can you keep this secret for the rest of your life without it ruining your marriage?"

That was worth considering. "Possibly, I don't know."

His mentor set the framed photograph back on his desk. His walls were decorated with more pictures of his wife and children. Unusual, considering businessmen generally framed professional certificates or articles about their accomplishments. Looking around, it would seem O'Connor considered his greatest accomplishment his family. That was another reason David liked him so well.

The family man folded his arms over his chest, a casual pose, but there was something in his face that hinted at strain. "When I met Amy, my life was one big lie. I knew if she discovered my secrets, she'd hate me. That was all there was to it. So I didn't tell her. But lies have a way of catching up, no matter how fast we run. Amy did find me out, and I was right, she hated me. For lying, for what she thought I'd done, for letting her care about me without knowing who and what I really was. I reckoned she would hate me forever, and I deserved it. But she didn't."

David turned back, riveted by the story. "Why not?"

"She forgave me."

Forgiveness? There had to be more to it.

"That sounds too simple."

"Oh, there's nothing simple about it." O'Connor strolled over and opened the door. "You let me know if you need any more advice. I'm not lacking in mistakes I could share."

David appreciated the man's dry humor, and was grateful for his mentor's willingness to reveal personal struggles. It took courage for a man to admit to being dishonorable and credit a woman for turning his life around. Before now, David had never misled a woman, much less lied. He'd done the right thing to the best of his ability. But when it came to love, being right hadn't gotten him very far.

He shook his mentor's hand again. "Thank you. This

isn't the first time I've come to you for advice, and I daresay it won't be the last. I'll try not to make the same mistakes."

O'Connor's eyes flashed with amusement. "Oh, you will. Just be sure you apologize properly."

VICTORIA POKED her head out from under the covers and blinked at the bright daylight. Maggie had left the room while it was still dark, which seemed like the middle of the night but was probably just an unholy hour of the morning.

Brrrr. Either the building wasn't equipped with gas furnaces, or the tightfisted shopkeeper chose not to light them. David didn't turn up the lamps. He doled out wood like it was gold. He was as miserly with his resources as he was with his smiles. How surprising that he'd proposed without asking the price first.

Shivering, Victoria dug through her suitcase and dressed quickly. She wouldn't want him to think she was lazy, as well as loose. Being so bold as to kiss him might've given him reason to question her judgment, but she hadn't imagined he would believe the worst about her.

If she didn't have his letters she might not believe he was the same person who'd asked for her hand. He couldn't write such moving prose and not have a romantic soul. For some reason, he'd kept it hidden since she'd arrived. Or somewhere along the way he'd changed his mind about her.

She lovingly tucked the packet of letters beneath the clothes in her suitcase. The man who'd written them existed, so that meant he must've had a change of heart. She had to find out why, and determine if she could fix whatever had gone wrong.

After finishing a covered plate of food left in the kitchen,

Victoria made her way downstairs. In the muted conversation drifting to the back of the building, she didn't hear David's voice, and when she entered the store, she didn't see him, either. He had mentioned having errands this morning, but he hadn't wakened her to say goodbye—another indication his ardor had cooled.

Maggie stood behind the counter waiting on a customer who held a fretful infant. Fannie, who'd been sitting at a small table near the stove, scurried over to her aunt.

Victoria's spirits sank further. Even David's daughter was not interested in greeting her. However, she could understand that reaction. She hadn't wanted a stepmother either—and hers hadn't offered gifts.

The pot-bellied stove, at least, offered a warm welcome. She stood behind it and held her hands near the radiant heat. The checkerboard set up on an overturned barrel remained untouched. Could Fannie be coaxed into a game? It was hard to know what might please her when she wouldn't speak.

The bell jangled as the customer left.

"Good morning, Victoria," Maggie called out. "How are you feeling today?"

"Human. Last evening, I'm sure I was a bear."

"Not a full grown bear. Maybe a snarly cub." Maggie smiled and handed Victoria an apron. "Here, put this on. That's a dressy outfit. You don't want to ruin it."

Victoria glanced down at her green wool jacket, plaid skirt and black button-up boots. Perhaps the silver clasp would qualify as *dressy*, but the rest of it? "This is one of my practical ensembles."

"Practical?" Maggie chortled. "This..." She gestured to a gray wool dress beneath the white apron. "...is what I call practical."

Victoria drew a similar apron over her head. "If you have one of those dresses available in the store, I'll take it. I didn't bring one along." Truth be told, she didn't have anything that drab in her entire wardrobe.

Maggie's smile turned wry as if she'd read Victoria's mind. "I'm sure we can find you something suitable."

David's sister could've made her feel foolish, but Maggie had been nothing but welcoming. That might be because she was eager to leave and therefore glad David had found someone who could take care of Fannie. Nevertheless, she deserved thanks.

"I appreciate all you've done, sharing your room, cooking." Victoria hugged her future sister-in-law. Maggie, at least, welcomed her affection. "The biscuits and ham were delicious. Thank you for leaving me a plate."

Maggie waved off her thanks. "It wasn't much. I would've done more, but I woke up late. David had to go meet our landlord this morning, and then it started snowing early."

"It's snowing?" Victoria eagerly crossed to the front window. Sure enough, a thin white layer covered the ground, and more delicate flakes drifted down. The snowfall didn't stop the shoppers here any more than in New York. They juggled packages on the sidewalks, and piled bags and boxes in wagons lined up along the hitching rail across the street.

"Sumner's Five Cent Store looks to be very popular."

"Yes, it is...unfortunate for us." Maggie picked up a cloth and began to wipe down the glass case. "He's taking away our business. Most items in his store are advertised for five cents or less. David is sure he must be stealing to keep his prices so low."

Victoria made a mental note to visit Sumner's store so she could investigate and possibly come up with helpful suggestions. She'd heard of similar institutions back east, which were reportedly growing fast. "What do you know of Mr. Sumner?"

Maggie's hesitation seemed out of character. David was the reflective one. Maggie said whatever was on her mind.

"I've seen Mr. Sumner around, and met him once, but I don't know much about him." Maggie continued cleaning without looking up. "He just moved out here last year. Rumor has it he closed a similar store in Philadelphia. No one knows why. This one seems to be doing well, but maybe, like David said, he's pricing things too low and he'll soon be out of money."

Victoria rearranged a display of ribbons that had gotten lost behind a tilting water basin shaped like a tulip. She sorted through a box of tortoise shell hair combs and set the prettiest one on top. "You think David's right?"

A troubled expression gathered on Maggie's brow. "I don't wish Mr. Sumner ill. But for David's sake, I hope he's right."

Fannie tugged Maggie's sleeve until she got her aunt's attention.

"Yes dear? What is it?"

Her niece pointed at the display case.

"Something in there?"

Fannie nodded.

Victoria observed the curious exchange. Perhaps Fannie's silence wasn't targeted at people she didn't like. "Does she ever speak?"

"Not a word in two years," Maggie said solemnly.

Two years? Victoria was shocked. In David's letters, he'd indicated his daughter had become withdrawn since her mother left, but not speaking at all? That was a great deal more than withdrawn. "She spoke before?"

"Perfectly. She started talking in full sentences when she was two. Didn't you, sweetie?" Maggie put her hand on Fannie's shoulder.

Her niece tapped on the glass.

Victoria walked over to examine the contents of the case: cheeses, meat pies, and a plate of pastries. "You could tell us what you want."

Without looking at Victoria, Fannie shook her head.

"The doctors examined her. They say she's fine, just stubborn. We've tried everything, even withholding food. She didn't eat a bite for two days. David refuses to punish her. He can't bear it. Neither can I."

So, Fannie wasn't incapable of speaking, in fact she seemed very bright, but for some reason she had cloaked herself in silence. Whatever the problem, it wouldn't be easily resolved. However, there was a way she could be helped, if she would cooperate.

Victoria bent down. "There is a better way to communicate what you want."

Fannie regarded her warily.

"I'm not offering you a snake."

The six-year-old scrunched her nose in disgust. The underlying meaning of the Biblical parable was lost on her.

"What I'm saying is, I'm not going to give you something worthless or harmful. Let me show you how to tell us what you want." Victoria curled her thumb and forefinger into the shape of a sideways C and then she brought her hand in front of her mouth and drew it downward, essentially an imitation of food moving into her stomach. "*Hungry.* That's how you say it."

Maggie stopped cleaning. "What's that you're doing?"

"People who can't speak—unlike Fannie, most of them can't hear either—use something they call sign language.

It's how they communicate." Victoria repeated the gesture. "I'm *hungry.*"

Fannie followed the motion with her eyes, and curiosity replaced wariness.

Maggie drew closer. "That's amazing, where did you learn it?"

"A good friend of mine had a high fever and as a result, she lost her hearing. Her parents sent her to a school for the deaf in Connecticut where she could learn sign language. I wanted to be able to converse with her, so I learned as much as I could during the times I went to visit."

Fannie turned and banged on the glass case.

"If you want a sweet, say *Please.*" Victoria demonstrated by placing her hand just above her left breast and making a circle. *"Please.* Then when your aunt opens the case, tell her *Thank you.*" Victoria held her fingers near her mouth and moved her hands outward and down.

Maggie's eyes sparkled with excitement. "That's wonderful!" She mimicked the motions. *"Hungry... Please... Thank you...."* The teacher had learned quickly enough. "Can you do that, Fannie?"

"Tell us you're hungry." Victoria repeated the sign.

With a frown, Fannie shook her head, stubborn, like her father.

Perhaps there was another way.

"What about your dolly? She might be hungry, too." Victoria took the doll before the child realized what she was about.

Fannie screwed up her face, priming the pump.

"No, don't cry. I'm not taking her away from you. I am only holding her so she can see you." Victoria turned the doll around. "Show her, Fannie. Show her how to tell us she's hungry."

A few tears escaped. When Victoria didn't budge, Fannie dragged the back of her hand across her face. Her dark eyes begged.

Smart girl. Knew all about how to use those big brown eyes to her advantage. No wonder her father had agreed to let her keep the kittens. Love *and* discipline were what she needed if she was going to learn how to get along on more than grunts and finger pointing.

"Show the doll, Fannie. Then we'll get you both something to eat."

Fannie curled her fingers and moved her hand up and down in front of her chest.

"That's very close. We'll practice later and get it perfect. Now, let's see what your doll has learned." Victoria took the doll's arm and made an effort to repeat the gesture, which wasn't easy considering the bisque fingers didn't bend and the stuffed arm was a bit stiff. "Hmm. She doesn't do it as well as you. But we understand her, don't we?"

The tears vanished and Fannie's lips inched into a shy smile. She curled her fingers and made the sign for *hungry* without hesitation. She had taken a big step and deserved a reward.

Victoria returned the doll. "I believe Fannie and her friend would like a treat from the case."

"Right away." With a wink, Maggie opened the display. The delicious aroma of baked goods wafted out. "What will you have, my ladies?"

Fannie pointed to a gooey pastry.

"That's bound to be messy. Here, I'll put it on a napkin..." Maggie handed her niece the pastry. "Now, you and your friend go sit at your table and eat."

After tucking her doll under her arm, Fannie carried the pastry to the child-sized table and chair set up in an area near the stove, close enough to be warm, but not so close she could reach the hot metal and get burned.

David had thought carefully about where to place the table. He showed how much he loved and valued his daughter by how he cared for her safety and his sensitivity for her feelings.

Victoria hadn't felt loved since her mother died. Her father had made it clear from the start that she wasn't valued. She'd thought her unhappy plight would change after receiving a heartwarming response from David O'Brien. But their first day together had been, for the most part, awful. Worse, she didn't know why.

Fannie propped the doll in the chair beside her and went to work on the pastry.

"Brilliant, Victoria," Maggie whispered. "Yesterday she giggled. Today she's talking."

"One phrase...in sign language," Victoria murmured under her breath.

"That's better than what she was doing before."

True. Victoria reveled in a rare sense of accomplishment. Not a huge victory, by any means, but enough to nudge Fannie in the right direction, and hopefully penetrate David's defensive shell. Though, from the look of things, it would be easier to get Fannie to open her mouth than it would be to coax her father to open his heart.

Maggie closed the door on the glass case. "We haven't sent Fannie to school because David fears the teachers might punish her or the students will make fun of her. So I've been tutoring her. I think you should take over Fannie's lessons, teach her sign language, along with everything else. I can answer any questions you might have."

The questions Victoria had didn't concern Fannie's

lessons. Maggie knew David better than anyone. She might have insight into why he'd changed suddenly.

Victoria motioned for Maggie to follow her to the end of the counter near the back door where they were less likely to be overheard. "Can you tell me what's wrong with David?"

Maggie appeared perplexed. "Wrong with him? What do you mean?"

"Ever since I arrived, it seems as if he's...well, hiding. He hasn't been forthcoming, even though I can tell something about this marriage, or me, is bothering him." Victoria didn't go into the details of the disastrous kiss. His doubts had started before that.

The ache in her heart was so great she could hardly bear it. Possibly, she expected too much, and yet the things he'd written had spurred those expectations. She couldn't accept something else...someone else.

She held out her hands, pleading for an answer. "I came out here because I fell in love with the man who wrote those letters. What happened? Why did he change?"

DAVID ENTERED the store through the back. Victoria and Maggie stood with their backs to him near the end of the counter. Victoria hadn't spoken very loud, but what he'd heard made his heart stumble. He stepped heavily on his damaged leg and the thick-soled shoe connected with a thud on the plank floor.

At the noise, the two women spun around.

"Oh! David, we didn't hear you." Maggie fiddled with the watch on her bodice, and her voice jumped several octaves. "Why did you come in through the back?"

"I stopped off at the flouring mill. Still have to unload." He motioned with his thumb over his shoulder, as if they couldn't figure out the wagon was in the ally.

Victoria's eyes remained wide, and her expression hopeful, as if she expected him to say something to reassure her. He couldn't. She was in love with a fraud.

His insides worked themselves into a knot. He'd been wrong to allow her to believe, even for a day, that he was the one who'd written those letters. That's why she was so unhappy now, and it explained why she'd thrown herself at him. As Mr. O'Connor had suggested, he ought to admit the truth and beg her forgiveness.

Fannie saved him from confession when she jumped up and ran over, lugging that damn doll. If Victoria decided not to marry him, the doll would be a painful reminder.

He took out a handkerchief, bent down and wiped his daughter's face. "You have crumbs around your mouth. Been eating pastries again, eh?"

Fannie's lips curved up, and she made a gesture in front of her with her hand.

"Two smiles in less than two days? What have I done to deserve that?"

His sweet daughter trusted him. He couldn't fail her a second time and marry a woman who might walk out of her life. Perhaps it was for the best Victoria left. The man she had come to find wasn't him.

Fannie made that odd gesture a second time, which seemed deliberate and something she wanted him to notice.

"What's that you're doing?"

Victoria ventured closer. She seemed a little skittish, and he felt bad that he'd caused her to doubt herself. It wasn't her fault he couldn't love her. "Fannie is telling you she's hungry."

He straightened, not understanding. "She didn't say anything."

"Yes, she did, in sign language. I taught her how to say, *I'm hungry*."

She'd stunned him, again.

"Victoria knows sign language," his sister explained. "That's what the deaf use to communicate."

Maggie smiled. And Fannie. And Victoria.

David frowned. They couldn't be *happy* about this. His daughter had to talk again, not wave her arms around in some useless gestures that nobody understood. She would be looked down on, shunned. "Why would you teach her a language she doesn't need?" he demanded of Victoria. "Getting her to talk, that's what you ought to be doing."

Maggie gasped. "David! She's just trying to help. The deaf communicate through—"

"My daughter isn't deaf."

Hurt flashed through Victoria's eyes a second before she narrowed them. "Sign language is used by people who are mute for whatever the reason, which is why she needs it."

"Fannie isn't mute."

Victoria's chin went up. Her sweetness hid a streak of stubborn. "She *is* mute, and as long as she remains that way, if she's willing to learn how to communicate through signing, we will better understand her needs."

Put that way, it sounded reasonable.

Wild emotions ricocheted against the walls of David's chest. He put his arm around his daughter's shoulders, unwilling to accept Victoria's judgment about Fannie's condition. That meant the end of hope for any kind of normalcy in his daughter's life. "You aren't mute, are you Fannie? Tell Miss Lowell."

The joy in Fannie's face fell away, replaced by the same

hopeless grief he'd seen in her eyes for the past two years. His child suffered, while he insisted on behaving worse than the backside of a mule. For all he knew, Fannie had some terrible malady that prevented speech. Even if she was perfectly healthy, she still wasn't communicating. Victoria had seen an opportunity to unlock the cage that kept his daughter a prisoner, and he insisted on locking it again.

He knelt in front of her. He'd held his sweet babe in the hours after she was born, completely enraptured. He loved her so much he would do anything to restore her, pay any price to bring her happiness.

He cupped her shoulder with one hand, and with the other touched her cheek. "*A stór...*" His voice grew rough with emotion. "My treasure. I'm proud of you for learning those signs."

He hugged Fannie, and ended up giving the doll a hug, too.

Afterwards, he glanced up at Victoria, rueful. He'd treated her poorly. No, worse than that. She had done nothing wrong. In fact, she'd done everything she could to help.

Slowly, he got to his feet. "I owe you an apology. For being a horse's a—" He couldn't say that in front of Fannie and the ladies, not even if the term fit. "For being difficult. If you'd like, you can keep track. Charge me a nickel every time I say something stupid."

"That might not be enough." The slight curl of her lip could mean she was joking.

He straightened his shoulders, and drawing Fannie against his side, prepared to right the wrong. "You're right. She does need to learn to communicate. Just took me by surprise, is all. You'll teach us more of those sign words, won't you? I'd like to learn, too."

She dipped her chin. "I would be glad to."

David exhaled with relief. She'd agreed, and without being demeaning. Nor had she made demands of him, except when it came to Fannie. Amazing, how she'd stood up for a child that wasn't even hers, and forced him to acknowledge what was in his daughter's best interests. She was the kind of mother Fannie needed. With her help, maybe one day his daughter would speak again. That is, unless he told Victoria the truth.

He didn't need *the sight* to know what would happen. After how he'd treated her, if he told her that he hadn't written those letters, she would pack up and leave. Even kind-hearted women had their limits. Already, she'd expressed disappointment, albeit mistakenly thinking she was the problem, which was laughable. She couldn't be more perfect.

"Is there a sign for...for thank you?" He'd almost said love. The biggest lie of all. Never again would he give a woman that kind of power over him. He didn't have to love her to convince her to marry him. All he had to do was to become the kind of man she thought he was, the one she'd found in those letters.

Victoria put her fingers to her mouth and made a gesture that almost looked like she was blowing him a kiss. "That's how you say, *Thank you*."

He mimicked the gesture, remembering how soft her lips felt and how sweet she tasted. She might even let him kiss her again, if he managed to pull this off.

Fannie's delighted smile cinched it.

He had to get his hands on those letters, and swear his sister to silence. Victoria could never find out. He could live with the lie. This wasn't a mistake. Protecting her from the truth was the only way he could be sure she wouldn't leave.

CHAPTER 7

One week later

"David's returned with the trees!" Maggie's shout echoed up the stairs, audible all the way to the kitchen where Victoria sat, helping Fannie with her lessons.

Fannie looked up from the primer and her eyes glowed. She used her fingers to spell.

Tree.

The little imp had picked up the sign language alphabet in a surprisingly short time, and could spell their names and simple words. Which just proved what Victoria suspected all along—Fannie was a very bright child.

Victoria closed the book and set it aside. Her charge was too excited to focus on studies this afternoon. "Enough reading. Let's go find our Christmas tree, shall we?"

Fannie didn't need to be told twice. She leapt up and raced out the door, pigtails flying, leaving Victoria to follow in her wake. The storeroom wasn't as frigid as usual. Maggie must've added extra wood to the stove while David was away.

Outside, the temperatures had dropped, and overnight, several inches of snow had fallen. After sweeping and shoveling parts of the walk not covered by the porch roof, David had left to collect a shipment of Christmas trees. He'd encouraged Fannie to stay with Victoria and work on her lessons. That suited Victoria just fine. She needed time to strengthen the fragile bond forming with her soon-to-be stepdaughter.

Her doubts about David had all but vanished over the past week. After their confrontation, he'd undergone a transformation. Instead of avoiding her, he sought her out at every opportunity. During the day, he would happen to brush up against her, or touch her arm or fingers as he passed by. Each night he spent time sitting with her on the sofa, sharing his dreams and talking about their future. Once, he'd cornered her when no one was around and had stolen a kiss.

She had written to her friend Roberta and told her all about David, and how she could hardly wait until Christmas Eve. It wouldn't be long now, and marrying him would be the best present she could receive.

As she entered the store, she smelled a sweet aroma. "Umm. Fresh baked pies?"

"Mrs. Murphy's pecan pies, to be exact. You just missed her." From behind the counter, Maggie gestured outside to where a stout woman bundled in a cape and bonnet was being assisted into a buggy.

Her burly companion turned to help David unload evergreens stacked in the back of the wagon. They lined up the lashed trees along the side of the building.

"This is the first year David has sold Christmas trees,"

Maggie said. "I hope they do well."

"I'm sure they will. They're very popular in Boston." A thrill of anticipation shot through Victoria. She caught up with Fannie near the front of the store. "We should go select our tree before the best ones are taken."

"David will want the best ones left for the customers." Maggie lifted a pie out of a box on the counter and bent down to set it inside the glassed display case. "Doesn't matter anyway, he won't allow a tree upstairs. It could possibly catch fire."

Anything could *possibly* catch fire.

"If one isn't careful, yes, the tree could catch fire, but..." Victoria's retort died on her lips. She would soon be David's wife, and shouldn't naysay his rules in front of his daughter. Later, she could speak to him about changing his mind. He'd shown he was willing to consider her opinions, and had even taken her advice a time or two. "Well, I suppose there isn't much space upstairs."

Fannie's shoulders slumped. She brought her hands to her face and drew them downward.

Sad.

Victoria nodded. "I know, I'm disappointed, too."

She'd promised Fannie they could decorate a tree. It would be great fun and a good way to bring them together. Thus far, there were few opportunities for family time because David worked all day in the store, and in the evenings took inventory and did bookkeeping. He explained he didn't want to spend the extra money to hire help. She wondered if he didn't have the extra money because the store across the street had cut into his business. If there was a way she could help, she would. But she knew next to nothing about running a mercantile. She was an expert, however, on little girls and Christmas trees.

"Maybe, if we move a few things, we could put a tree in the store," she suggested.

"Move things?" Maggie's muffled laugh came from behind the display. "To where?"

Good question. Victoria propped her hands on her hips and considered the possibilities. Only a narrow path remained between the counters, cases and tables, not to mention the stove and those large barrels. In front of the window, snow shovels were displayed.

Who wanted to look at shovels?

"There," Victoria said, pointing to the dangling shovels. "We can set it up in front of the window."

"What are you putting in front the window?" David asked as he entered the store. Off came the cap. He removed his gloves and ran his fingers through his hair to smooth it.

Her heart tripped, as she recalled plunging her fingers through his dark hair. She'd ask him not to cut it before the wedding. "We want to put up a Christmas tree in front of the window."

"A tree, in here?" He made it sound as if the idea had never occurred to him. "There's no room for it."

He didn't allow a Christmas tree upstairs or have space for one in the store. The term Scrooge came to mind.

Instead of arguing—which only made him dig in his heels—she propped up her elbow in her hand and placed her forefinger on her lip to appear thoughtful. He responded well to reason. "If you don't put up a tree, how do you celebrate?"

"Celebrate?"

"You do celebrate Christmas."

"Of course we do. We have a big dinner."

"But what about decorations? It doesn't feel like Christmas without decorations."

He gestured to the door. "We could put up a wreath with the extra boughs."

For a man who could pen pure poetry, he wasn't displaying much creativity.

"David, we could do more than just a wreath." Thankfully, Maggie had switched sides.

Victoria took in Fannie's woebegone face and knew she couldn't let the child down. "You could make room for a small tree in front of the window."

"A Christmas tree is frivolous." He might as well have said, *Bah, humbug*. "Besides, we have snow shovels on display. Shovels are more practical."

Victoria released a frustrated huff. "Ebenezer, this isn't the time of year for practicality. People want to be frivolous and extravagant."

"And you know this because you've been running a mercantile...for how long?" He challenged her with an arch of his left eyebrow.

Her father had perfected the arrogant eyebrow, so she wasn't the least bit cowed. In fact, it made her twice as determined. She would appeal to David's business sensibilities, the surest path to his heart.

"I'm not saying I'm an expert, but what about Mr. Macy? He certainly knows something about running a store. Every year when my father took us to New York, we'd rush over to see what Macy's had in their window display. Talk about extravagant. People flocked to his store to buy Christmas gifts and decorations. You can't say the owner of the most successful store in the country doesn't know what he's doing."

David hung his cap on the hat tree by the door. She might've suspected he was ignoring her, except he wore a thoughtful expression, which meant he was considering her suggestion, or thinking of how he would refute it. His tendency to reflect seemed strangely at odds with his spontaneous decision to wed her after exchanging only three letters.

Speaking of, she had misplaced those letters. Or... Her gaze slid to David's daughter. She'd caught the little girl digging through her clothes earlier in the week. "Fannie, have you seen a packet of letters?"

"Why did you go to New York every year?" David asked.

Victoria returned her attention to their discussion, which at the moment was more important than locating her letters. "We did our Christmas shopping in New York."

"But you lived in Boston. Aren't there shops there?"

"Plenty of shops, but..." She propped her hands on her hips as she deduced his strategy. Oh no, he wouldn't. "You're changing the subject."

He shrugged off his overcoat. "I'm just curious about your travel. Did you stay in a hotel?"

"No, we had a—" She stopped before she stumbled into admitting they had a house in New York. There was no need to talk about how many houses her father owned, or ships, for that matter. David had already taken issue with her wealthy background. "That has no bearing on the point I'm trying to make."

The way he looked at her, almost accusingly, triggered a flood of guilt. She hadn't lied about her family's wealth, just hadn't dwelled on it. Doing that would only emphasize her and David's vast differences in upbringing, rather than draw them closer.

"My point is, Mr. Macy puts out decorations so people will see them and want to come inside and shop."

David's dark, intense gaze held hers until she shivered.

His lips tightened in a slight smile as if he knew very well his effect on her. That wasn't fighting fair.

He wandered over to a table where a variety of knickknacks and ornaments were piled in boxes. More were in crates on the floor. "These trinkets are out where people can see them."

"But they can't see them from outside." She crossed to the large window in the front and gestured at his competitor's store. That would get his attention. "Mr. Sumner has a Christmas display."

"That doesn't mean he knows any more than I do about selling trinkets."

"I didn't say he does. I'm suggesting that if you decorate a tree with those ornaments, then people will see we have *better* trinkets than that fellow across the street."

"She does make a good point," Maggie called out from behind the counter.

Fannie ran over, tugged his sleeve and signed, *Please*.

"You too?" David's stern expression eased. His eyes softened and his lips twisted in a wry smile. "Ah well, because you ask so nicely."

When he looked up at Victoria, his smile broadened. The dimples appeared, and her heart took off at a wild gallop. "I can't fight all of you. Help me move these shovels and we'll bring in a tree."

"I'll help, too." Maggie practically leapt over the counter in her haste. His sister's smile said he had made her happy, along with his daughter, not to mention his bride-to-be.

The old David would've stood his ground and refused to rearrange the store to make room for something he considered frivolous. But he had vowed to become the man Victoria had fallen in love with so she wouldn't leave. He suspected that man would put up a Christmas tree.

They selected a stout pine, brought it inside and untied the branches. David secured the trunk in one of the ornate metal stands on display. The tree would've sold quickly, the stand as well, and taking them for personal use seemed a waste of merchandise. Then again, he couldn't put a price tag on joy.

His daughter skipped as she fetched ornaments from a box. Maggie laughed. Victoria didn't stop smiling. The very air seemed charged with happiness. He couldn't recall being in such good spirits since...well, he couldn't remember.

He kept busy waiting on customers while the others decorated the tree. More people began to wander inside. Everyone remarked on the Christmas tree, and most purchased decorations. He hated to admit it, but Victoria was right. Even his business had benefited from her touch.

As more customers arrived, she kept up cheerful conversation and directed them to merchandise. Her easy manner and friendly nature drew people to her, not to mention her beauty. Her eyes sparkled like gems and her skin glowed with health. That velvet skirt and jacket fit her like it was made for her, and probably had been.

She'd given up wealth and social standing to come out here and marry him. He felt humbled and proud, even if he hadn't been the one who'd convinced her. He could never have penned those heartwarming letters, and he wasn't as fine a man as his sister made him out to be. But that was the man Victoria had fallen in love with, and the man who loved her. Surprisingly, it wasn't as difficult as he thought it would be to keep up the pretense.

When the time came to close the store, he couldn't wait to lock the door so he could spend time alone with Victoria.

Maggie herded his daughter toward the rear of the store. "Why don't I take Fannie upstairs and we'll get supper on the table. You can help Victoria finish decorating the tree." She threw a quick look over her shoulder, and winked.

David pretended not to notice her laughable attempt at subtlety. His sister had kept Fannie out from underfoot so he and Victoria could spend precious time together. To her credit, Maggie hadn't breathed a word about her part in arranging their wedding.

Victoria circled the adorned tree, studying the handiwork. Ornaments hung from every branch, a wide lace ribbon had been looped around the tree from top to bottom. It looked like someone had dressed it for a ball.

David folded his hands behind his back. "Anything left for me to do?"

She handed him a hand-painted angel with a hoop skirt fashioned from paper and decorated with ribbon. "We need something on top. I think this would do nicely."

"Here?" He positioned the angel over the uppermost vertical branch.

"That's perfect."

"Just what I was thinking." He didn't take his eyes off Victoria. "A perfect angel."

She averted her gaze with a pleased smile. "I believe that's all we need. I should go help Maggie with supper."

She'd leave? Now? Just when he'd gotten a moment alone with her? He nabbed her arm. "That's not all I need."

Her eyes widened as he bent to kiss her parted lips. She gasped, drawing his breath into her mouth, and it seemed she took his heart with it.

He hauled her into his arms and forgot about everything

except kissing her. She apparently shared his hunger because she clung to him, returning his ardor.

A knock sounded on the door. He pulled back at the same time she did. The old David would've opened the store rather than disappoint a customer. To hell with that.

"Whoever is outside can't see us through the Christmas tree," he whispered, keeping a tight hold around Victoria's waist. "They'll soon figure out we're closed and leave."

Her lips were rosy from his kisses, and a deep flush spread across her cheeks, making her eyes appear lighter, clearer. Her beauty took his breath away. He tried to find the right words to tell her, but he couldn't. He couldn't even recall any of the flowery nonsense Maggie had written. All he could come up with was an endearment his father had used with his mother.

"A mhuirnín," he murmured.

She leaned against his chest, and he pressed a kiss to her temple. "What does that mean?"

"Darling."

"It sounds romantic when you say it like that. Will you teach me?"

"More fun to show you." He covered her mouth and gave her a demonstration.

Only two more weeks, he couldn't wait. Her eager response told him she didn't want to wait either. They could slip away and tie the knot tonight, but for the fact that the justice of the peace wouldn't appreciate being dragged away from his supper. There was something they could do, though, to declare their commitment before they made it legal. In fact, she might find the ancient ceremony romantic. He trailed kisses to her ear. "Are you ready to be married?"

She drew back in surprise. "Now?

"Why not?" He picked up a handful of silk ribbons from

a table display and then tugged his shirtsleeve to expose his wrist. Capturing her hand, he pushed her jacket sleeve up her arm before bringing their wrists together. "We'll hand fast."

She gazed up at him trustingly. "What is a handfast?"

"An Irish tradition. Back in the old days, a man and woman would come together in front of witnesses, exchange vows and bind their wrists to symbolize they'd be united for a year."

"Only a year?"

"They could stay together for as long as they wanted."

"Is forever permissible?"

She was adorable. David couldn't resist dropping a kiss on her pink lips. "That ought to be long enough."

David wrapped the first ribbon around both of their wrists. He'd seen the handfasting ceremony several times, mostly at friends' weddings. He hadn't followed tradition with his first marriage, which had been rushed and without much fanfare. That had turned out to be a good thing. It made this ceremony special.

He looked deep into his bride's eyes, "Victoria Lowell, do you willingly come to this marriage?"

She nodded.

"You're supposed to say, *yes*."

"Oh. Yes. Yes, of course."

Caught off guard, she was understandably nervous. He was, too. It wasn't every day he got married. The ceremony wouldn't be recognized as legal, they didn't even have witnesses. However, in his mind, this was as binding as any piece of parchment. He would commit his life to her, right here, right now.

"And I come to this marriage willingly, as well."

David wrapped a second ribbon around their joined

wrists. He couldn't recall the precise vows, so he spoke from his heart. That was all that mattered anyway. "Victoria, I vow to honor and respect you, and to remain by your side through times of pain and sorrow, as well as in times of laughter and joy. Now you..."

Her eyes never left his as she repeated the vows.

The place where their wrists were joined grew warm, and her pulse throbbed against his until their hearts beat together.

David's hand trembled as he added a third ribbon. "Through this ritual of handfasting, you declare your intention to be my wife and promise to keep your commitment."

Her eyes grew bright, and her throat worked convulsively before she finally answered. "I do, and I will."

"And I declare my intention to be your husband, and to provide for you and protect you."

Bending down, he kissed her. Not like the hot, hungry kiss he'd given her a moment earlier. This was a sacred kiss, the memory of which would remain on his lips long after it ended.

She opened her eyes, looking dazed. "Does this mean we're married?"

"Far as I'm concerned, it does. We still need to make it legal, and for that, we'll need a witness."

"How about two witnesses?" The question came from the across the room.

Maggie and Fannie stood just inside the doorway. How long they'd been back there, he had no idea, but it was long enough for his sister to start crying. Tears of joy, he'd guess. The crease between Fannie's brows was more difficult to decipher.

"Two witnesses would be even better," he agreed.

Without releasing the bonds, he threaded his fingers with Victoria's and lowered his arm to his side, bringing hers down with it.

Maggie beamed. "We'd love to stand up with your father and your new mother, wouldn't we Fannie?"

Fannie yanked her hand from Maggie's grip. She signed something he didn't catch, but Victoria did, and based on her expression, it hurt. For the first time in his life, David was sorely tempted to take a strap to his daughter's backside. He didn't get the chance before Fannie ran away.

"What did she tell you?"

Victoria turned her head, her eyes brimming. "She doesn't want a new mother."

CHAPTER 8

That night, Victoria lay beside Maggie, unable to sleep. After the impromptu wedding ceremony, David hadn't suggested they share a bed. Of course, they weren't officially wedded, not yet. Just handfasted, which meant... Well, she wasn't certain. He'd assured her they were as much as married, but hadn't he also told her the agreement was only good for a year? Although he'd seemed happier with her this past week, he still might not be sure she met his requirements for a wife, and handfasting was his way of determining whether she would work out, rather like a trial period for a new maid.

Doubts wouldn't plague her if he'd found a way for them to be alone, even just to talk. Throughout most of the evening, he had been dealing with Fannie, who was skillful at finding places to hide when she didn't want to be found. Still...

Victoria turned over. She shifted onto her side and faced the dark room. Rather than toss and turn and wake Maggie, she ought to get up. No reason more than one of them should miss sleep.

Opening the door, Victoria tiptoed into the parlor and was greeted by a soft snore. David had turned down the light, but not turned it out completely, perhaps so he wouldn't trip over something if he got up in the night. He'd wedged himself onto the sofa, still wearing his trousers and shirt, hugging a blanket that looked far too thin to keep him warm in this cold apartment.

Shivering, she knelt beside him, taking advantage of the opportunity to study him close up while he slept. *So tempting.* She curled her fingers closed to keep from smoothing the dark, tousled hair off his forehead. His eyes remained closed. Thick, inky lashes shadowed his cheekbones, and his breath puffed through slightly parted lips.

If only he would kiss her again and hold her close like before, and reassure her that he cherished her, then she wouldn't be so afraid. He had promised to honor and respect her. He'd vowed to provide for her and protect her. He'd said nothing about love.

Another shiver passed through her. She stood, hugging herself.

David wouldn't have gone to such lengths to obtain a temporary wife. Not only that, he wouldn't marry her if he wasn't willing to give love another try.

The torsion clock on the mantle chimed five.

She'd cook him breakfast this morning. The way to any man's heart was through his stomach. Every woman knew that—even the ones who didn't know how to cook.

Victoria headed into the kitchen, grabbing an apron from a drawer. She examined the range. This stove burned coal. Several times a day, Maggie would empty the ashes and add enough fuel to keep a fire going. Through the night, it would burn down to embers and would have to be stoked early in the morning so it would be hot enough for cooking. Not wanting David to think she was useless, Victoria had never admitted to her ignorance of ranges or her lack of knowledge in cooking. How hard could it be?

Humming quietly, she adjusted the dampers and scooped the amount of coal she'd seen Maggie use, and then added another large shovelful, reasoning it would make the fire hotter and warm the rooms faster. Once she got the fire in the range going, she turned her attention to making biscuits. She'd brought along a cookbook, but had learned more by helping David's sister.

After sliding the pan of biscuits into the oven, she stood and wiped perspiration off her forehead. Flour drifted into her eyes. Oh dear, it was on her hands, and now, all over her face.

Frying bacon turned out to be more difficult than it looked. When the bacon started sizzling, she realized she needed something to wrap around the hot handle. By the time she'd located what looked like a sleeve, bacon grease was popping out of the pan onto the stove.

Beads of moisture formed on her upper lip. The stove had certainly heated up the room. At least David wouldn't be cold when he got up.

The grease started smoking something awful.

She jerked the frying pan off the burner. Hot grease leapt over the edge and a few drops splashed onto the back of her hand. She bit her lip at the pain, but had no more time to think about it because a gray haze filled the kitchen, along with smell of something burning.

Smoke slipped out from around the edges of the oven door.

"The biscuits!" She used her apron to open the oven door. Smoke billowed into the room. Grabbing a cloth she'd tucked into her waistband, she pulled the pan from the oven. Her first biscuits resembled chunks of coal.

"Oh no. No," she groaned.

"What the hell!" David appeared in the kitchen almost as if he'd flown there. The upper buttons of his shirt were undone, revealing he did have dark hair on his chest. His trousers hung dangerously low on his hips without the aid of suspenders to hold them up. He had a wild look in his eyes, and his untamable hair stuck out in every direction.

"Did I wake you? I'm sorry. Everything's all right." Flustered, she stammered. "I-I just thought I'd cook breakfast and...well, it seems the fire got too hot..."

"Get out of here!" He snatched her by the arm and flung her out of the kitchen, still yelling. "Get Fannie and Maggie and leave the building."

She stumbled, barely catching herself before she fell over the table. "Leave? Why? I can start over. I can make more—"

"Shut up! Do as I say." He vanished into the smoke-filled kitchen.

Victoria remained rooted to the floor for another moment. A pungent cloud wafted into the parlor and hovered just below the stamped tin ceiling.

Oh dear, oh dear, oh dear.

She had failed, horribly, on her first attempt at cooking. Worse, David wasn't just unhappy with her, he was furious. Panicked, even. Had she unwittingly caused a disaster? She had to do as he said. Even if it seemed somewhat ridiculous to run from a smoky oven, what did she know? If she didn't get Maggie and Fannie to safety, she'd not only be ignorant, she would be irresponsible. At this rate, the handfast marriage might not last longer than a day.

AFTER GETTING the overheated stove under control and airing out the room, David went looking for Victoria. She had herded his sister and daughter outside as ordered, and they stood huddled together on the sidewalk, shivering, despite having wrapped up in blankets.

He felt damn foolish for panicking. Now guilt stabbed him for sending them out into the freezing weather. They were more likely to catch their death from cold than to expire in a fire. Victoria had only burnt the bacon and biscuits; she hadn't burned down the building.

Poor thing. She had flour on her face, her apron was stained with grease and soot, and her hair hung in limp strands around her face. She'd gone white as milk and looked thoroughly shaken. He tried to comfort her, but she pushed him away.

"I'm useless," she muttered.

"No, you're not. I overreacted." Didn't matter how many times he repeated himself. She didn't appear to believe him.

After ushering everyone upstairs, he told Victoria to go wash up and help Fannie get dressed while he and Maggie cleaned the kitchen. It didn't strike him that Victoria would take his suggestion as a slap at her competence, but the defeated slump of her shoulders told him she did. They would have a long talk later, once he'd put things back in order.

David wiped the grease off the range top, and dumped the charred remains of their breakfast into the garbage bin. Thank God it hadn't been worse. There was no permanent damage, nothing that couldn't be remedied. Even still, he couldn't stop trembling.

At the smell of smoke, he'd woken, reliving the

nightmare. The awful cracking sound just before the porch roof collapsed. Terrible pains shooting up his leg, which somehow got twisted beneath him as he tumbled into the pile of shingles and broken timber clinging to his little sister. Someone had snatched her away and pulled him, screaming, away from the rubble and the suffocating smoke.

He couldn't breathe.

Somehow, he'd managed to suck in air and drag his mind out of the past long enough to get off the sofa and get Victoria out of danger—had she been in danger, which now appeared unlikely. A smoky kitchen wasn't disastrous, and closing the dampers had suffocated the fire. However, a rational analysis of the situation didn't make his heart stop racing.

"The fire got too hot and the food burned. It's nothing." Maggie muttered from behind him. Was she trying to convince him or herself?

As she cleaned flour off the worktable, her long black braid swung against the quilted wrapper she'd donned before dashing out of the apartment.

It was freezing outside. Burning up in here. David used his sleeve to mop sweat off his forehead. His shirt had gotten dirty while cleaning up so he'd have to wash it anyway. "Will you make us some breakfast?"

"Yes, of course." Maggie sounded calm, yet distracted. She held something in her fist. He turned her hand over. Her fingers opened. The gold watch pin, she must've retrieved the heirloom before fleeing. The elegant watch had belonged to their mother and was one of the few personal items recovered from the fire that had killed their parents.

Maggie had been four at the time. She claimed she couldn't recall anything. Whenever she tried, her heart raced, her skin grew damp, and dark, inexpressible emotions clouded her mind. He'd urged her not to try to remember if it upset her. Locking away the terrifying memories was the only way he'd been able to deal with them.

Today, those memories had rushed back with the force of a flash flood.

He swallowed the knot in his throat and closed her fingers around the watch. "Are you sure you're all right?"

"Right as rain." She pinned the watch to the front of her wrapper. "Is the stove hot enough for me to cook eggs?"

He'd been so panicked he had doused the fire even after he'd shut the dampers. Starting it again would take awhile. Rather than admit to his overreaction, he suggested an alternative. "Don't bother. We can have some of Mrs. Murphy's pastries. She'll be here by seven. Look after Fannie while I see to Victoria."

Maggie's shoulders relaxed, indicting she was glad to be released, even if she had agreed to cook. "I'll take her downstairs. The milk delivery should be here."

As she passed by him, she brushed her fingers over his sleeve. Her gaze reflected sympathy and understanding. "Tell Victoria everything is all right. She feels very bad about it, and I...I was too upset to talk to her."

He nodded. Although he dreaded it, explaining the cause of his panicked reaction was his responsibility. Sometimes, even without triggers like smoke, he woke up in a panic, reliving the fire, and he didn't want to scare her if that happened.

A moment after Maggie left with Fannie, Victoria emerged from the bedroom. She'd changed into a dark green skirt and jacket, had gathered her hair up and fixed it with decorative combs. She looked very neatly put together.

He wouldn't guess anything had happened, except for the lack of color in her face and the dazed look in her eyes.

"Sit down." He gestured to the sofa. As much as he didn't want to sit in a room still smelling of smoke, there was nowhere else to go to have a private conversation. "We need to talk."

CHAPTER 9

$\mathcal{V}$ictoria trembled so badly she had to thread her fingers together to keep her hands from shaking. This must be how a condemned man felt when facing the gallows. As requested, she sat on the sofa. David had to be so disappointed in her.

Tears gathered along her lower lids. She had no skills in homemaking or knowledge about the mercantile business. Even Fannie had rejected her. She was as useless as she feared. "I'm sorry. I just wanted to cook you breakfast. I didn't mean to...to make so much smoke. Do you want me to leave?"

The cushion sank as David sat beside her. Dark smudges marred his cheek. His white shirt was ruined from cleaning up her mess. He leaned forward, and reaching over closed his hand around her tightly clasped fingers. "We're handfasted, Victoria. Pledged to each other."

His warm brown eyes didn't have that wild look anymore, and his tone sounded tender, not angry. The terror squeezing her heart eased.

"You're not sending me away?"

"No. Why would you think that?"

Victoria sagged with relief. Thank goodness, he'd forgiven her for nearly burning down the building, and he hadn't even asked how it happened. Her conscience prodded her to tell him the full truth, so he would know what sort of wife he was getting. "I don't know how to cook."

One corner of his mouth curled upward. "I do. If you still haven't learned by the time Maggie leaves, I'll teach you."

Cooking was only one of her failings. She risked another confession. "I don't know how to sew, either. Even my cross-stitching is abominable."

Amusement reached his eyes. "Most of the clothes we wear are readymade, the ones I carry in my store. What I don't have, we can find elsewhere."

"And the laundry?"

"We'll use a laundress. You'll be busy giving Fannie her lessons and helping me in the store."

She released her fear on a long sigh. "I thought after last night, when you said I should sleep with Maggie…"

"Last night?" He shook his head, half smiling. "You think I don't want you? That's not why I suggested we wait. You questioned me about whether we were actually married, so I figured you had reservations about, well, sleeping together before we made it legal. We can stand in front of the judge today." He squeezed her hands. "You can't leave. I need you, Victoria."

Her heart fluttered in her chest. That was as close as he'd come to a declaration of love.

He wasn't rejecting her at all. He wanted her, but he'd been honoring her by waiting, and in saying he needed her, he'd confirmed what she had come to believe from his letters. He had seen something in her no one else had seen, something special.

She gazed at him, filled with wonder. "No one has ever said they needed me before."

"How's that, a lady like you?" he declared with astonishment. "You're beautiful, educated, refined..."

The burst of joy fizzled as he ticked off her pedigree. It was all she really had to recommend her, when it came down to it.

"But I no longer have money, or status."

"Is that what you think I want?" A thoughtful crease appeared between his sable brows. "I don't recall asking for those things."

"You didn't." She'd remind him of what he'd written and maybe that would spark whatever had compelled him to tell her she was the *perfect choice*. "You asked for a woman of good standing who would be a kind and loving wife and mother. Someone willing to overlook scandal and open her heart to a divorced man; a woman of strength and courage."

His lips twisted in a rueful smile. "Is that all she asked for?" Alarm flashed across his face. He released a laugh that sounded nervous. "I mean, all *I* asked for?"

Victoria caught the odd slip. Based on his reaction, it wasn't a matter of misspeaking. He'd unwittingly given something away.

The letters. He must've had help crafting them.

Come to think of it, he'd told her the other night that he'd quit school to go to work to support his sister, who had gone on to college. He might've worried that his limited education would show in his writing and hurt his prospects,

"You don't recall what you wrote?" she prodded.

"Sure, I recall most of it. The important parts." The fear on his face gave him away.

So, Maggie had helped him. Disappointing perhaps, but not the end of the world. The exact words might not be his, but they reflected what was in his heart, and his sentiments meant the world to her.

"You don't have to remember. I could tell you everything in those letters."

"Memorized them, did you?" David rubbed his forehead, as if the thought of memorizing made his head hurt. She didn't want him to feel lacking in that area, as well.

"There were only three, so it wasn't as difficult as memorizing whole Bible passages."

"Hopefully not as boring." Without smiling at his own quip, he shifted forward and braced his arms on his knees. "Do you recall what I told you about the fire that killed my parents?"

"You told me they died, but not how you managed to escape."

"The stairs were on fire. My father put Maggie and me out on the porch roof to get us away from the smoke. Then he went back for my mother. The porch roof collapsed."

She shuddered. "That's awful, terrifying. Is that how you were hurt? How did Maggie escape injury?"

"I held onto her and my body cushioned her fall. Broke my leg in three places. I couldn't save my folks." He stared off in the distance, somewhere else or in some other time. His sadness broke Victoria's heart.

"You saved your sister."

He shook his head, as if to clear the morbid thoughts. "Sorry. That's not why I brought this up. I wanted to apologize for yelling and frightening you and sending you out in the freezing cold. I overreacted."

"You didn't overreact. I nearly set the kitchen afire," she laid her hand on his knee to reassure him.

His larger hand came down over hers and his warmth reached all the way to her cold toes. "The fire got too hot. All I had to do was shut the dampers."

"I should've thought of that. I feel foolish."

"Don't." He patted her hand. "It takes time to learn how to adjust the fire to the right temperature. You just burned the bacon and biscuits, that's all. Everyone burns food when they're learning how to cook."

He was being too kind.

"I didn't just burn it. My biscuits turned into blackened bricks."

"Those were biscuits?" He gave her a quick smile, and just as quick, it vanished. "The smoke, sometimes it wakes up old memories...and, I'm living it again, and the panic."

Victoria laid her hand on his unshaven jaw, longing to comfort him. She also loved touching him, loved how warm his skin felt; even loved the roughness of the dark bristles that grew so fast. "It's hard for you to talk about this."

"Very."

"Then you needn't if it hurts too much."

He lifted her hand and kissed the center of her palm. "Thank you. I worried you might not want a man with a damaged mind, as well as a damaged body."

"I want you," she said simply. Truthfully.

He curled his fingers around her hand. "And I want you."

Victoria searched his eyes, saw hunger reflected in the dark depths and her body quaked with desire. He wanted her. Needed her. Perhaps he even loved her. Yet, something held him back from admitting it, something he might think she wouldn't understand. She had to make him see there was nothing so terrible it could stand between them.

E.E. BURKE

She clasped their joined hands. "We must have honesty between us."

He regarded her with a puzzled frown. "That's why I told you about how the smoke affects me. Why I overreacted."

"Yes, and I'm glad you trusted me with that. Now you can trust me enough to tell me about those letters. Maggie wrote them, didn't she?"

Worry gathered around his eyes. "You figured it out."

"It wasn't hard after you misspoke."

He dropped her hand. Leaning his arms on his knees, he put his head down. His slumped posture conveyed resignation. "I was going to tell you."

Eventually. Perhaps. But she'd been right to bring this up now, so they could remove the last barrier and he wouldn't feel as though he had to hide. Maybe the almost-fire had been a blessing because it forced them both to be truthful and to realize they didn't have to be perfect. They just had to be themselves.

She couldn't resist rubbing his back. "It's all right, David. Who wrote them doesn't matter."

His head turned, revealing his astonishment. "You don't care that Maggie wrote to you?"

Her heart went out to him. His lack of education meant nothing to her. "I wouldn't hold that against you. Who penned the words isn't what's most important."

"I tried...but I kept putting it off." He threaded his fingers through his hair, as he did when he was frustrated or struggling to express himself. "I don't write so well. No, that's not why. I was afraid to go into another marriage. At first, I was furious with Maggie for posting a personal ad without telling me. Amazing, it's turned out for the best. I just wish she'd shared your letters sooner."

Victoria drew her hand from his back. No, that couldn't

be. "What...what are you saying? Maggie posted the advertisement? *She* answered my letters?"

David's gaze remained fastened to the floor. "You said you'd figured it out."

"I deduced she penned the letters, yes, but I assumed it was under your instruction."

His silence plunged a dagger into her heart.

David hadn't picked her above all others. She wasn't anyone special. He hadn't even read what she wrote. When she found her voice, she managed a rough whisper. "When did you see my letters?"

He still wouldn't look at her. "The morning before I met you at the station."

The cold blade twisted. No wonder he'd acted as if he didn't know what to do with her and seemed resentful of her presence. An unwanted bride had been foisted on him.

"Why didn't you tell me immediately?"

He shook his head, seeming at a loss. "I thought it might work out."

Dear God, the truth was awful. Much worse than she thought possible. Everything she'd believed had been a fantasy. "What might work out? You just said you didn't want a wife."

He jerked his head in her direction. His neck and lean cheeks darkened. "I didn't want to get married again, but I needed a wife. I intended to post an advertisement, just never got around to it. So Maggie did it for me."

Victoria curled her hands into fists, wishing she had his conniving sister's neck in her grasp. "How can you defend her?"

"I'm not defending her. I'm telling you what happened. Being honest, like you said." His voice had gone as wooden as his expression. She longed to slap him, so at least he would *feel* something. He should hurt as much as she was hurting.

She flushed with anger and humiliation. "*Why?* Why did you let me believe you'd written those letters?"

"If I'd told you the truth, you would've left." He came to his feet and began to pace. "I'm sorry, Victoria. Sorry I wasn't truthful. But I couldn't take the chance. I thought you'd leave, and you're so good with Fannie..."

His stumbling explanation sank in, right down to the pit of her stomach. Fannie's needs, not his, that's what this was about. What it had always been about, only Maggie had carefully colored the truth with romantic prose.

"You didn't...didn't ever want..." her voice wavered. He hadn't wished to marry her, and even if he did now, he still didn't value her as anything more than a caretaker. She held onto her composure by getting angry. "That's the only reason you need me, so I can watch Fannie."

VICTORIA'S OUTBURST CONFUSED DAVID. He'd expected her anger when she found out she'd been deceived about the letters, but that wasn't what seemed to bother her the most. She sounded more insulted about why he'd decided to marry. It was a valid reason, and something many a man had done before him. "Not just to watch her. Fannie needs a mother."

This explanation didn't seem to help. Victoria still looked as if she might burst into tears. She could be worried Fannie wouldn't accept her, and she would disappoint him. She'd tried so hard to learn the business, and her foray into cooking was another example of her determination to be a good wife. Earlier, she'd kept muttering about being useless. Maybe she thought she'd somehow failed at mothering.

"Victoria, I know you care about Fannie, and she trusts you. She only ran away because she doesn't want Maggie to leave, and she thinks if she likes you, it's somehow disloyal. I explained Maggie is leaving anyway and it has nothing to do with you." David held out his hands, appealing to reason. "Look how far you've come. She's communicating with signs. If you keep working with her, she might overcome whatever prevents her from talking."

The high color drained from Victoria's face. She gripped the curved arm of the sofa. "You expect me to cure her?"

The weight always present in his chest grew heavier. If only she knew how little faith he had in anything. "That's not what I expect, although I admit to having hope."

He spied Fannie's favorite rag doll in the toy crate beside the sofa. Bending down, he picked it up. No bigger than his hand, threadbare from being hugged so much. "Rachel gave her this doll. She used to carry it around all the time. I haven't seen her with it lately. Not since you gave her the other doll. That's a good sign, I think. Means she isn't clinging to false hopes. She's accepted you, at least as a friend. One day, I'm sure it'll be more."

Victoria looked away, wiping at the wet streaks on her cheeks.

He wasn't making his point very well. "Do you understand what I'm trying to say?"

"Oh, yes. I understand perfectly." Her lips twisted into a cynical smile, not at all like her. "You don't want a wife. You want a miracle worker."

His face grew hot. He knew he wasn't good with words, but she wasn't listening. "That's not what I—"

"That *is* what you want."

"That's all you took from what I said?"

The way she'd turned away from him, the stiffness in her posture, the hurt on her face, gave him the answer.

He wrestled with uncertainty. If he didn't get this right, he might lose her.

David paced the length of the room and back, rubbing his forehead, analyzing the problem. He'd attempted to explain why he needed her, and how much faith he had in her. Maybe if he convinced her he wanted her she'd have no other reason for doubt.

He rejoined her on the sofa. He longed to kiss her tears away, but he didn't think she'd welcome that just now. She hunched her shoulders and held her hands together, a sign she didn't want to be touched.

Resting his arms on his knees, he spoke in a low, soothing, tone. "Victoria, listen to me. We can have a good marriage. You said yourself you want me, and I want you."

"You want a willing woman in your bed." The bitterness in her voice let him know just how much he'd hurt her, and she probably hadn't forgiven him for suspecting she was promiscuous.

"Not just any woman," he said softly. "I haven't been with anyone. Not since Rachel left."

With the admission came the realization of how solitary and empty his life had been before Victoria had come into it.

"You loved her." Victoria stated it as if it was a fact, not a question.

He had loved his wife, much as he hated to admit it because she sure as hell hadn't loved him. Now, though, he felt nothing. Like she had died without leaving any good memories. "She killed whatever love I had for her."

"But that's why you won't let yourself care. You think I'm like her."

Half of what she said was true.

"You're nothing like her. You're honest and generous and selfless. You have more kindness in your little finger than she has in her whole body."

"If she was so bad, why did you love her?" Victoria's expression seemed less cynical. There was an anxious tone to her voice, as if the answer meant a great deal to her.

David had no desire to talk about his past. He only wanted to discuss their future. However, Victoria made it clear she would go no further until he opened that door. For her—only for her—he'd do it.

"Rachel wasn't bad at first, or I couldn't see it. Her family was dirt poor. Her father spent what little he earned on whiskey. Her mother passed on when Rachel was sixteen, and she ran away from home. I gave her a job because I wanted to help her..." That wasn't the whole truth. "It didn't hurt that she was pretty and vivacious. But then the old man came after her. He just wanted the money she made, but he took a strap to her when she refused to give it to him. She begged me to protect her. The only way I could do that was to marry her."

Vulnerability, he'd discovered, was a strong aphrodisiac. Rachel had sensed and exploited his protective streak. He hadn't blamed her for manipulating him, and had been foolish enough to think love would change her, soften her and make her less grasping. He'd been wrong.

"It wasn't long before she complained about being bored with working in the store. I thought having a baby would help, and for a while it seemed to settle her down. Then she got restless again. When she started taking Fannie out all the time, I worried. I had crazy fears about something happening to them. We fought over it, constantly. Then she started sneaking away after I went to sleep. One night, I tracked her down and found her in bed with another man. She left with him the next morning."

He would've killed the gambler had he not feared he'd be jailed and Rachel would leave town with Fannie.

"The most generous thing she did was to leave Fannie with me instead of taking her. But that might be because her lover didn't want a child along."

Victoria had been watching him, weeping. "She took something with her just as valuable. She stole your trust."

David's throat closed. He wanted to deny Rachel had gotten away with anything, but he couldn't. Victoria had it right. He'd let his faithless wife steal away with part of his soul. What was left might not be worth salvaging.

That wasn't what he should say. Not if he wanted Victoria to stay with him.

First, he had to dry those tears. He took her hand and checked beneath the hem of her sleeve, found a lacy handkerchief tucked away in the spot women kept them for emergencies, and then he wiped away the evidence that she cared too much.

She'd become important to him, too, in some ways, necessary. But he couldn't for the life of him put what he felt into words. All he knew for certain was that he wanted to marry her.

He tucked the handkerchief into her palm. Cupped her small, delicate hand in his, holding it like he'd once held a baby bird, fearful he'd crush it if he didn't take care. "I do want you as my wife, and not just because of Fannie."

She searched his eyes with a kind of desperate hope that sent a shudder through him. "Can you love me, David?"

The simple question struck with the force of a hard

punch. He leaned back, staggered. This shouldn't come as a surprise. He'd known from the start what she expected, what she'd come out here to find. Only, he had fooled himself into thinking he could satisfy her with physical passion. But no, she would accept nothing less than love.

Sadness pulled at her eyes. "I didn't think so."

When she stood, he shot to his feet, panic setting in. As she walked to the door, he followed in her wake like a shadow. When she crossed the threshold, he stopped.

He watched as she descended, battling the urge to dash down the stairs after her. When she reached the bottom of the stairs, he called her name.

"Victoria."

She paused.

If he told her what she wanted to hear, then she might stay.

Yes, but for how long? A month? A year? How long would it take before she realized she had married a different man than the one she'd fallen in love with?

"Don't leave." His agonized whisper must not have reached her because she stepped off the last riser and kept going. Even if she'd heard him, he had nothing more to say.

The night before Rachel had left, she'd told him that he was a bore, a tedious fellow who didn't understand a woman's needs and cared for nothing but work. He wasn't the man she thought she'd married, and he couldn't give her what she wanted.

He couldn't give Victoria what she wanted, either. He couldn't offer her what he didn't have—a whole heart.

*V*ictoria drew her cape around her shoulders. Her arms, legs, chest, even her heart, felt numb. The walls of the storeroom closed in on her, overwhelming darkness threatened. It seemed as if she was walking through a dream, or a nightmare.

She'd heard David call her name, had stopped at the bottom of the stairs, waiting. Hoping. But when he said nothing more, she decided it was only her mind playing tricks on her. He hadn't said a word when he'd followed to the door, and then he had stopped following. He wouldn't call her back just to tell her what she already knew.

He couldn't love her.

His silence at her question only confirmed what she suspected. When he'd told her about that wretched woman who'd ripped his heart out she'd known. Her hopes had collapsed in that moment.

Still in a daze, she entered the store. They hadn't opened yet as it was still early.

Fannie sat on the counter, swinging her legs as she devoured a pastry. The excitement of the morning had given her an appetite. She'd dressed herself, right down to the mismatched stockings and patched frock. Victoria had tried to plait her hair, but the result looked like a cross between a misshapen snake and a porcupine. Why on earth David thought she would make a good mother was beyond her. She couldn't even manage a proper braid.

Questions swirled in her mind. Should she go home? Unthinkable. Take the next train west? Irresponsible. Devise a plan? She'd thought she had a good one when she answered David's advertisement.

She needed to get away. Have a few moments alone to think about what she'd done, and what she should do next. If she didn't leave *right now*, she would do something foolish, perhaps break down. David had kindly wiped her tears, but he wouldn't know what to do with a flood.

Bottles of milk rattled in the tray as Maggie carried them to the icebox. "Would you like something to eat? I've put out pastries. Help yourself..." Maggie's head turned, and her gaze followed, topped by a perplexed frown. "Victoria? Are you all right?"

She floated past the potbellied stove, which had been stoked to just the right level of heat, something she would have to learn how to do, especially if she ended up on her own. "I'm not hungry just now. I think I'll take a walk."

"A walk?" Maggie's reply was incredulous. "It's freezing outside. Are you sure you're feeling well?"

Victoria drew the hood over her head and cut off Maggie's concerned voice by closing the door. She squelched a spurt of regret at her rudeness. David's sister could stew for a while. If not for Maggie's interference, he wouldn't have an unwanted bride to deal with.

On the other hand, he could've put a stop to the travesty at any time. Instead, for some reason he'd played along.

Even to the point of taking her through an Irish handfasting ceremony, which conveniently offered the option of a limited term.

David might desire her. He might even be fond of her. Yet in the end, he wouldn't commit his heart, which meant she couldn't trust him with hers.

The wind buffeted her as she walked down the sidewalk. Her cape served as a poor shield. David was right about the wind never ceasing. It blew in across the plains and barreled into town, defying everything in its path. The unstoppable wind could knock down any barrier.

She could be persistent, too. She would blow down walls if she thought it would make David love her. But he was impervious to the cold, and unmoved by her efforts. He'd let her walk away. He'd let her go, without a word. Perhaps it was time she let go.

As she wandered aimlessly, her teeth began to chatter. Maggie was right, it was too cold to stay outside, and despite being devastated, she had no wish to freeze to death. She crossed over and started back. Her hands, despite gloves, grew numb, as did the tip of her nose. That was nothing compared to the frozen wasteland inside.

Without giving it much thought, she stopped in front of a window with a display of Christmas toys set up in a scene from the first Christmas. Even the hopeful message didn't help. She'd followed a false star to a false promise.

"Excuse me, miss. May I be of assistance?"

It took Victoria a moment to realize the man was talking her. She dipped her chin politely. "No, thank you. I'm just out taking the air."

He kept a firm hold on his black hat as the wind picked up. "Pardon me for saying so, but the air might take you." His sky blue eyes shone with amusement and a mustache the color of cinnamon lifted beneath a smile. "Could I persuade you to come inside out of the cold? Offer you a cup of coffee, or tea. Whatever you prefer."

Going somewhere with a stranger wasn't part of her plan. Not that she had a plan, but that wouldn't be part of it.

"We've not been properly introduced."

"Let me fix that." He swept off his hat. The wind ruffled ginger hair as he dipped his chin in a smart bow. "Gordon Sumner, at your service."

Her gaze moved from the dignified gentleman to the window where gold letters spelled out the name he'd given. Her short trek had taken her nearly full circle, and she'd ended up across the street from David's store. No sign of him, though. Hard evidence he didn't want her, which left her feeling more bereft.

The nice gentleman waited politely. Being miserable didn't mean she had to be rude. "Mr. Sumner. You're the owner of this establishment, I presume?"

"You presume correctly. However, you have me at a disadvantage. You are...?"

"Victoria Lowell." She held out her hand and he took her fingers briefly. Fine manners, elegant suit, and glib tongue, he showed signs of a gentleman. Whether he possessed other gentlemanly traits remained to be seen. She'd thought David O'Brien a man of great sensitivity with a romantic soul. Come to find out, that was his sister.

"Lowell. The name is familiar," Mr. Sumner murmured.

Her family was well known in social circles up and down the East Coast, so it was no surprise the erstwhile Easterner might've heard the name. "As you said, we've never met."

"That's a Boston accent. *Brahmin*, if my ear serves me well."

Victoria hated the term Oliver Wendell Holmes had

given the tight-knit Boston aristocracy. Brahmins were the highest caste in India's rigid system. She thought the epithet very un-American. "I am formerly of Boston."

"About that cup of coffee?" Mr. Sumner rubbed his hands up and down on his arms. Perhaps he was getting chilled after having come outside without an overcoat.

The eastern merchant didn't look like a rascal, as David had dubbed him. Actually, he seemed rather nice...and utterly uninteresting.

She cast a longing glance over her shoulder across the street and tried to tell herself she didn't expect to see David.

"That's a nice tree O'Brien put up. I wouldn't have expected it," Mr. Sumner mused.

Nor would she have expected it a week ago. But since then, David had given her glimpses of the man she'd imagined him to be, the man he probably was before he was wounded. Last night, he had created magic with nothing more than a handful of ribbons.

"Mr. O'Brien can be very creative when he chooses to be."

He could also be amusing and thoughtful and caring, and upon occasion, romantic.

Still, he refused to give his heart. Perhaps he was afraid or he no longer possessed one. That awful woman had taken it. Whatever the reason, there was no changing him. No matter how much she longed for love, she would never find it with a man incapable of giving it. It was time she approached her life with more practicality. If nothing else, David had taught her that.

For now, she would remain in town. Find a place to live, and she'd need a job. She wouldn't abandon Fannie, though. As difficult as it might be, she would continue Fannie's lessons until David found another teacher, or a woman content to wed him without love. That woman wouldn't be her.

She turned to the waiting gentleman. "A cup of coffee sounds nice.

DAVID CHANGED out of his grease-stained shirt and trousers into clean clothes. His nerves jumped every time he heard a sound. He kept listening for Victoria's voice, expecting her to walk in and take him on like she had when she'd challenged him over Fannie's lessons. His wife was small, but mighty. She didn't back down. She wouldn't give up and walk away from her vows. Not unless she thought he'd given up by letting her go.

Even so, Victoria wasn't like Rachel. Even if he hadn't spoken words of love, she knew the depth of his commitment. He'd pledged his devotion and protection for the rest of his life. There was nothing more binding than that. Once she was over being upset, she would realize this. She wouldn't leave him.

Heading downstairs, he checked his watch. Seven. She'd been gone less than an hour. She was probably in the store having pastries with Maggie and Fannie.

Victoria wasn't downstairs, and she wasn't in the store.

Fannie sat next to a tray of pastries on the countertop with jelly on her face, playing with her doll, the one that looked like Victoria. An invisible band tightened around David's chest.

"Have you seen Victoria?"

His daughter nodded.

Maggie's head popped up from behind a display case and she shook out a cleaning cloth. "Victoria went for a walk, at least that's what she said she was doing. I thought she acted strange. Distracted. Like she was in a daze. Is she still upset about burning the biscuits?

"The biscuits, no." His heart pounded harder. He didn't want to admit, or even acknowledge, that he'd burned more than biscuits. "Did she say where she was going?"

"She didn't, but it's too cold to go very far."

Which meant she wasn't on her way to the depot, which was several miles away. No one would walk that distance in this weather.

His hardheaded wife might.

David's heart raced as a sense of urgency overtook him. He threw open the door and ran outside. Stupid, pigheaded fool. That's what he was, for letting her walk away without convincing her to give their marriage a chance. He had to tell her he trusted her, and that he needed her for more than what she could do for Fannie.

She wasn't on the sidewalk in either direction.

He dashed past the hitching rail, slipping in an icy patch alongside a tarp-covered wagon. One of the ropes keeping the tarp down proved to be his salvation. He clung to it until he got his feet under him.

She couldn't have gone far in this cold.

David scanned the street. He nearly jerked his neck out of joint doing a double-take when he caught sight of her standing outside the Five Cent Store, talking with the owner.

Victoria smiled, took Sumner's arm and allowed him to escort her inside.

Anger roared through David faster than a wind-blown fire. By God, he'd kill the bastard. At the very least, he'd punch Sumner in the face for making off with his wife.

Before he reached the opposite sidewalk, he halted. Why

would Victoria go over there? If she got cold, she could've crossed the street and come home. Instead, she'd sought refuge with his competitor, a man she couldn't know very well. There could be only one reason. She knew that Sumner's would be the last place on earth he would think to look for her. Therefore, she must not want him to find her. Which meant she was hurt, or furious, or more likely, simply done with him.

Cold dread pooled in his gut.

Forcing himself to turn around, David retraced his steps. Barging into Sumner's store and hauling her across the street wouldn't prove anything, except to show her he had a bad temper. If Victoria wanted to come home, she would do so. If not...

Reaching his store, he threw open the door so hard it banged against the wall.

Fannie twitched as if someone had fired a gun.

Maggie jerked up from behind the counter. "David? Are you all right? What's wrong?"

"Get the cash drawer," he ground out. "We're opening."

His sister checked her watch. "Not for half an hour."

David stuffed his anguish deep down inside. He would focus on work and not think about Victoria being over there with another man. Reason told him it didn't mean anything. However, reason wasn't preventing his gut from churning with anger.

He lifted Fannie off the counter. For a split second, he considered taking the doll and throwing it away. Seeing it every day would be pure agony.

Who was he kidding? He couldn't shut Victoria out of his mind that easily.

With a lump in his throat, he handed the doll to Fannie.

She gazed at him with a question in her eyes.

"Victoria's gone."

Maggie put something on the shelf behind him. "Gone for a walk, you mean."

"I mean she's gone." He might as well tell his sister the truth. "I let her go."

Maggie grabbed his arm and jerked him around to face her. "What did you say to her?"

David resisted the urge to take hold of his sister and shake her, tell her this was as much her fault as his. That wouldn't accomplish anything except to drive a wedge between them, and he didn't want or need the extra tension.

"The truth. That you posted the ad and wrote the letters and I had nothing to do with it until the day she arrived. She was understandably upset." He didn't add that the last straw was his refusal to assure Victoria of his love. That was between him and Victoria and no one else.

His sister began to shake her head about halfway through his curt explanation. "Why in the name of St. Michael would you do that? You didn't have to tell her. I would've kept our secret."

"It's not our secret." He lost the battle with his temper and exploded. "I can't live a lie, Maggie. She'd find out sooner or later and it's best she found out sooner."

He went to the back and grabbed his apron. "Just let it be. You've done enough. She's made her choice."

"Don't be ridiculous, she hasn't chosen to leave." Maggie's tone reached a shrill note. "She only said she was going for a walk."

"She just went into Sumner's...with the owner."

Maggie rushed to the front window. "Maybe she just wants to see how the store is laid out. She mentioned being curious about it. I'm sure she'll be back before we open."

He wasn't so sure. Not after he let her think he couldn't love her.

The tenuous hold he had on his emotions slipped. David splayed his hands on the counter and hung his head, fighting tears. Victoria wasn't to blame. She'd come out here believing in him, had willingly come to him with open arms and an open heart, and he had betrayed her in ways he'd never betrayed Rachel. It was no wonder if she despised him.

"I'll sweep the walk," Maggie offered. So she could watch for Victoria, no doubt.

He drew a deep breath. Let it out. Regained his composure. He couldn't fall apart. The store would open soon, and he had his daughter to think about.

Fannie had wandered over to the Christmas tree. She hugged the doll Victoria had given her. Every night, he had to tuck it into bed and even kiss it goodnight. That doll had become his daughter's constant companion. Maybe because she knew it couldn't walk away on its own.

David crossed to where she stood, lost in her own world. He loved her beyond all reason, but he hadn't been a very good father these past two years. It was about time he started. His daughter wasn't Victoria's responsibility, or Maggie's. She needed his time and attention more than she needed another mother.

He dropped onto his haunches next to her. "You did a good job decorating the tree. Would you like to have a small one upstairs? I think we could fit it in."

Fannie accused him out of the side of her eyes. She knew it was his fault Victoria had left and she wasn't happy about it. Even if she'd been reluctant to accept Victoria as her new mother, the two had become fond of each other.

"You want me fix things, don't you?" He heaved a heavy sigh as he stood. "I'm not sure I can."

The bell jangled as Maggie opened the door. She returned the broom to its usual place, and though she shot a worried glance in his direction, she didn't say anything. He could guess what was on her mind.

"I won't ask you to stay. Fannie can remain with me in the store, like our folks did with us, and I'll hire a tutor." He didn't add that it had been a stupid idea to think marriage would solve anything. They would get along without Victoria. He'd help his daughter adjust to another person walking out of her life, and he wouldn't put Fannie through this again.

Maggie's troubled gaze locked with his. "Will you go after her?"

"No."

His sister's eyes grew sad. "I know I told you I don't remember anything about the fire, but I do remember one thing. I remember you holding onto me. Even when the roof collapsed, you didn't let go. You held on. Don't let go this time, David."

*V*ictoria sipped coffee from a steaming cup and peered over the edge. From where she sat on a stool in front of a counter, she could observe shoppers in Sumner's Five Cent Store, and possibly deduce why it was so popular, which gave her something to focus on besides her misery. She shouldn't have come in here. This wasn't helping her mood at all. But while she was here, she might as well make good use of her time. Even if David didn't want her, there was no reason she couldn't help him by passing along whatever she learned.

Overhead, etched globes glowed brightly and the light reflected off wood floors polished to a high sheen. The aisles were free of clutter. Items placed on display were clearly marked with prices, most being a nickel or less, although there were costlier goods as well.

David had the same goods—actually it seemed he offered more—and by expanding to the building next door he could open up space and make it easier for shoppers to get inside and look around. She could help him organize merchandise. Before she left.

"Would you like more coffee?" Mr. Sumner, who'd taken a seat next to her, lifted a silver carafe. He seemed content to let clerks take care of the customers while he saw to his guest, and the customers appeared happy with the arrangement.

Not only was Sumner's store better lit and less confusing to navigate, he also employed women. The clerks dressed in crisp white shirtwaists and black skirts. The fact that they also happened to be pretty and young might have something to do with his store's popularity.

David didn't need to hire pretty young women to work in his store. Men made perfectly competent clerks.

Victoria set her empty cup on the counter and gave the host a polite smile. "Thank you, I'm much warmer now. You've been very generous."

"That's what I'd like for you to think. I don't typically find beautiful strangers on my doorstep and I couldn't resist."

Perhaps she shouldn't have come in for that cup of coffee. She didn't wish for Mr. Sumner to be misled into thinking she'd come looking for him. "Your window display caught my eye."

"Did it?" His russet eyebrows arched with interest. "Are you looking for anything in particular?"

"Nothing I can purchase, I'm afraid."

"Anything I can help with?"

"No, though I appreciate the offer." She wouldn't insult him by telling him his interest did nothing but increase her melancholy. The only man's affections she wanted to attract were David's, and he seemed determined to guard them.

Mr. Sumner reached inside his coat, withdrew a flyer and handed it to her. "Here's a better offer. There's a reading of Dickens' *Christmas Carol* tonight. If you'd consider attending, I'd be honored to escort you."

If only David were so persistent.

Her heart constricted in a spasm of longing and regret. David hadn't been the one to walk out. He had pledged his life to her, whether or not he'd spoken the words she wanted to hear. She in turn had promised fidelity. Yet, moments ago she'd been ready to abandon him because he couldn't give her the kind of love she wanted. How could she demand love when she wasn't willing to give it?

Love was patient and kind, longsuffering and hopeful. Love honored its vows, even if it didn't get its own way. If she turned her back on David, she didn't deserve those things she had hoped for, because love, true love, didn't give up.

With a polite smile, she returned the flyer. "I'm very sorry if I've misled you, sir. I am promised to Mr. O'Brien."

"Indeed? I must say that comes as a surprise." Mr. Sumner folded the paper, and his smile turned wry. "Scrooge is a lucky man."

Scrooge? The name did fit insofar as David being miserly and up until lately not having much Christmas cheer. But if someone as hardhearted as Scrooge could change, so could David. He just needed an angel to show him the way back to his true self. And hadn't he called her a *perfect angel*?

She set down the cup. "Thank you for your well wishes. I do look forward to being Mrs. Scrooge. Now, I need to get back."

"Yes, you do." A shadow fell across the counter.

Victoria's heart leapt with joy even before she looked up. David hadn't let her go. He'd come after her.

He looked windblown without his hat. He'd forgotten his overcoat, as well. His dark eyes flashed with anger, which was directed at his competitor. When he looked at her, his gaze turned anxious. "Come home, Victoria."

Her home was with him, that's what he was saying. What her heart already knew.

"O'Brien." Mr. Sumner greeted his guest without enthusiasm. "Seems I stumbled across your bride-to-be. Did you notice she'd gone missing?"

The jab wasn't amusing, even if it was meant to be.

"Don't be ridiculous. David knew I went out for a short walk." Victoria slid off the stool, smiling at her husband. She had no intention of embarrassing him, and had she been thinking more clearly, wouldn't have ventured inside his competitor's store without him. "Mr. Sumner was kind enough to offer me a cup of coffee."

David secured her arm firmly through his, addressing the other man in a flat tone. "Thank you for your thoughtfulness."

"Anytime." Mr. Sumner turned to her and dipped his chin. "Good luck to you, *Mrs.* Scrooge." He touched his forehead in what looked like a salute and strolled away.

"What was that about," David grumbled.

She shrugged. "Maybe he thought I had a part in tonight's reading of Mr. Dickens' Christmas story."

"Scrooge wasn't married."

"No? Mr. Sumner must not know his literature."

David circled his arm around her, a possessive gesture that thrilled her. He guided her past shoppers and out the door. Wagons and buggies lined up along hitching rails on both sides of the street. Women bundled in coats and capes crowded the sidewalks. Men on horseback thronged the street. Despite the cold, more people were out shopping the closer it was to Christmas.

She huddled against David to share her warmth. "I'm

sorry if I worried you. I didn't intend to remain gone for so long."

"Did you intend to go to Sumner's?"

His bland tone didn't fool her. He hadn't been happy about where she'd stopped. If fact, he couldn't get her across the street fast enough.

"Mr. Sumner offered me a cup of coffee to warm up, and I was cold, so I accepted. I've always been curious as to why his store is popular." She'd made a mental list of improvements they could make, which wouldn't include pretty clerks.

"Did you find what you were looking for?" David's set expression made it appear he was braced for some bad news. He assisted her up to the sidewalk in front of his store, and then turned her to look at him.

Her heart constricted. She couldn't be angry with him for having doubts after she'd walked out without a word. There was so much she wanted to tell him, but not out here. When they went inside where it was warm, she would explain a few things about love. Better yet, she'd show him. "You should know, Mr. O'Brien, I won't find what I desire there."

DAVID DIDN'T GET the chance to ask Victoria if she might find what she desired with him because Mrs. Robinson and her daughter stopped to offer greetings.

"Merry Christmas Mr. O'Brien, and to you, Miss Lowell," said the elder of the two.

The younger woman peered through the window from beneath a fur-trimmed hood. "Oh mother, look. What a lovely Christmas tree."

"Victoria's idea," David bragged, and wrapped his arm around her waist. She'd done more than bring Christmas into his store, she had brought hope back into his life, and he wasn't letting her take it away.

"Any of the ornaments on the tree you may purchase," Victoria told the two women. His wife was a natural at sales. She was, as Maggie had promised, *perfect*.

"We'll be sure to take a look," Mrs. Robinson said. "Come along, Nancy."

A frigid gust swirled down the sidewalk. The two women pulled their cloaks tight and hurried into the store. David clamped his teeth together, the cold cut right through him because he'd forgotten his coat in his rush to get to Victoria. The fact was, he loved her, and keeping silent about it wouldn't change that, no more than his daughter's silence would change the past. They had both been silent for too long.

Victoria hugged his arm. "Let's go inside with the others."

"Not before I tell you—"

Fannie scampered outside. She threw her arms around Victoria's waist, and clung to her like she'd never let go. Victoria's surprised expression became tender, regretful. She put an arm around Fannie.

"Were you afraid I wasn't coming back?"

"She was. So was I." He'd been terrified. On top of that, angry enough to spit nails. When he'd barged into Sumner's store and saw her having coffee with the owner, it had taken every ounce of willpower not to grab Sumner by his shiny black coat, drag him off the stool and beat him to a bloody pulp.

Victoria gazed at him and her eyes spoke for her. She understood his fears, and loved him in spite of them. He'd been an idiot to think he could resist loving her.

Fannie raised her hand, stared at it, apparently trying to think of how to sign something. Then she looked straight at Victoria. "How do you say *I'm sorry*?"

Good God. She'd spoken.

David was so stunned to hear his daughter's voice, he couldn't think of what to say. Victoria appeared just as astonished.

"Fannie?" he said, when he found his voice. He knelt before her and gently grasped her hands, and then it hit him what she'd said, the first words out of her mouth in two years, and it broke his heart. "You haven't done anything wrong. I'm the one who needs to apologize."

His daughter nodded solemnly. "You're sorry, too. Tell her, Dada."

She'd started calling him "Dada" when she was tiny, and he'd point to himself and say, "Da." By the time she was two, she'd been chattering all the time. She was so smart, and she was right. Still on one knee, he turned his attention to Victoria. "How do you say, *I'm sorry*?"

Victoria's eyes glistened with tears. She formed a fist and made a circle over her chest. "I'm sorry," she said softly.

He gestured. "I'm sorrier."

Her lips twitched into a smile. "That's not a word."

"It's an apology."

"Are you coming back?" Fannie's voice still surprised him. Lilting, clear, as if she'd never stopped talking.

Victoria bent down, hugged Fannie and kissed her cheek. "Yes, dear."

"And you won't be leaving," he added, and then waited, anxious for her confirmation.

Victoria's cheeks turned bright pink. Could be because

he'd put her on the spot, or it might be the cold, or due to the audience they'd attracted. A gaggle of women looked on from a few feet away. Two old farmers hitched their rigs with more slowness than could be accounted for on a frigid day. Everyone appeared to be waiting on Victoria's response.

"We're handfasted, David. Pledged to each other," she said loud enough for all to hear. "I seem to recall you said forever."

He shot to his feet and dragged her into his arms. "*Mo chroí. I should've told you before, I love you.*"

She hugged him. "And I love you, my darling."

"Me, too. I love you, too!" Fannie pressed into his side. He drew her up against him, and Victoria put her arm around his daughter's shoulders, bringing her into their circle. If possible, he loved his bride even more.

Victoria had brought him and his daughter out of a dark place where they'd retreated, back into the light. Now they would become a family, and God willing more children would follow.

A few claps sounded, and then the applause swelled. There were a few hoots, as well.

Maggie had slipped out the door and stood nearby, with her arms crossed over her chest and wearing a big smile. "My, my...you three are putting on quite a show."

David glanced around at the growing crowd. He could care less if everyone in town knew he loved Victoria. In fact, he'd hang a sign. "We should charge an admission."

"Or invite everyone in for cider," Victoria suggested.

"Better idea." He made wide, welcoming gesture. "Come on in, everyone. Join me in a toast to my bride, Victoria."

EPILOGUE

July 1, 1891, Fort Scott, Kansas

"Yᴏᴜ bought the last one." David handed the customer her receipt.

"I'm eager to try it out," replied Mrs. Robinson. The elder matron cast a furtive glance over her shoulder at her unhappy daughter, who held onto the handlebars of a bicycle. "Nancy doesn't want me to have one. But I say, I'll only be this young once."

Victoria smiled at Mrs. Robinson's cheeky wink. The woman had to be sixty if she was a day. Everyone should be as spry and sassy at that age.

"Let me help you load it," David offered. He circled the counter and walked the bicycle to the door.

Business had improved since they'd been able to expand to the next building and add larger items to their inventory, as well as reduce the clutter. David had also turned up the lights.

"Do be careful," Victoria called after the older woman. She would be remiss if she didn't issue the warning.

Mrs. Robinson gave a wave of her hand, as she and Nancy followed David outside. "I've been careful all my life. It's time I had a little fun. You take care of yourself, now, and that baby. We're eager to meet the little tyke."

Victoria stood from the stool where she'd sat to take a short rest. She stretched the tight muscles in her back, and felt a movement low in her belly, a kick, which brought on a delighted smile. Her hand curled protectively around her swelling middle. Their baby had become very active. The doctor said that was a good sign.

Fannie looked up from a stool at the end of the counter, where she sat working on her handwriting. She'd been able to start school, and in fact, was far ahead of her classmates in her reading, writing and ciphering skills. She grinned, revealing a space where her front teeth had been a few months earlier. "Is my brother jumping rope again?"

"Feels like it." Victoria put her hand on Fannie's shoulder and gently warned her. "We can't be sure he's a boy."

She nodded with grave authority. "Uh huh. We can. You've been dropping things a lot, and if you get clumsy, it's a boy. That's what my teacher says."

"What if I'm just prone to clumsiness because I'm getting bigger?"

Fannie pointed with her pencil. "Maybe you got *two* boys in there."

"Good heavens." Victoria placed her hands on her rounded belly. She wasn't sure whether to be thrilled by the idea, or terrified.

Fannie pushed her paper aside and jumped down. "I'm done now. Can I go find Pumpkin?"

"He's probably in your father's office."

David had allowed Fannie to keep one kitten, as well as the mother. He claimed he wasn't fond of cats and only put up with them because the two were "good mousers." The lazy orange tabby loved to slip inside his office and curl up in his chair. He'd placed a cushion on the seat. For his own comfort, he said. But Victoria suspected he'd provided it for the cat.

That was another thing she loved about him, his soft heart.

The bell jangled as David returned. He flipped the sign around to *Closed* and locked up. "It's been a good day. We've sold all our bicycles—and didn't have to charge a nickel."

She smiled at his reminder of her insistence they price more items at a nickel to better compete with the Five-Cent Store. "We took in a good number of nickels, as well."

"Thanks to you." He gave her a kiss, and then he put his hand on her protruding stomach, smiling when he was rewarded with a sharp kick. "They say boys are more active in the womb."

"Have you and Fannie been comparing notes?" Victoria's smile faded. Her father made no secret of his disappointment in a female child. David wasn't like that. He might prefer a boy, however. "What if it's a girl?"

"Then Fannie will have a feisty little sister." He wrapped his arm around Victoria and pulled her into a tight hug. "Boy or girl, all I care about is that our baby is healthy."

She leaned her head against his shoulder. "I love you."

"And I love you, *mo chroí.*" The Gaelic phrase rolled off his tongue. He'd told her the meaning of the Irish endearments he used, which expressed his feelings so beautifully. Hearing him speak them warmed her heart.

Speaking of warm hearts... "My friend Roberta wrote to me again. She's expecting, too."

"Two?" David held up two fingers.

"Oh my, no. She has two stepsons, one baby on the way. At least, I don't recall that she said anything about twins."

David splayed his hand over her stomach.

She felt a flutter and then a kick. "There's only one in there. I'm sure of it."

"We could accommodate two. There's an empty drawer in the bureau."

"Very funny. No more talk of twins. It's making me nervous." She reached into the wide pocket of her apron and withdrew a letter she'd received earlier in the day. "My father's reply."

She'd written shortly after her wedding to let him know she was well and happily married. However, she hadn't expected her father to write back. His response had, in some ways, surprised her.

"What does he say?" David asked.

"You want to read his letter?"

"Give me the high points."

"I'm not sure there are high points. He says he's known all along where to find me. I assume he hired a private detective. He said chose not to contact me, to *honor my wishes*."

"Sounds like he's acknowledging your right to make your own choices."

She twisted her lips in a wry smile. "Maybe if it came from your father that's what it would mean, but from mine, it means he's scolding me for not honoring *his* wishes."

"What else does he say? Did you tell him about our marriage?"

"Yes..." This was where it got sticky. "He calls you an

Irish peasant and a Catholic pagan all in the same paragraph."

David rubbed his hand down her arm. "He's warming up to me."

She laughed. "Do tell me how you managed that interpretation."

"He's acknowledging my existence. If he rejected our marriage, he wouldn't bother to comment because he wouldn't care. He's annoyed you married below your station. That's understandable. What else does he say?"

"He enclosed something." She drew the tissue-wrapped gift from her pocket and showed David the delicate filigreed gold ring, which she'd recognized immediately. "It belonged to my mother. He said I'm just like her."

"What was your mother like?"

"Loving and kind. But she was very willful, too. She never forgave my father for telling her I should've been a boy."

"That was a stupid thing to say. I'm sure somewhere along the way, he regretted it. But it's clear to me he loved your mother, and he's trying to say he loves you, and don't tell me I'm interpreting that wrong."

"No, oddly enough, I think you're right."

"Of course I'm right. I'm always right."

She cocked an eyebrow. "Always?"

He turned her in his arms and dropped a tender kiss on her forehead. "Almost always. Except for when you're right."

Victoria gazed lovingly into his eyes. "I was right when I selected you from among the prospective grooms who were advertising."

"Selected me? You didn't know me until we met."

That's where he was wrong, and where he'd always been wrong. "Oh yes I did. I knew you through your sister's eyes, and she knew you better than you knew yourself. I'm glad she introduced us."

David heaved a sigh of mock resignation. "Oh, all right, I admit it, she did me a favor. But don't ever tell her I said so... and let's not encourage her to do anymore matchmaking."

The End

SANTA'S MAIL-ORDER BRIDE

E.E. BURKE

Maggie O'Brien plays matchmaker again. This time, for the local Santa, who also happens to be her brother's fiercest competitor. She's in for a surprise when he helps her a craft the advertisement for Santa's perfect bride.

CHAPTER 1

December 7, 1892, Fort Scott, Kansas

"*E*very child deserves a Christmas present." Maggie O'Brien paced the length of her brother's general store with her fifteen-month-old nephew propped on her hip. The gleeful toddler tugged at loose strands of her hair, no longer in an artful arrangement.

She tickled him to distract him. "Isn't that right, Paddy?"

The cherub laughed and said something that sounded like *Mama*.

"Yes, your Mama is busy now. Look at all the people buying presents. Wouldn't it be nice if some of these gifts could be sent to the orphans? Don't you agree, Victoria?"

Her sister-in-law finished wrapping a stuffed toy in brown paper, smiling as she handed it to a customer, while Maggie's brother David waited on a gentleman purchasing a hobbyhorse.

"I do agree," Victoria answered, after the customer walked away. "Every child deserves to be shown love."

Hugging Patrick close, Maggie sidestepped a distracted couple accompanied by three children. The youngest, a boy, stopped to examine a sack of marbles, while two older girls wandered over to a display featuring paper dolls with crepe paper clothing, a gift that would appeal to her niece Fannie. Customers were packed like sardines into O'Brien's, taking advantage of the unexpected sunshine to do some Christmas shopping.

Not every child had someone who loved them purchasing hobbyhorses, marbles and dolls, and Maggie's heart ached for those orphaned children. Worse, homeless children in Kansas were put to work on poor farms or languished in dingy facilities crowded with impoverished adults.

This year, Maggie had come home on a mission—to collect gifts for orphaned children in the area and distribute them by Christmas Eve. How she'd accomplish this, she wasn't sure. She had a list of fifty names. Collecting that many gifts in roughly three weeks boggled the mind, but she was determined to show these children they were not forgotten.

David looked over the next customer's shoulder. "It's not us you need to convince, Maggie."

"I know. You've been very generous."

Not surprisingly, her brother had agreed to aid her. They both had a soft spot for orphans, having lost their parents at an early age. They had been fortunate to be taken in by friends, but David had been forced to drop out of school at twelve to go to work so he could support them.

Homeless children also needed schooling, as well as to have their basic needs met. Sadly, she didn't have the wealth or the influence to make that happen anytime soon. She could, however, provide Christmas presents—if she could find enough backers.

Maggie passed by the large glass window overlooking the street. Wagons and buggies lined the hitching post in front of O'Brien's. Mr. Sumner's Five Cent Store also appeared busy, as usual. The two stores, opposite each other, engaged in heated competition. David had nearly been forced to close his doors two years ago, until he'd made changes to the store. The merchant across the street had few scruples, and he would undoubtedly come up with some new way to harass her brother.

She continued walking with her nephew, looking for ways to keep him entertained, paused at a table with a display of mechanical toys. When Patrick reached for a wind-up train, she did a quick turn on her heel and headed for safe territory. How his parents kept him from turning the store upside down was beyond her. She didn't dare put him on his feet. Forget bull in a china shop, he was a frolicking calf.

"Is this Patrick, or do my eyes deceive me?" One of the customers, Mrs. Robinson, waylaid them. The stately matron had more lines in her face than last year and her steps seemed slower. There was nothing slow about her mind. Her eyes snapped with intelligence and curiosity. "Miss O'Brien, it's good to see you again. You're home for good, or just for Christmas?"

"Only through Christmas, and then it's back to the schoolroom."

"How do you like Kansas City? I hear that cow town will soon be more populous than Fort Scott, though I can hardly believe it."

"Oh, that's a fact, what with all the railroads and the

stockyards." Maggie loved the bustle and excitement of the growing city, but she missed home far more than she'd thought she would. She'd been gone two years, off teaching, which was what she'd always wanted to do. She would be forever grateful to her older brother, who had scrimped and saved to send her to a teacher's college. He'd sacrificed so much for her. She would never let him down.

Mrs. Robinson patted Patrick's back as he bounced on Maggie's hip. "You're getting to be a big boy."

"Yes, indeed." Maggie lifted her nephew's compact weight higher and smiled at him. "How big is Paddy?"

With a huge grin, he lifted his arms in the air and stretched them out as far as he could.

"*Sooo* big," Maggie dragged out the first word, to the delight of her nephew.

Patrick giggled and patted her cheek. She'd earned an *A* with the correct response. *So big* had become his favorite game, next to pulling the cat's tail.

"What a sweet-tempered child," Mrs. Robinson cooed. "And he looks just like his father."

"That he does." Maggie had rather hoped her brother's child would have his mother's striking aqua eyes and golden hair. Not surprisingly, Paddy had inherited the black O'Brien eyes and hair, as had his father and his aunt and his half-sister Fannie. But, oh, he was a beautiful boy, healthy and happy, just as every child should be.

Mrs. Robinson gave Patrick another fond pat. The wealthy matron served on the board of St. Andrew's Episcopal, the oldest church in town, and had her finger in every pie when it came to local charities. She would be a perfect person to ask for help.

"Have you ever seen a *poor farm*?"

The widow appeared puzzled by Maggie's question. "No, can't say that I have."

"It's a sad place, I can tell you." Maggie couldn't get the images out of her mind. *Poor farm* was an appropriate moniker for those awful places. "They work the children like slaves, and still there's barely enough to feed and clothe them. I have a list of fifty orphans just from this area alone that won't have a Christmas if we don't do something about it. I'm collecting gifts for them. David and Victoria have been very generous, but their contributions won't be enough. Could you suggest others who might help? Churches, perhaps?

The elderly lady's face folded into a sad smile. "That's very kind of you, my dear, but I wouldn't count on the churches for more than what they've already committed to doing. They all have collections this time of year to help needy families. You'll have to look elsewhere, I'm afraid."

Maggie's spirits dipped. She thought it would be easy to gain support, especially around Christmastime, but this was the message she'd heard from several other people.

"You say your brother is donating goods?" the older woman asked.

"Yes, clothes and toys."

"What about asking that nice gentleman across the street for donations? Mr. Sumner ought to be willing to match his competitor." Mrs. Robinson's eyes twinkled. "If you make a personal request."

Soliciting donations from the owner of the second largest store in Fort Scott would be a good suggestion, if it didn't require talking to him. Not to mention, Gordon Sumner would be unlikely to help the sister of his chief competitor, even if she made her plea *personally*.

Maggie shifted Patrick to her other hip, and lowered her

voice so others in the store couldn't hear her. "I doubt Mr. Sumner would be open to any request I'd make. He and David don't get along."

"My dear, if you're determined to have those gifts, you may have to mend a few fences." Mrs. Robinson kissed Paddy's cheek and then took her leave.

"She's right, you know," came a soft voice from behind.

Maggie turned to meet her sister-in-law's knowing gaze. Victoria didn't have a mean bone in her body, not even one reserved for her husband's archrival. "Not you, too."

"Contrary to what you and David seem to think, Mr. Sumner doesn't have fangs and claws. He's very civil, and I suspect he would be happy to help you."

"You're the soul of kindness, Victoria. The man could be a wolf in disguise and you'd invite him to dinner."

Maggie would never admit she'd taken notice of the handsome Mr. Sumner. What woman wouldn't? However, the eligible Easterner flirted with every young lady in town. He wouldn't be interested in her in particular, even if she wanted him to be, which she didn't. Not even if he did have lovely auburn hair and the bluest eyes she'd ever seen.

Victoria glanced over at her husband, who'd started frowning the moment Sumner's name was mentioned. "We needn't extend a dinner invitation. All you're asking for is a donation." She reached for Patrick. "Here, I'll take him. It's time for his lunch and a nap."

Patrick began to fuss the moment he heard the word *nap*.

Victoria rubbed his back soothingly. "Thank you for watching him, Maggie."

"I loved every minute," Maggie pressed a kiss on the toddler's head. He smelled warm and sweet, just like a baby should smell. She adored her nephew and her eight-year-old niece and missed being around them.

She had lived with her brother and looked after Fannie for a troubled two years after David's first wife had abandoned them. He'd been miserable until Victoria came along.

Maggie took no small amount of pride in her matchmaking efforts. Thanks to her, David had found his true love. She longed to discover that same rare connection. Growing up, she dreamed of finding her soul's mate, but at the advanced age of twenty-four, she had yet to meet a man who made her heart race.

"I'll walk over to the school and meet Fannie," she told Victoria. "There's a Christmas tree exhibit at Convention Hall I'd like to show her."

"She'd love that, I'm sure." Victoria stroked her son's silky hair as he laid his head on her shoulder. "And do consider Mrs. Robinson's suggestion. You'll need all the help you can muster if you're determined to collect fifty gifts by Christmas."

Maggie sighed with resignation. She had avoided the charming Mr. Sumner because her loyalty would always be to her family, and heaven forbid she might actually like the man. But her sister-in-law was right. Nothing should get in the way of collecting those gifts, not even her reluctance to do business with a dapper carnivore.

She straightened her shoulders. "I'll pay Mr. Sumner a visit this afternoon."

CHAPTER 2

Gordon Sumner slammed the account book shut. Another round of calculations wouldn't improve the numbers. He glared at a stack of letters on the desk next to the lamp, then jerked open a drawer, crammed the unopened envelopes inside and shut it. Why bother reading them? He knew Sikes had passed the point of impatience six months ago. Sales had better be stellar this Christmas, or he was in big trouble.

He grasped the gold fob and drew his watch out of his vest pocket. Six o'clock. Time to lock up. For the month of December, he'd kept the store open an hour later than usual, in hopes of snagging his competitor's customers. O'Brien's always closed at five sharp. Had the other store folded last year as anticipated, his problems would have been solved. Somehow, the stubborn Irishman hung on. He'd even expanded and improved the interior, and his efforts had paid off. By all signs, O'Brien's was doing well.

Sum swore. He would win this battle. This time he wouldn't fail.

Standing, he pocketed the watch and left his office. He'd

go downstairs, collect the day's proceeds from the till and tell the clerk she could go home, if she hadn't left already.

When he'd first opened his Five Cent Store, he anticipated needing only a single clerk to manage the cash register. Unlike an the old fashioned shebang, his store featured goods displayed in clear view and marked with prices, eliminating the necessity of clerks having to memorize prices and quote them to customers. He'd hired Anna Smith, and then discovered having pretty women around helped his business. So he hired a few more like her, mostly as window dressing.

Even with the improvement in sales, he could no longer afford window dressing. Over the past year, he'd let go of all but one clerk. After the Christmas rush, he would, regrettably, have to do without Miss Smith. He hated to dismiss the hardworking young woman, knowing the girl was her family's only source of income since her father had been killed in a mining accident and her mother had fallen ill. After his debts were cleared, he would rehire Miss Smith.

Downstairs, the overhead lights burned brightly, although the store appeared to be empty...except for a woman standing in front the Christmas display. That wasn't his clerk. But he would recognize her anywhere, even from the back. The Irishman's sister.

Sum's mood immediately improved. He'd wanted to get to know the black-haired beauty ever since meeting her on his first day in town. Sadly, she had avoided him like he carried a plague. Then she'd moved away. She must've come home for Christmas. That didn't explain what had brought her into his store. Why speculate when he could ask?

"Miss O'Brien. May I help you?"

She turned, her brown cloak swirling around a green plaid skirt. The woodsy colors complemented her dark hair and gypsy eyes. "Ah, Mr. Sumner, good evening. I thought the store might be closed, but I saw your lights were still on."

"We've extended our hours this season. Did Miss Smith let you in?"

"Your clerk said to tell you she had to leave to pick up some medicine for her mother. She...she said it was all right if I looked around while I waited." His lovely visitor flushed a becoming shade of pink and clutched a small handbag to her chest. Had the Irish lass ever shown a smidgeon of interest, he might've interpreted her reaction as a virginal woman's response to a man who fired her blood. He didn't presume that to be the case with Miss O'Brien. Still, he couldn't help being pleased she'd sought him out for some purpose.

"You're welcome in my store anytime." He reached up to straighten his tie before remembering he'd pulled the bow loose and unbuttoned his collar, deciding he might as well be comfortable as he reviewed the books—a process that made every item he wore feel as if it pinched. Not only that, he'd left his coat upstairs. Greeting a lady wearing a wrinkled shirt and waistcoat wasn't how one made a good impression. Though impressing Miss O'Brien shouldn't be high on his list of priorities. She was his adversary's sister, therefore, not to be trusted.

If he had the sense of a clam, he'd close his shell.

Clams weren't known for their intelligence.

She made a brief assessment of the store before regarding him quizzically. "You've invested a great deal into furnishings. Where did you find the etched globes and maple display cases?"

A laugh bubbled up his throat. "You came in here to talk about my furnishings?"

"No..." She fussed with the drawstrings on her bag, twisting them around her fingers, looking everywhere but at him. "I came over here to ask you for money."

His ego took a hard fall. "Money?"

"Or goods, either would do." The tip of her tongue sneaked out and moistened her lips.

He had the most insane thought that if she offered a kiss in exchange, he would grant her wishes. However, he couldn't imagine why she'd ask him for money, unless her brother was in financial straits.

Sum arranged his face in a look of concern to hide a very uncharitable reaction to the possible *bad* news. "May I take your cloak? We can sit down and have a cup of coffee while we discuss your, um...needs."

Her blush deepened to crimson. "That's not necessary. It's not my needs I'm concerned with at the moment. The gifts are for the orphans."

"The orphans?" Not what he'd expected her to say, nor was it a fascinating topic. Given the choice, he'd rather talk about her. "You can spare a few minutes, surely? After all, you've made a rather curious request, and should I grant it, I'd like to know more."

Unease flickered across her face. She had no desire to linger, and if his guess was right, she loathed the very idea of seeking him out.

His self-confidence was taking a beating.

"Very well. I'll stay...for a *short* visit."

She turned, allowing him to take her wrap. As he drew the cloak off her shoulders, an intriguing scent teased his nose. Peppermint. How delightful...she smelled of candy. His mouth watered.

With no small effort, he dragged his mind away from inappropriate longings. Sweet or not, she didn't belong to him. Therefore, he had no business kissing the back of her neck, no matter how good she smelled.

Sum draped the cloak over his arm. He gestured in the direction of the back counter, where stools were set up for shoppers who wished to tarry and indulge in pastries or a sandwich. "All the baked goods have been purchased, or I would offer you something to eat."

"Thank you, I'm not hungry."

"Coffee or tea? I could make either.

"No, thank you. I'm not thirsty."

Not easy to please, apparently. But what beautiful woman was? He could be smitten if she sent him one tiny signal that she shared this insane attraction.

Sum waited until she sat down before he slipped onto a stool next to her. His knee brushed against her skirt. She twisted to one side to open space between them. Modesty? Or she might fear he would pounce. He found her skittishness charming.

"Just who are these orphans? They must be important to have compelled you to enter my lair...I mean, store."

Her lips didn't so much as twitch.

He adopted a droll tone. "Rumor has it, you have a sense of humor."

"I do, when something's funny."

He smoothed his mustache to wipe away a smile. She probably wouldn't appreciate him saying he found her amusing, as well as alluring.

Her gaze became very direct. Not just brown, her eyes were nearly black, yet her skin glowed with pale opalescence. The contrast made her beauty all the more exquisite. "I won't waste any more of your time..." she started.

"You aren't wasting my time. I can think of nothing I'd rather being doing at the moment."

"Have you ever been to a poor farm, Mr. Sumner?"

She was about to play on his heartstrings with a sad tale. Thus far this season, he'd heard no less than a dozen pathetic stories, and had spared all the good will he could afford. She should've shown up earlier. Nevertheless, he would listen to her plea, especially if it meant she would stay longer.

"No, I haven't been to a poor farm, if by that you mean one of those places they put homeless children to work. I presume you have?"

Her expression grew somber. "Yes. Fortunately, I was never sent to one. After our parents died, my brother and I moved in with an elderly shopkeeper and his wife. I suspect we would've ended up on a poor farm had David not gone to work to support us."

Sum frowned at the surprising revelation. He'd heard her brother had reopened his parents' business, but hadn't known the couple died early. "How old were you when they passed away?"

"They were killed in a fire when I was four and David was ten." She looked down at her lap, fiddling with the fringe along the bottom of her purse.

Sum wanted to know more about her past, but he wouldn't probe if it made her uncomfortable. She appeared achingly young and vulnerable, and he had a sudden urge to put his arms around her. He was certain the gesture wouldn't be welcomed. "That explains why you have a heart for orphans."

She looked up with surprise. "I hope you share my concern, Mr. Sumner. I've committed to providing gifts for fifty orphaned children. That's why I'm asking for your contribution."

Contrary to what she'd heard, he did have a heart. She might have better luck than most with breaking it, if he wasn't careful. "Of course I share your concern. Only a hardhearted brute wouldn't."

Miss O'Brien rewarded him with a warm smile. "I'm relieved to hear you are a man of compassion. Victoria felt sure you would help."

Another surprise. He hadn't imagined the wealthy Boston Brahmin-turned-shopkeeper's wife had a soft spot in her heart for him. Two years ago, he'd flirted with Victoria when she'd ventured over to his store, something O'Brien hadn't appreciated if the murder in his eyes gave any indication. "How nice to know Mrs. O'Brien speaks well of me."

"Oh, I wouldn't go that far. My sister-in-law only said she expected you to match my brother's contribution."

Clever girl. Miss O'Brien had thrown down a gauntlet, his competitor's generosity.

Sum wouldn't be bested. "How much do you need?"

"My brother is donating generously. He's providing gifts for five children. Would you be willing to do the same?"

He would, except he had no excess inventory. He couldn't afford to give away goods, and he had no extra cash on hand. Being woefully behind on repaying his debts, he didn't dare give freely.

"Mr. Sumner? Can I count on you for a contribution?"

He forced a smile, inwardly chiding himself for walking into an ambush. She'd used unfair tactics to distract him, her lovely face and form, and her delicious scent. "You'll need more than clothes and gifts for ten children."

"Yes, we need gifts for fifty. Could you manage more than five? I have a list." She eagerly dug into her purse.

He couldn't manage two. But, if he could figure out a way to get other people to pitch in to meet her quota, then that would solve her problem...and make him look like a hero.

Sliding off the stool, he began to pace. Thinking was easier when he moved. "There's not much time left."

"I know, I should've started earlier," she bemoaned.

"Don't lose hope. We'll come up with something."

"We?" She withdrew her hand from her purse. "I haven't formed a committee, nor do I recall asking you to be on one."

"Good. Committees take too long. If your volunteers are as difficult as those fools in charge of the Christmas parade, you'll never get anything done."

He came to an abrupt halt as his mind latched onto an idea. Oh, it was a good one. Not only would she gain the necessary contributions, but he would garner additional publicity, even more than what he'd hoped for in agreeing to don a costume and play the part of old St. Nick.

"The parade," he murmured. "Yes. That would be perfect."

"Parade? Perfect?" She shook her head. "I'm sorry, I'm not following."

"*Sumner's Five Cent Store* is sponsoring Santa's sleigh, and I'm dressing the part. What if, instead of giving gifts, Santa Claus requests contributions to his list, all of which will be delivered to the orphans by Christmas Eve."

Miss O'Brien's lovely lips parted and her eyes widened with surprise. "Oh! Oh, Mr. Sumner, that's brilliant!" She clapped her hands together like a delighted child, and then leapt off the stool and threw her arms around his neck. "How can I ever thank you?"

Oh, he could come up with several suggestions.

He leaned down to hug her and ended up crushing her soft breasts against his chest. Every muscle in his body tensed as desire buried him in an avalanche. Throwing caution to the wind, he picked her up and twirled her around. Before he released her, he stole a quick kiss.

"We'll get your orphans gifts, Miss O'Brien. I promise you."

She stared at him, dazed, and a rosy blush stained her cheeks. Her hands floated up to her mouth. At least she didn't slap him.

As for him, the brief touch only whetted his appetite for more. He vowed to get a longer, deeper kiss before Miss O'Brien waltzed out of his life again, and he knew just how he would engineer it.

"You...you..." she sputtered.

"Kissed you? Yes. That's what a man does with his wife."

She scurried backwards, the high color draining from her face. "What are you talking about? I'm not your wife."

"Not mine, Santa's. You, my dear, will be Mrs. Claus."

CHAPTER 3

*T*hree days later, Mr. Sumner showed up to escort Maggie to a meeting of the Christmas Parade committee, where they would present his idea. Not the part about Mrs. Claus. The flirtatious rascal would never convince her to be his pretend wife. The whole town would think she'd set her cap for him.

The day had dawned sparkling bright, the kind of winter morning when the sun lights up a clear blue sky and temperatures drop down low enough to freeze smiles into place. Just walking the short distance to the offices of the *Fort Scott Monitor and Tribune* turned her hands and feet into blocks of ice.

Mr. Sumner appeared unfazed by the cold and talked the entire way.

Maggie hadn't realized he could be so chatty, although it ended up being a good thing because she was nervous and it spared her from having to converse much. "Are you sure they'll approve your recommendation?" she asked as they neared the brick building at the corner of Wall Street.

"If we're in agreement, I don't see why not."

Maggie hesitated, and not for the first time. David hadn't liked the idea of his competitor's personal involvement in her project, but he'd gone along with it for her sake. She couldn't let him down by doing anything that would embarrass him, such as posing as Mr. Sumner's parade wife. "I'm agreeable to Santa Claus collecting gifts," she clarified.

When they reached the newspaper offices, Mr. Sumner indicated a bench in the front hallway. Taking her cloak, he hung it on a brass hook and then sat next to her.

"We're to wait here until we're summoned."

Maggie couldn't resist returning his impudent smile. The parade committee included Fort Scott's most influential citizens and some of the members acted like royalty.

Mr. Sumner squeezed in next to her on the bench, which had armrests carved into the shape of lion's claws. Somehow this seemed fitting, given her companion's predatory nature. After last night, she would be on guard for any unexpected attacks, such as that kiss he'd given her. To her mortal shame, she couldn't stop thinking about it. What had possessed him? Or did he go about kissing every lady he met?

She removed her gloves and flexed her fingers. "My hands are frozen. Hard to believe it can be so bitterly cold when the sun is shining."

"Appearances can be deceiving," he noted.

Indeed. By all appearances, Gordon Sumner would qualify as a gentleman. But *gentlemen* didn't kiss ladies without permission.

As a distraction, Maggie arranged the folds in the sumptuous velvet skirt. She'd put on her most festive outfit, which had a pine green jacket trimmed in red braid, and a matching figured bonnet. Mr. Sumner had complimented her so effusively she'd gotten embarrassed. Resisting the charmer would be easier if he weren't so amusing, not to mention handsome as sin.

He'd unbuttoned his double-breasted overcoat to reveal a fashionable gray suit with a contrasting waistcoat. The points of his starched white collar were neatly turned down, and he wore a colorful four-in-hand tie. *Looking savage*, as David would say. To impress the committee, no doubt about it. Then again, she couldn't recall a time Mr. Sumner didn't look impressive.

Her gaze drifted upward to his lips, which were framed by a cinnamon-colored mustache. Their kiss had lasted no more than an instant. Yet, in that moment, something inside her had shifted, and she had the strangest impression that her life had been altered, like a train switching tracks. Ridiculous, because nothing had changed. The kiss hadn't meant anything, even if it had made her lips tingle. That must've been on account of his mustache. She hadn't expected it to be so soft, and the tickle surprised her.

Drat, the tingling had started up again.

He smiled.

She met an admiring blue gaze and blushed. He'd caught her staring.

Flustered, she blurted the first thing that came to mind "Are you cold?" She formed a core with her hands and blew into it. "I should've brought thicker gloves."

"Give me your hands," he commanded.

Instead of waiting to see if she would comply, he reached over and took what he wanted, sandwiching her fingers between his palms, creating gentle friction. After a moment, delicious warmth penetrated her chilled skin. Then, the heat crept up her arms and spread throughout her entire body, reaching as high as her face.

"Thank you. Much better now." She tried to remove her hands.

He wouldn't let go. "You're still cold."

That wasn't why she was shivering.

"I'm not cold. Not anymore."

One of the men who worked for the newspaper strode down the hallway. He glanced over, eyeing them with a quizzical expression. Alarmed, she tugged her hands free and then flattened them on the seat. Whatever Mr. Sumner was up to, she wanted no part of it.

In fact, he'd surprised her when he suggested the gift collection idea and then offered to help her implement it. What could he possibly gain, save getting more coverage in the newspaper? "Why are you doing this?" she whispered.

He rested his hand on the bench over hers. "Warming you up?"

His touch did more than warm her; it sent alarming quivers across her skin and made her heart do sprints. The dratted man drew her off balance. Somehow, she had to find her way back to equilibrium. First, she must acknowledge reality. He wasn't her beau, and she would never be his bride, pretend or otherwise.

She removed her hand from beneath his and curled her fingers in her lap. "What I mean is, why are you helping me? Not out of sympathy for the children."

"You think I'm not sympathetic?" His tone implied she'd wounded him, though it was difficult to tell if he was teasing or serious.

"I only wondered if you might see this as an opportunity to polish your reputation."

"So, you believe me to be mercenary, as well as heartless." This time there was no mistaking his reaction. He looked puzzled, even a little hurt.

Her conscience took her to task. "Forgive me if I misread your intentions." That wasn't good enough. She had insulted him. "You've been very kind, and I do appreciate your help."

"My pleasure."

His smooth baritone, low and resonant, reminded her of the purr of a very large cat. He hadn't curled up beside her, but he sat very close—close enough to make her heart beat faster, and her breathing quicken.

Footsteps sounded on the hardwood floors. Mr. Marble, the newspaper editor, approached with a pencil tucked behind his ear. "Mr. Sumner, Miss O'Brien. The committee is ready to discuss your proposal."

"Excellent." Her companion stood and offered her his hand. Maggie allowed him to tuck her fingers into the crook of his arm because that was the polite thing to do. Had she been able to avoid touching him, she would have. The effect was far too stimulating.

They entered a large, dim room, made darker because of the wood paneling on the walls. Heavy curtains had been drawn over the windows to keep out the cold. Light from a gas chandelier illuminated an oval table and twelve committee members sitting around it.

The gentlemen stood as she entered. Feeling ridiculously shy, she clung to Mr. Sumner's arm. She knew every person sitting at that table, had known most of them all of her life, but that didn't make her any less nervous. David was the one who had business dealings with grownups. She was more comfortable in front of a roomful of children.

"Good morning, ladies and gentleman." Mr. Sumner sounded confident and at ease, as if he presented in front of important people all the time.

Mr. O'Connor, who insisted everyone call him Buck, gestured to two chairs. "Mr. Sumner, Miss O'Brien, please sit down."

The elder businessman cut an intimidating figure at well over six feet, with rugged features, flowing white hair and pale blue eyes. Seated next to him was his wife. Strands of gray marked her rich brown hair, yet she had an ageless beauty. Although petite, she exuded authority, which made her nearly as intimidating as her husband.

Mr. Sumner pulled out a chair. He laid his hand on Maggie's shoulder in a brief, comforting touch, before taking the seat next to her.

Mrs. O'Connor sent her an encouraging smile. "Good to see you back in town, Miss O'Brien. How long will you remain?"

Before Maggie could respond, Mrs. Mueller interrupted. "Miss O'Brien, we understand you wish to *collect* gifts this year instead of giving them away."

The disdainful tone sent Maggie's hackles up. Oh, she had seen that one in the store a few times, although the rich lady didn't purchase readymade items. Mrs. Mueller ordered her dresses from Eastern designers, along with fashionable hats, including the one she had on, which featured stuffed birds pasted to the side. She and her hat were equally gruesome.

"That's right, Mrs. Mueller, we wish to collect gifts for a charitable purpose." Mr. Sumner spoke before Maggie could make her tongue move. His wry smile made her wonder whether he shared similar feelings about the woman and her hat.

He'd remarked earlier that they might meet resistance from the town's wealthiest patron, who'd come up with the idea for the Christmas parade and considered it her personal project. Even her nickname, *Old Ironsides*, implied trouble.

"Miss O'Brien, would you like to explain our cause?" With that, Mr. Sumner gave her the floor.

"Yes, of course." She dug into her bag and retrieved the list. "I have the names of fifty orphans across Bourbon and Linn counties who won't receive gifts for Christmas unless we provide them. Most live on poor farms. Have any of you ever been to a poor farm?"

Mrs. Mueller's nostrils flared like she smelled something offensive. "No, I'm not in the habit of sticking my nose into other peoples' business."

Only telling them what to do.

With effort, Maggie put on a pleasant face. "But mankind *is* our business, is that not what Mr. Dickens wrote in his fine tale? These children's lives are miserable. They work like slaves, they're barely fed and clothed, and provided with no education. It breaks my heart."

Her voice wavered with emotion. She longed to improve the plight of orphaned children in Kansas, and this small, yet meaningful step could draw attention to the problem. "Giving them Christmas presents isn't nearly enough, but it's a start."

The matron glanced around at the somber expressions, and then cleared her throat. "That does sound like a very serious problem, but it's not something we can solve with a parade. Our Santa is supposed to bring gifts, not take them. If he doesn't distribute presents, the local children will be disappointed."

Charlie Goodlander leaned back in his chair, his substantial weight making it creak. He twirled one end of a walrus mustache, looking thoughtful. "Of course we love our traditions, but what Mr. Sumner and Miss O'Brien are suggesting is for a good cause."

Maggie's spirits lifted. The outspoken president of the Citizens' National Bank, one of the town's original settlers, was exactly the kind of person they needed behind this project.

"The idea is worth considering," he went on. "We might even be able to establish an orphanage right here in Fort Scott, if we can raise money every year during the parade—"

"There are *many* good causes, Mr. Goodlander," Old Ironsides insisted. "If we allowed every one of them to pre-empt our event, it would be a disaster. The people of Fort Scott love the Christmas parade and Santa arriving to bless the children. It's the most popular attraction of the year. I vote we keep things the way they've always been."

The old biddy didn't care about blessing anyone. She only wanted to exert control, as if her vote was the only one that counted.

Perhaps it was, considering how quiet everyone became.

Mrs. O'Connor broke the silence. "We're not voting yet, Mabel. Our rules call for discussion first."

God bless Mrs. O'Connor. She'd put Old Ironsides and her dead birds in their place.

The committee commenced to *discuss*, which ended up being more of an argument. The O'Connors and Mr. Goodlander supported the proposal, two other members supported Mrs. Mueller, and the rest remained undecided.

Mr. Sumner leaned her way. "This is ridiculous," he whispered.

He scooted his chair back and stood, which got everyone's attention. "Honorable ladies and gentlemen, consider how it might look if you *don't* support this effort.

Should Miss O'Brien's request be rebuffed, the leaders of the community will look like Scrooges."

Mrs. Mueller's florid face turned a deeper shade of red. "How do you suppose that? Santa arriving with gifts reflects the soul of generosity. The children in Fort Scott, including those from needy families, should be our first concern. We won't look miserly—unless you fail to provide the donations you promised."

Old Ironsides narrowed her eyes as if spotting a weakness she could exploit. "Mr. Sumner, you did agree to sponsor Santa's sleigh this year. That sponsorship includes providing toys and other items to be given away. Or are you saying you don't have them."

"We'll have what we need," he stated with uncustomary brevity. Then he sat down. Being close, Maggie could see the hard set of his jaw.

Her stomach somersaulted. Now it was clear why he'd suggested a Santa gift collection. He'd promised gifts for the parade and wasn't in a position to make another generous contribution, and this was his way of making up for the deficit. But now, his plan might backfire. For certain, he wouldn't benefit from being at odds with these influential people. He really was a kind man, but he didn't have to shoulder this responsibility.

She dug in her bag for a peppermint to calm her queasiness. The fragrant scent wafted upwards. Apparently, Mr. Sumner could smell it because he'd turned to look at her, wearing an apologetic smile.

"Do you have any ideas for how we might keep our tradition, and still be able to collect gifts for the orphans?" he asked.

"She doesn't have an idea. Let's vote," Mrs. Mueller demanded.

Maggie rolled the candy between her thumb and forefinger. "Actually, I do have an idea." She stood and held up the candy. "This is what I propose."

"Peppermints?" Old Ironsides huffed.

Mr. Goodlander leaned forward. "I'll have one, thank you."

Maggie retrieved another candy and passed it to the bank president. She prayed her brother would support her and made a silent promise to find a way to repay him.

"Every year, Santa gives gifts, but there are never enough to go around to all the children. What if this year Santa arrives with candy instead? If Mr. Sumner and my brother pool their resources, we can provide an ample amount of candy to go around. And we can post Santa's list and ask people to bring gifts for the orphans."

"Santa doesn't collect gifts," Mrs. Mueller insisted.

Mr. Sumner splayed his hands on the gleaming table surface, looking as if he'd like to leap across and throttle the wretched woman. "Then have a *Mrs. Claus* do it."

Maggie shot him an alarmed look, which he didn't catch and kept talking.

"Mrs. Claus can post a list of gifts she needs for the orphaned children. You, Mr. Marble, can write a column about it, include the items, and ask people to bring them the day of the parade. Mrs. Claus will collect them at my store and at O'Brien's."

Maggie released a slow breath. At least he hadn't committed *her* to playing the role.

"That's a wonderful idea," Mrs. O'Connor declared. She snatched up her husband's gavel and smacked it on the table. "Let's vote and call it done."

"We've never had a Mrs. Claus," blustered the naysayer.

"There's always a first time." Mr. O'Connor retrieved his

gavel. "And I think it adds a nice touch. It'll appeal to the women, seeing Mrs. Claus riding beside her husband and helping him pass out candy, and gathering the gifts together. I vote for it, too."

He cradled the gavel and peered around the table with a challenging look.

"Count me in." Mr. Goodlander, who appeared amused by the gavel-wielding duo, lifted a forefinger. The rest of the committee quickly voiced their agreement, all but Mrs. Mueller.

"Who will play the part of Mrs. Claus?" she challenged. "I certainly won't."

Maggie couldn't imagine anyone asking her. She had the sourest personality. Victoria might. No. David would have a fit.

"Miss O'Brien, of course." Mr. O'Connor smacked the gavel, making Maggie jump. "After all, it's her project, and her brother is helping supply candy. Just makes sense."

"The two of us together..." Mr. Sumner turned to her, his cerulean gaze questioning. "What do you say, Miss O'Brien?"

He made it sound as if she had a choice. Of course she didn't, unless she wanted another round of arguments, which might end up burying the entire proposal. She'd backed herself into this corner, and had committed her brother too. Not only that, if she refused, she would embarrass Mr. Sumner. She couldn't do that. Not after all he'd done for her.

Knowing full well she'd regret it, Maggie nevertheless gave in with gracious smile. "Yes, I'd be delighted to play the part of Mrs. Claus."

CHAPTER 4

*I*t took Sum two days to dislodge Miss O'Brien from her brother's store so they could go to a seamstress and have costumes fitted for the parade. A winter storm had moved in and dumped a foot of snow on the ground—that was her excuse anyway.

"Stay close to me so you don't become chilled." He wrapped his arm around her waist to steady her on the snow-packed sidewalks as they mushed along for six blocks.

"I'm not cold."

So she said, but she didn't pull away. At least she'd bundled up in a hooded cloak and scarf, with thicker gloves and sturdier boots, which looked warmer than the button-up shoes she'd worn the day of the meeting. Still, he didn't want her to get chilled and come down ill.

"We could hop aboard a street car." The one lumbering past had passengers in every seat and overflowing the aisles. Two men standing on the steps clung to outside rails.

Miss O'Brien shook her head. "Too crowded. We'll get there faster if we walk briskly."

Her legs were much shorter than his, but he had to press

his pace to keep up with her. When they reached their destination, he checked his timepiece. "Your brisk walking set a new record. We made it in less than ten minutes."

"Does it normally take you longer?" She regarded him with a look that said he must be a lazy fellow if he couldn't make the distance within that time.

They sought warmth inside the cozy shop. The tailor and his wife who ran the business together appeared to be doing well, if the multiple racks of clothing in various stages of completion were any indication.

After Sum explained what they wanted, Mrs. Bowman shooed them into separate dressing rooms. The buxom brunette had years and energy to spare, compared to her stooped, elderly husband. Rumor had it, the old tailor was a single widower for nigh on twenty years, and then one day, a young woman showed up in his shop. He'd introduced her as his new bride, ordered from back east.

Despite being in the merchandising business, Sum considered the practice of ordering a wife ludicrous. Brides and grooms routinely misrepresented themselves, and someone was bound to be disappointed. He suspected Mrs. Bowman hadn't gotten the virile husband she'd expected, but she put on a good show of being happy with her lot in life.

Mr. Bowman muttered under his breath as he took Sum's measurements. He tottered off to the back room, still muttering. Assuming the fitting was done, Sum ducked back into the shop, hearing cheery conversation.

The two women chatted about the inclement weather, a favorite topic of late, as the tailor's wife measured her customer's trim waist. Sum considered offering his assistance, but the seamstress stood up and put away her measuring tape. Maybe another time.

He propped his arm on the doorframe, admiring Miss O'Brien's unguarded profile. No falsely represented female here, she was the real thing: beautiful, kind, gracious, and, as an added bonus, educated—a schoolteacher, no less.

He could think of no reason why he shouldn't pursue her, save his financial uncertainty, which would be resolved after Christmas with any luck. He wasn't getting any younger. Having a wife would gain him more respectability —and admiration, should his wife happen to be the lovely and gifted Miss O'Brien. Granted, she was his competitor's sister, but he would find a way to manage the consequences. If he had let thorny moral dilemmas stop him when he was younger, he wouldn't have gotten anywhere in life.

He didn't need O'Brien's permission, and his sister was old enough to make her own decisions. In fact, Maggie presented the bigger obstacle, having told him, point-blank, they could have nothing to do with each other after the parade. Come the first of the year, she would leave for Kansas City and that was that.

He wouldn't let her escape so easily.

Above his head hung a sprig of mistletoe. The first step in his plan crystallized.

"How long before the costumes are ready?' he asked Mrs. Bowman.

"Two weeks, I'd say."

"Then we come back for a fitting?"

"That's right."

"Can you come over here a moment?" he asked the unsuspecting Miss O'Brien.

Holding his gaze warily, she approached. Over her shoulder, he saw the seamstress glance upwards, and then cover her mouth. She didn't make a sound, God bless her.

Miss O'Brien hadn't noticed the mistletoe, as she had her attention trained on him.

He'd seen her watching him whenever they were together; studying him, as if trying to work out some difficult equation. He wasn't that complex but was flattered she thought so. He also took courage from her trembling response each time he touched her. It meant she was susceptible to him, and that meant he had a chance.

His heart accelerated as she drew near.

"What is it?" Her expressive eyes conveyed hesitant curiosity. He sensed she could be adventurous if he could coax her out of her disciplined shell, and get past her suspicion.

He crooked his finger, urging her closer. "After coming up with a brilliant compromise, you aren't having second thoughts are you?"

Her finely arched eyebrows drew down in a doubtful frown. "I'm still not sure why there's a need for Santa to have a wife. I've never read about a Mrs. Claus, or where she came from."

"Who's to say he didn't order her out of a newspaper?"

Miss O'Brien looked askance at what he considered a hilarious remark. The seamstress, at least, giggled.

"Thank you for agreeing to be Mrs. Claus."

"You're welcome."

God knows he owed her more than thanks. Her inspired compromise had saved his skin. Instead of donating merchandise he couldn't afford, thanks to her, all he had to do was split the cost of candy with her brother and toss in a few items for the orphans. Her project couldn't have come at a better time. However, he couldn't say that without sounding miserly, and he didn't want her to think poorly of him, or more poorly than she already did.

"You saved me a great deal of embarrassment." He could risk that much honesty.

Her suspicious gaze melted into sympathy. "I wouldn't have embarrassed you in front of the committee. You've been very generous."

She misunderstood because he hadn't explained, thought he meant she would've shamed him by refusing to go along as Mrs. Claus. Her concern for his feelings burrowed deep into his heart. He didn't deserve her. Then again, he hadn't deserved most of what he'd gained. The deserving rarely prospered.

"Not generous enough." He slipped his arm around her waist and bent his head. Alarm filled her eyes the instant before he covered her mouth.

She tasted of peppermint and tea, a delicious combination, somehow sweet and seductive at the same time. Holding her tight against him, he sampled the flavor on her lips, which softened and parted beneath his. He longed to linger, to feast...but not here, in front of a giggling dressmaker. He'd only intended a brief kiss, just enough to let her know what it could be like between them, as well as to make it clear to the rest of the world that he'd laid claim to her.

Regretfully, he lifted his mouth.

She blinked, appearing dazed, then with a shocked gasp, stepped backwards, her cheeks flaming. "H-have you lost your mind?"

Perhaps. Coming to a decision as important as marriage within a few days was madly spontaneous, even for him. He hoped he wouldn't regret it. But at the moment he couldn't dredge up one ounce of caution. "Can't Santa kiss his wife under the mistletoe?"

Her horrified gaze lifted.

The seamstress gave a peculiar little snort. "He's got you there, miss. That's mistletoe. You get caught under it, and a fellow can kiss you."

The giggling recommenced.

MAGGIE GRABBED HER BAG, swung her cape over her shoulders and started out the door. Before she left, she thanked Mrs. Bowman, saying she would return in two weeks to collect her costume. She would go through with this farce because she didn't back out of her commitments, but she would not spend one more minute than necessary in Mr. Sumner's company.

Instead of taking the sidewalk, she veered off across the park on a shortcut. Despite the cold air, her face burned. He'd taken advantage of her in the worst way, called her reputation into question and humiliated her after she had gone to great lengths to save him from embarrassment.

Her boots sank in the soft snow, slowing her down. She picked up her skirts and plowed a path up an incline. She'd reached the top when he caught her arm.

"Miss O'Brien... Margaret, wait..."

She spun around, and lost her footing in the slippery snow.

With the quick instincts of a cat, he caught hold of her and halted her fall by hauling her up against his chest. However, instead of releasing her, as proper, he wrapped his arms around her...out in the middle of the park, with people wandering around, watching. He would ruin her before he was through.

Panic flooded her mind, drowning out rational thought.

Flailing him with her fists, she yelled, "Let go! Stop tormenting me!"

"Margaret wait, I'm not... Don't push me, we're on a—"

Her shove sent him backwards.

His arms circled in a windmill as he attempted to right himself, but then he stepped back and lost his footing. She reached out to save him, ended up on top of him, and the force sent him sliding, upside down, to the bottom of the rise. Somehow, he kept her from falling off.

As they coasted to a stop, he began to laugh.

Maggie lifted up on trembling arms, still sprawled atop him, surprised, but not hurt. She wasn't even cold, although he must be freezing, with snow piled up around his head and shoulders. His blue eyes seemed brighter, clearer, enhanced by the heightened color in his cheeks. "Are...are you all right?" she asked breathlessly.

Still chuckling, he laid his hands on her shoulders. "I've never been a sled before. Would you like another ride?"

Saints above. Did he ever think before he spoke?

"Of all the..." She tried to get up, but got tangled in her cloak so she could only manage to roll off, and toppled onto her back. Thankfully, her hood remained up so she didn't get snow beneath her collar.

Really, it wasn't his fault she'd ended up on top of him. He had used his body as a cushion to keep her from injuring herself. Her brother had done that once, many years ago, in much difference circumstances, and with a far less amusing outcome.

Still flat on her back, Maggie gazed into the sky, surprisingly clear, the same pure blue as his eyes. How irritating that she should notice. "Mr. Sumner, you are more annoying than the worst-behaved boy in my classroom."

"No more sledding, then?" He reached for her hand and

laced his gloved fingers through hers. "We could make angels in the snow if you'd prefer."

The last of her anger and frustration came out in a breathless laugh. "You must've struck your head."

"What makes you think that?"

"Because something knocked you silly."

He squeezed her hand. "Do you like me when I'm silly?"

"No."

"Do you like me when I'm serious?"

Another laugh escaped in spite of her determination not to laugh, which only encouraged him. Whether she liked him or not was beyond the point. Mr. Sumner was off limits.

Maggie untangled their fingers, holding hands with him made her breathless. She lifted her cloaked arms to form the shape of angel wings. The childish game worked as a temporary distraction to prevent her from thinking about her attraction to the aggravating man.

He moved his arms and legs. "I haven't done this in years."

"Me neither. My students love it. I thought joining them would be beneath my dignity."

"Your secret is safe with me." He sat up, brushing the snow off the sleeves of his overcoat. With an easy hop, he got his legs under him, stood and held out his hand. "I won't tell a soul you turned me into a sled and forced me to make snow angels with you."

She tried to fight the smile, a useless effort. Sitting up, she put out her hand and let him haul her to her feet. "This isn't funny."

"Why are you laughing?" He brushed snow off her cloak. The scoundrel took every opportunity to put his hands on her, and fool that she was, she actually enjoyed it, and longed for him to kiss her again. This couldn't go on, something had to be done before her reputation was compromised beyond repair.

Gordon Sumner behaved outrageously, but his flirty teasing could be a cover, a defense mechanism he used to hide deep loneliness. Her peculiar sensitivity to his feelings might be because she shared them and understood how difficult it was to find the right person. In fact, she did better at matching others than she did making her own match.

Two years ago, she'd helped her brother find Victoria. Granted, her approach had been unconventional and rather deceitful. But she'd had great success pairing him with the perfect wife. There was no reason she couldn't help Mr. Sumner, too, and in doing so, it would free her from this unwanted attraction.

She brushed loose strands of hair away from her face. By now her hair must look hopeless. "Are you in the market for a wife?"

He stared at her as if she'd suddenly blurted something in a foreign tongue.

"I've rendered you speechless. That has to be a first."

"You're not joking?"

"Not at all. I'm in earnest. If you want a wife, I believe I could help you."

Beneath the snow-dampened mustache, his lips twisted in a wry smile.

"You'd better not laugh at me."

"I wouldn't dream of laughing at you." Gathering her hands, he gazed down at her with a mixture of amusement and tenderness. "Do you have someone in mind, Margaret?"

She winced at his use of her formal name. "I dislike Margaret. It sounds old."

"All right, then...Maggie." The way he said her name, low and edged with sensual promises, sent shivers racing across her skin. He'd misunderstood her intentions. He thought...

"Mr. Sumner, that's not what I—"

"Sum. That's what my friends call me."

"But we aren't friends."

He tightened his hold on her hands, reproaching her with a look. "Of course we are. We're going to be very good friends."

Whether he'd meant to or not, he had just provided the escape she needed without getting into a discussion that would be humiliating for both of them.

"All right then, we will be friends. *Only* friends. Nothing more."

Disappointment, she'd swear it, flashed across his face before he was back to smiling. "Friends? I thought you were proposing to me. Or are we still talking pretend?"

A hot blush seared her face. "Heavens no, I'm not proposing. I meant only that I could help you search out someone who suits you. I helped my brother find Victoria." She didn't add that she'd been the one who posted the personal advertisement, wrote to the Boston miss and actually proposed, pretending to be her brother. That's not how she would do it again, even if everything had worked out wonderfully.

Sum gave her a puzzled, if affable, smile. "How will you help me find a wife?"

"I'll assist you with writing a personal advertisement for a bride, and you can post it in the matrimonial newspapers."

The laughter that followed made it clear he didn't take her proposition seriously.

"You want me to advertise for a bride?"

"Why do you find this so astonishing?" She folded her

arms across her chest. "Hundreds of men do it, and with great success."

"You've taken a poll, then?"

"No, but I know several men who've found brides this way, my brother being one of them."

For a moment he just stood there, smiling. When she didn't respond to his amusement, his smile diminished. "You are serious."

"Very."

He didn't come back with a tart response. He might not want her help, or...

The possibility that he might actually care for her shouldn't thrill her. There could be nothing between them, not so long as he remained her brother's competitor, and he wouldn't give up his store, nor would she ask him to do so. She would find him a more appropriate wife...even if the thought made her heart ache.

Maggie drew her cape closer and shivered. The damp cold had seeped through her clothes. "If you wish to discuss it further, m-maybe we can talk about it over a cup of tea?"

He wrapped his arm around her shoulders. "I'll make a pot. Sounds like we'll need one if we're going to convince some lovely young miss that I'm the man of her dreams."

CHAPTER 5

Sum tried to hold on, but Maggie shied away from his arm.

"On second thought, I really should get back to help Victoria with the children. You could come over for tea later, after the store closes, and we can discuss your advertisement then."

"Very well." Growing frustrated, but not wishing to show it, he brushed the snow off his coat and walked over to pick up his hat from where it had landed after it rolled away.

He'd been having a fine time up until the point when she'd offered to find him another wife. Being coy didn't seem to be her nature, so it would appear she couldn't wait to be rid of him. Or perhaps desperation had driven her to make the offer because she was beginning to like him. Being an optimistic fellow, he chose to believe the latter.

This diversion of hers would make courting more difficult, but he could adjust. He'd use the opportunity as an excuse to see her, and by the time they finished the ad, she would come to her senses and realize there was only one bride who met his requirements.

At five minutes past five in the evening, he crossed over to his competitor's store. The bell jangled as he entered.

O'Brien appeared to be waiting for him. He turned the sign around to *Closed* and locked the door as soon as Sum got inside. "You can use the stairs in the back. Maggie will let you in."

Sum hid his irritation behind a smile. Granted, he'd made no effort to befriend the man, and truth be told, he'd rather have a tooth pulled than spend time in O'Brien's company. For Maggie's sake, he'd attempt to make amends. He held out his hand. "Tis' the season."

The Irishman's handshake turned out to be surprisingly firm, almost painful. Maybe his annoyance stemmed from more than having to host his competitor for tea. Doubtless, Maggie had reported the outcome of their meeting with the committee, and her brother might resent being committed to spending money.

Sum flexed his hand as he withdrew it. "Thank you for pitching in on the candy for the parade. This means a great deal to Maggie."

If possible, O'Brien's expression grew darker. "You don't have to tell me what it means, and I know Maggie better than you do. Practically raised her." He turned and walked to the rear of the store with that curious gait, as if one leg might be a hair shorter than the other, hung his apron on a peg and rolled down the sleeves of his white shirt.

Sum removed his hat. The host hadn't offered to take it, or his overcoat, and made it clear there would be no polite conversation. Just as well. It wasn't O'Brien he'd come to see, and he wouldn't waste energy on feeling guilty about how things had worked out.

He followed the storeowner through a rear door. The storeroom looked as large as the one in the building he rented and was filled with boxes and crates, some stamped with the names of well-known manufacturers. O'Brien looked to be planning a big Christmas sale. Sum suppressed a groan. That meant another price war he couldn't afford.

"Right up there," O'Brien gestured to a stairway leading to living quarters on the second floor.

"You aren't joining us?" Sum inquired to be polite.

"Too much work to do."

Sum didn't lie and say he was disappointed. "I'll leave you to it, then."

He grasped the rail and started up the stairway. The place felt chilly. Should've left on his coat. O'Brien disappeared into a small office tucked beneath the stairs. Sum shuddered at the thought of being closeted in a windowless rat hole. Thankfully, he had plenty of room upstairs for an office. O'Brien needed the extra space for his growing family.

Sum slowed as he reached the landing. When he and Maggie married and had children, they would need more living space. That would be a while, enough time to resolve debts and start saving so he could expand, or better yet, purchase a proper house. With more than one to provide for, he'd have to be more frugal. That didn't mean he had to scrimp on coal to heat the place.

Facing the door, Sum smoothed down his hair, straightened his tie and then switched his overcoat and hat to his left hand and knocked with his right.

After a moment, the door opened. A young girl gazed up at him. She could've been an eight-year-old version of Maggie. He'd seen the child around, but he'd never been struck by the thought that he might enjoy having a daughter with luminous dark eyes and sable braids.

His breathing became constricted. He cleared his throat

and made a bow. "Good evening, Miss Fannie. I'm Mr. Sumner."

"Aunt Maggie told me you'd be here. She's in the kitchen with Mama. She said to let you in and tell you to sit down and wait."

"Were those her precise words?"

Fannie's raven brows gathered in thought. "She might've said something else, but I forget."

Fighting laughter, Sum followed the girl inside.

The apartment setup appeared similar to his, with a large parlor flanked by bedrooms in the back and a kitchen and dining area in the front.

He smelled something sweet baking, mingled with a woodsy scent. *Pine.* Coming from a Christmas tree tucked into a corner. On its dark green boughs hung a hodgepodge of decorations, a combination of store-bought ornaments and handmade treasures. The cozy family room, with its worn upholstery and intriguing scents, had an inviting atmosphere that his well-appointed rooms lacked. Must be the Christmas tree. That was another thing he'd add to the list after Maggie moved in.

"You've put up a tree," he noted to his short hostess. "That reminds me, I'll need to get busy and put mine up, too."

Fannie crossed to a stuffed chair pushed aside to make room for the tree and picked up a doll, which looked to be a miniature of a child her age, only blond and blue-eyed. She flounced onto the chair and swung her feet. Her shoes had gone missing and her woolen stockings, visible by several inches beneath her plaid frock, sagged around her ankles.

"Alice helped me make the angels," she explained in a mature tone. "Patrick tried, but he kept eating the crepe paper and Mama had to put him to bed."

Sum smoothed his mustache to hide his amusement. Fannie wasn't trying to be funny. "After eating crepe paper, I should think I would want to crawl into bed, too."

"Is Fannie keeping you entertained?" Maggie entered the parlor, carrying a tray with a tea set and two cups. She'd changed into a crisp striped shirtwaist and dark wool skirt. Her pretty velvet suit must've gotten damp from rolling around in the snow. Maybe she'd mentioned something about their mishap to her brother and that's why he was so out of sorts.

"Miss Fannie is an excellent hostess," Sum assured Maggie.

"That's good to hear. We'll have warm sugar cookies out in just a minute."

Catching Fannie's eye, he put his hand to his middle and smacked his lips. "My stomach's growling already."

"Mine, too!" Fannie hopped down with the doll hugged to her chest. "Alice wants a cookie, so I'll have to get two," she informed her aunt.

Maggie nodded agreeably. "Of course. We wouldn't want to deprive Alice."

Fannie skipped off to the kitchen, he assumed to make sure she and Alice received their due.

Maggie set the tray on a table in front of the sofa, which appeared to have been shortened to make it suitable for serving coffee or tea to guests. Most of the furniture in the room reflected a popular mid-century style, overly fussy in his opinion. It might not be Maggie's choice, being her brother's home. Her clothing reflected simpler tastes, less flamboyant. Sum hoped she liked Eastlake's designs. Redecorating wasn't in his budget.

She took his coat and hat, hanging both on the hall tree, and after pouring tea, fled to a wing-backed chair closest to the settee. This would be so much easier if she would cooperate.

"You might sit over here..." He put his hand on the sofa cushion as he sat down. "Easier to compare notes on the advertisement."

Maggie placed her cup and saucer on the marble tabletop next to her chair. "I can discuss it from here. Once I know what you're looking for, I'll put something on paper and you can come back tomorrow to take a look."

Little minx thought to avoid being alone with him.

"Not during the day, too busy. After the stores close, you can stop by. We'll have time to work on it together." Sum lifted the teacup, having to pinch the delicate little handle to hold it. Rather than risk dumping hot tea in his lap, he cradled the china base.

She peered suspiciously over the rim of her cup as she took a sip. "You could come back over here."

And face her glowering Irish guardian? *No, thank you.*

He shook his head. "It's bad enough we're disturbing your family tonight. You don't wish to do that every night. The parade is only two weeks away. We need time to discuss revisions to the parade posters, and a newspaper article, maybe a column from Mrs. Claus about the orphans and what they need. We can work on my personal advertisement in between."

Maggie sat straight in the chair and put on her best schoolmarm expression. "David and Victoria don't mind. If it bothers you to meet here, we'll use the store. There's a counter down there where we can spread out the papers."

"My store has a larger counter, and less noise." He glanced meaningfully in the direction of the laughter coming from the kitchen. "That's only from one, the louder one hasn't roused from his nap yet."

She didn't have a comeback.

Sum restrained the urge to throw his hands up in the air, declaring himself the winner of round one. He'd win the next round, too. Not on brute strength. He'd learned quickly in a short-lived stint in the boxing ring that he wouldn't get far with his fists. He won more often by using his wits—and when it came to Maggie, he'd need to exercise a fair amount of self-control. At least as long as he could hold out until he got the chance to kiss her again.

MAGGIE GREW tense facing off with Sum. Noise aside, his point about bothering her brother and sister-in-law had merit. Sometimes she felt like an interloper. David had his own family and didn't really need her anymore. Before remarrying, her brother had depended on her to help him with Fannie, and she had put aside a teaching career for two years to assist him. He'd done so much for her, she wanted to do what she could for him, which was why she'd sent off for a mail-order bride on his behalf.

Sum wouldn't need to order a bride if he could find one locally. She might be able to come up with a suggestion, once she knew his requirements. Either way, she wasn't letting the sly fox trick her into being alone with him again.

"Cookies anyone?" Victoria announced, entering the room with a platter of warm treats in the shape of Santa Claus. They'd used one of the new cookie-cutters David had ordered and then sold out of within a fortnight.

Maggie set her cup aside. "Umm, they smell delicious."

"Of course they do. You made them." Victoria set the platter on the table in front of Sum. "Maggie would never brag, but she's the one who taught me how to cook. My cookies aren't nearly as good as hers. She's also a master at pies and cakes...and biscuits." Victoria tossed an amused glance over her shoulder. "Isn't that right?"

Maggie loved how her sister-in-law could laugh at herself. "Your biscuits have gotten much better since that first time."

"I should hope so." Victoria handed a cookie on a napkin to their guest. "My first attempt at cooking biscuits resulted in nearly burning the building down."

"Oh, now that's not so." Maggie found the memory of the incident amusing, though at the time it had been anything but. "You didn't come close to burning anything down. It was just smoky."

"Coal chips," Victoria declared. "That's what my first biscuits looked like."

"How did they taste?" Sum's polite inquiry elicited laughter.

"They were *awful*." Fannie sidled up to Victoria, who wrapped an arm around her and gave her a hug. The sweet affection between the two, forged through Victoria's patience and persistence, put a lump in Maggie's throat. She missed her niece something fierce. But she was glad Victoria had become Fannie's mother and given David another child. Maggie wasn't sure what Sum would be looking for, but this, this kind of love, that's what she wanted.

His questioning gaze met hers, like he'd picked up on her thoughts, but then he returned his attention to Fannie, scrunching his nose in an exaggerated expression of distaste. "You ate the coal chips?"

Fannie went into a fit of giggles. "They were biscuits... and no, we didn't *eat* them...not even Alice would eat them."

Sum leaned forward, as if intrigued. "What does Alice like to eat?"

Fannie eyed the platter longingly. "Oh, she loves Christmas cookies."

"If it's permissible, she may have half of mine." Sum broke the cookie in two and held it out. The charmer. He would win Fannie's heart, as well.

Victoria nodded her approval. "Put it in the kitchen, then, to save for after dinner."

She brushed her hands off on her apron. Her hips were slender, even augmented with a bustle. Still, she had an enviable figure. Did Sum prefer willowy women or full-figured ones?

Maggie glanced down at her oh-so-average form. Looking up, she met his gaze, and blushed. Saints above, had he seen her examining her bosom?

Fannie inched toward Sum to retrieve her prize. For some reason, she appeared reticent to approach him, even though she'd had her eyes on him the entire time. She might think it strange that a man had come by to see her Aunt Maggie.

Heaven knows her callers had been few and far between. Then again, she hadn't found a man she wanted to encourage, not until she'd met the one man she shouldn't encourage.

Her niece took half the cookie out of Sum's hand. "My Da says you aren't nice—"

"Fannie!" Victoria called sharply, at the same time Maggie sucked in a sharp breath. Maybe the child didn't realize what she said would offend Sum because David had made the disparaging remarks in her presence. It was time to put an end to that.

However, Sum didn't react like a man who'd been insulted. In fact, he smiled kindly at Fannie. "Your father must've read the naughty list and seen a name that looked like mine."

Maggie breathed easier.

Victoria managed to hide her displeasure behind a calm façade. "Fannie, please take the cookie into the kitchen, and then I'd like for you to meet me in your room."

Fannie's eyes grew wide and bright with tears. "I didn't mean to do anything wrong."

"Don't fear, your name isn't on a naughty list," Sum assured her. "Old St. Nick allowed me to help out this year for the parade, and I've checked. You're definitely not on that list with the other naughty children, and neither is Alice."

Faith, what a sweet man... Maggie withheld her applause. Had she been sitting next to him, she might've given him a hug.

Fannie offered him a tremulous smile before obediently heading into the kitchen.

Victoria waited until Fannie had completed her task and disappeared down the hallway and they heard the sound of her door closing. "Thank you, Mr. Sumner, for your kindness. I hope you'll accept my apology on behalf of my daughter...and my husband."

"No need to apologize," Sum replied in his usual friendly tone.

Victoria excused herself and went after Fannie. As soon as she left the room, he stood.

"Probably best if I leave," he said.

So he had been offended but was too much of a gentleman to admit it.

Maggie came to her feet. "I'm so sorry." She followed him to the door, retrieving his coat and hat. What a fiasco. She should never have invited him to her brother's home, not with the high probability of conflict. "Please forgive me for bringing you here, and for any embarrassment it caused."

Sum's smile turned rueful. "If I'm suffering from embarrassment, I have no one to blame but myself. Fannie's right. I haven't been nice to your brother. That's something I intend to correct—within the bounds of friendly competition."

Maggie's eyes stung at a sudden welling of gratitude. There had been a time when she'd viewed him as poorly as David did. Sum had proved them wrong. Today, he'd handled an uncomfortable situation with humor and understanding, and put Fannie at ease.

He would make a good Santa, being easy to approach and good with children. Being a single man, he didn't have any children. Not as far as she knew. Then again, she knew very little about him. She must get to know him better, in order to write his advertisement of course. That meant she would need to go to him.

"I'll be over tomorrow to discuss the article for the parade." She handed him his coat.

"And you promised to help me with a personal advertisement, don't forget that." He maintained a straight face, so she couldn't tell if he intended the remark as a joke, or simply as a reminder. Either way, she didn't back out on commitments, and she was determined to find this remarkable man a very good match.

"I haven't forgotten. I'll write something up, and you can take a look at it. We want it to be perfect."

"If you're writing it, I'm sure it will be." He replaced his hat, tugging the brim in a brief farewell. He didn't kiss her.

She shouldn't have been surprised...or disappointed.

CHAPTER 6

The week before Christmas couldn't have started out better, in Sum's opinion. Shoppers turned out in hoards and sales were better than ever. The parade costumes had been finished on time. Best of all, Maggie would arrive at any moment.

He checked a pot of tea on the stove. His personal preference was coffee, but he'd take up tea if it meant he could drink it with Maggie. He'd spent a blissful two weeks in her company. Each evening after the stores closed, she would come over to work on parade posters and nitpick his article about the fundraising drive. Each time she brought up the personal advertisement, he put off discussing it. If things progressed as he hoped, he wouldn't need it.

One night, Victoria O'Brien had invited him to dinner. Her husband remained polite, if not talkative, perhaps deciding he shouldn't say anything if he couldn't say something nice. Maggie acted nervous. To relieve her tension, Sum spun tales about Santa Claus and his wife and the reindeer and everything else he could recall reading about the jolly old elf. He succeeded in making

Maggie and Victoria laugh, and even O'Brien had seemed less dour.

The fact that he'd be concerned about gaining the good opinion of his competitor confirmed his pathetic condition. The worst part, he didn't mind taking the head-over-heels tumble and had no interest in getting over it. He hadn't planned on this, wouldn't have gone out looking to catch it, but ever since Maggie had come into his life, he couldn't imagine going on without her.

A knock sounded. She was never late. That was a good sign. Try as she might to hide it, he could tell she was as eager to be with him as he was to be with her. This nonsense about finding him a bride was just her quirky way of resisting the inevitable. He adored her quirks.

He opened the door, and a swirl of cold air followed her inside. "Come in and get warm."

She drew back her hood. "It is warm in here. You must use more fuel than David does."

Sum frowned, not liking the image of her shivering in the cold. "He allows you to freeze?"

"Of course not. He's just frugal. I can always put on a coat."

Maggie turned to allow him to take her heavy cloak. She'd pulled her thick hair up with combs, leaving a few silky curls to escape down the back of her neck. He couldn't resist a quick kiss just below her hairline.

She whirled around, startled. "No kisses, we agreed."

"Did we? I don't recall." He wasn't promising any such thing.

Her fingers moved up the tiny jet buttons on a fitted jacket, as if she were checking to make sure each one remained fastened. He imagined undoing them and following the trail with his lips.

God, he burned for her, and she wanted him as well. All signs pointed to it: her eagerness to be with him, her secret smiles and adorable blushes, the way she watched from beneath her lashes when she thought he wasn't looking.

"No more kisses," she said sternly. "I have my reputation to protect, and you'll soon be marrying someone else."

Her remark didn't fool him. It did, however, irritate him. She kept insisting they were just friends, reminding him that after the first of the year she would go back to her teaching job in Kansas City and he would send off for his bride.

The only bride he wanted was Maggie. Whatever the obstacle—be it her brother, her job, or her own uncertainty—he would overcome it. Nothing would stand in the way of getting what he wanted, not even Maggie.

"Come sit down. I'll pour you a cup of tea." He ushered her to the rear of the store where he'd set cups out on the counter. She refused to go upstairs to his office or apartment, for propriety's sake. Fine, he'd wait until they were married to bed her.

"Are you hungry?"

She settled onto a stool and adjusted her skirts. "I had dinner before I came over. No need for you to feed me."

Why not? It was an excellent idea, slipping her morsels in between kisses...something to look forward to.

She fished out a folded sheet of paper and a pencil from a serviceable leather bag she'd placed on the counter. "I took the liberty of working on the advertisement..."

Sum poured tea into two cups. He unbuttoned the front of his tweed coat and took the neighboring stool. Seeing as she wouldn't be dissuaded, he would play along. "Can't wait to hear what you've come up with."

Maggie's attention remained on the paper. She

smoothed it out on the counter and studied it, almost too intently. Annoying, how she refused to look at him. He could make her notice.

With his forefinger, he smoothed a silken strand away from her face. The touch drew a reprimanding look, which softened at his smile.

"You take too many liberties." She scolded in a voice too soft for her to be put out.

"Do I?" He considered taking more, such as drawing her to him and kissing her thoroughly. But then she would accuse him of violating his promise and that would give her a convenient way out. No, he had to remain patient. Seduce her by inches, not yards.

Without apology, he picked up his cup and took a drink. He'd work with her on this silly advertisement and in the process make her admit she was his perfect match. At least, that was the plan. His biggest worry—his plans, like his father's, had a way of going awry. He wouldn't allow that to happen this time. "Read what you've written so far."

"Successful merchant in fast-growing Western community seeks educated young woman with exemplary reputation for purposes of marriage. Applicant must be willing to work long days and will need patience—"

He laughed, nearly spitting his tea, and set down the cup. "Patience? Am I that trying?

"You didn't let me finish. *Will need patience with children.*" She glanced at him with a wry smile. "I assume you'll want children, and your wife will need patience if you expect her to work in a store and look after them."

Her assumption would've been wrong a mere few weeks ago. "Children? When did I start wanting those?"

"I don't know." Maggie searched his eyes, as if she'd find

an answer there. She would if she looked very hard. "Have you been married before?"

"Never married. No children." None that he knew of, and he'd been careful.

"Was it after you agreed to play Santa?"

"That decision had nothing to do with children, entirely selfish. I wanted to wear the green robe." He loved the little fluttering and eye roll she did when he made a joke.

"Maybe it was after you met Fannie?"

"Your niece's bluntness endeared her to me, but no...it had to be after I met you."

"Ah, because I'm a schoolteacher." Maggie sidestepped his blatant admission with admirable dexterity. She must be practicing at home.

Undaunted, Sum gazed into her eyes. This close, he could see they weren't black, but a deep, rich brown, the way he liked his coffee. "What about how she looks?"

Maggie's lips parted like she might say something, but forgot what it was. She jerked her attention to the sheet of paper on the counter. "You mean to say, you want an *attractive* bride. We can add that. Remember, the personal advertisements run forty words. It'll cost you extra for every word thereafter."

"We're not to forty words yet." Didn't matter, at any rate. By the time he finished listing his requirements, there would be no question in her mind as to which bride he wanted.

She sighed, and picked up the pencil. "I haven't even gotten to the part about you."

"I like what you wrote about me being a successful merchant." That's what he wanted her to believe, and it would be so, once he'd cleared his debts. He saw no reason to enlighten her as to his current financial instability. She might let something slip. Not to hurt him, but because she seemed to think her brother would qualify as a saint.

She bent over the paper and scribbled something. "The difficulty in writing a personal advertisement is effectively selling yourself while remaining completely honest."

Sum leaned in and inhaled her scent. "Honest, yes... You smell of peppermint."

Maggie glanced at him with alarm and slanted away. She reached into a pocket on her jacket. "I forgot I had these in here. Would you like one?"

He plucked a red and white candy out of her palm. "Thank you. I love peppermints."

"You do? They're my favorite."

"Mine, too." They'd become his favorite ever since he'd started associating the smell with Maggie. Who knew candy could be so provocative? He would keep a jar in their bedroom. "Include that in the advertisement. Favorite candy must be peppermint."

She laughed, revealing white teeth that were, for the most part, even. One tooth near the front slightly overlapped another. The imperfection endeared her to him even more. He couldn't meet the standards of a perfect woman. "Sum, be serious. Only include what's most important."

He rolled the sweet minty candy around in his mouth, remembering the taste on her lips. "That's pretty important, don't you think?"

"I can think of other things more important."

"Such as?"

Maggie lifted her cup and blew across the tea, sending ripples over the dark surface, before taking a careful sip. That he found everything she did fascinating concerned him because she didn't appear to suffer from the same condition. He could tell she liked him and even desired him, but as for being smitten... Well, if she'd fallen, she did a good job hiding it.

She set her cup down and picked up the pencil. "We need to list your good traits so your bride knows what she's getting."

That would be a short list. "You said I was successful."

"That's not a trait."

He ventured out on a limb. "What, in your opinion, are my good traits?"

She tapped the pencil on her pursed lips. Perhaps that helped her think. He hoped she didn't have to think too hard to come up with something.

"Your sense of humor," she said at last. "It's not always proper, but you can make me laugh, even when I'm vexed with you."

"That's self-preservation."

She smiled, and wrote *witty* on the paper. More words followed: *engaging, affectionate, generous...*

He felt each stroke of the pen across his heart. "Are those traits appealing enough?"

"I would think so, but I'm not the one you need to convince."

"Your opinion matters." In fact, her opinion was the only one that mattered.

She ignored another clear hint and went on. "We need to describe you. You'll send a photograph, but that doesn't tell her the color of your hair or eyes."

He made a face. "I thought you said this list needed to impress her."

"You know you have impressive looks, don't act so humble."

His lips tugged into a foolish smile at her praise. He did

try to make the best of what God had given him, but he had never considered his looks *impressive*. "Some women don't appreciate red hair."

"Your hair isn't red. It's..." She eyed the top of his head. "It's more the color of sassafras leaves in the fall. Only deeper, richer."

He passed his hand over his hair. Up until this moment, he'd despised the color. "I've never heard my red hair described quite that way.

Maggie shook her head at him. "I told you, it's not red. More of a deep orange with rich umber tones, auburn perhaps, though I don't think that word does it justice. And your eyes aren't just blue. They're the color of a winter sky after the clouds have cleared and the sun comes out."

His heart lodged in his throat. She couldn't describe him in those soaring terms and not want him. "What about her traits?"

"We listed those. Educated, hard-working, patient, attractive..."

"That's not specific enough."

"All right, then. What specifically do you want?"

Now, he would make his requirements crystal clear, and they could stop this nonsense about mail-order brides. Although if she wanted to wax poetic about his looks, he'd encourage her, preferably while they lay in bed together.

Holding her gaze, he reached out and captured a curl dangling near her ear. "She has to have black hair that glistens and feels like silk, and gypsy eyes, dark as coffee."

Maggie's gaze widened. Her delicate nostrils flared, and her tongue slipped out to moisten her lips, all signs of sensual awareness and mutual desire. Her reaction made his body tense and his heart pound harder.

She shook herself and batted his hand away. "Stop this."

Her expression shifted from angry to anxious to regretful. "You aren't making this any easier by teasing me."

Sum's smile fell away. To hell with these games. He grasped her arms and drew her to him. "Who's teasing? You asked for my requirements."

BEFORE HE COULD KISS HER, Maggie turned her face. His lips landed on her cheek. Without missing a beat, he blazed a trail to her ear. "Write it down," he whispered. "Then add that I want her to smell like peppermint, and to roll her eyes at my jokes, and go along with my crazy scheme to put Mrs. Claus in the parade—"

She slammed her eyes shut, but that didn't block out his words, or keep her skin from tingling as his breath gusted in the shell of her ear. He delicately traced the edge with the tip of his tongue, sending another spasm of quivers rippling through her.

"Please, Sum, stop...I don't want this..." Liar. She wanted him more than she'd wanted anyone or anything.

"You do want this, so do I." His mouth moved to her neck and he grazed his teeth against her sensitized flesh. The shivers became trembles, and an urgent ache started deep in her core. She couldn't break free of his tight grip on her arms without dragging them both off the stools, and the possibility of ending up on the floor on her back put the fear of God into her.

Desperate, she braced her hands on his heaving chest, trying to push him away so he'd stop tormenting her. "For the love of St. Michael," she whispered.

"Gordon," he murmured, "and I'm not a saint."

Blasphemous sinner. She should've heeded the signs,

ever since he'd kissed her under the mistletoe. However, this wasn't flirting or teasing, he was doing his level best to seduce her. She stammered, trying to remind him, to remind herself, they had agreed to be only friends. "You... we...we can't be..."

When his hands moved upward and into her hair, she somehow found the strength to leap off the stool. She backed away, reaching up with shaking hands to keep her hair from falling. The devil had taken her combs.

He dropped the heavy tortoise shell combs on the counter and advanced toward her, looking every inch the predator she'd once imagined him to be. Beneath the sensual heat in his eyes gleamed another emotion, one that looked like desperation. He held out his arms. "Maggie, why are you resisting what's between us? I know you feel it. I feel it, too."

She shook her head. "No, I can't become your...your concubine, and face myself in the mirror."

"Concubine? Where do you find these words?" He huffed a soft laugh, sounding incredulous. "You think I'm asking you to be my mistress? I wouldn't dishonor you, Maggie. Good God, woman, I all but dictated your measurements for that bride advertisement."

Her resistance wavered.

Sum had her in his arms before she could blink. He must've sensed her weakness, and pounced. His mouth silenced her protest.

The moment his lips touched hers, the fire inside reignited. Ablaze, she wound her arms around his neck and kissed him with all the pent-up longing in her heart.

He wanted her, she wanted him, and in this moment, nothing else mattered.

She didn't fight when he dug his fingers into her hair,

pulling her head back so he could trail hot kisses down her neck. He murmured love words mixed with obscene suggestions, but the way he said them didn't sound repulsive.

He returned to worship her mouth while at the same time moving his hands over her, stroking her back, following the swell of her hips, his every touch taking her to greater heights. "You know we're meant to be together," he murmured against her lips.

Yes, she knew they'd fit like puzzle pieces, their bodies and their hearts. That thought triggered an abrupt return to reality. If she gave Sum her heart, it would be the ultimate betrayal of her brother. Conflicting loyalties would tear her apart.

Squelching her selfishness, she pulled away, and before Sum could stop her, rushed to the counter, scooping her combs into her bag. Springing away from him, she grabbed her cloak. "I have to leave."

"The hell you will." Glowering with frustration, he stopped her at the door, dropped to one knee and grasped her free hand. "Marry me." He didn't ask. He demanded.

Her head grew light and she feared she might swoon—for the first time in her life. "Sum, I...I..."

He gazed at her with an intensity she'd never seen before. "We get along famously, and I know I could make you happy...if you'd let me."

His plea tightened a vise around her heart. She tried to find her voice so she could plead with him not to beg for her hand, tell him she wasn't worth crushing his pride. Her vision blurred as tears gathered along her lower lids. "I'm honored, so very honored, I can't express how much it means to me. But, I can't accept."

His face grew stiff. "Yes, you *can*. Don't let anything stand in the way of what you want."

She couldn't act that way, and if he could, then maybe they didn't belong together. The painful realization sent streams coursing down her cheeks. "I could never betray my brother by marrying a man who could put him out of business."

Sum stood, looming over her. "This isn't about your brother. Whether or not his business survives isn't up to you."

"I'm not talking about his business." Her voice cracked with emotion. She tried to stop crying, but it was no use, her heart was breaking. "This is about love, loyalty, being part of a family."

The fierceness in Sum's expression softened. He cupped her face, wiping the tears away with his thumbs. "That's what I'm offering you, a family. You said you were orphaned."

She clasped his wrists, meaning to pull his hands away, but instead she clung to him. "Orphaned, yes, but I wasn't alone. My brother took care of me. You understand, don't you? Didn't someone take care of you?"

His gaze turned glacial. "No, I took care of myself. My father was too busy chasing his wild ideas. My mother never came out of her self-pity long enough to notice I was around. My brothers died when I was four."

Every word fell like a hammer blow to her heart. "I didn't know. I'm sorry."

"Don't be sorry. It's not your fault, and I didn't tell you that to gain your pity. Not sure why I blurted it out. Maybe because you keep talking about family as if everybody has one."

She had grown up painfully aware that not everyone had a family. Her brother had been the only family she'd had for years. She didn't remember much about their lives beforehand. Except, she knew they'd been loved. Sum hadn't even had that much. No wonder he grasped at affection and held onto it so tightly. He was afraid to let go, fearful no one would be there for him. This painful letting go, it was her fault. She'd let him believe she could be his family.

"Please. forgive me," she whispered.

His angry frown turned to one of unhappy confusion. His hands fell away from her face, he dug a handkerchief out of his vest pocket and offered it to her. "Here, I always carry a clean one in case I happen across a crying woman."

"Thank you." She dried her eyes. He'd offered her far more than a handkerchief, but that was all she could accept. However, she owed him more than gratitude. She owed him honesty.

"I wish things could be different, with all my heart I do. But David would never do anything to hurt me, and he knows I would never betray him, and it would be a terrible betrayal if I married you. It's bad enough we've become friends."

"Our friendship is bad? So you'll end that, too?" The hurt in Sum's eyes sent pain knifing through her. Couldn't he understand she had no choice except to cut the ties?

She gathered her cloak around her, and with it, her resolve. "You must see, we can't be friends anymore. Not now. We can't be anything to each other."

He opened the door, his movements jerky, and when he turned to her, his gaze had hardened. "Then good night, Maggie. I'll see you the day of the parade."

CHAPTER 7

*S*now fell early on the day of the parade. A soft white blanket covered the streets and sidewalks and collected in canopies and on tree branches. Come noon, the festivities would commence, with or without clear skies. Life went on, regardless of storms.

Maggie stood in her brother's store next to a Christmas tree he'd put on display and stared across the street. Sum wouldn't open his store for another hour. He and David both opened at eight, and, until recently, had closed at exactly the same time. They offered many of the same goods, priced them similarly. There was no need for two stores. One would fold, eventually. Regardless of which one failed, her heart would break.

She held the handkerchief Sum had given her to her face, inhaling the clean smell of soap along with a faint masculine scent. A fierce yearning wrung her heart. She'd never meant to hurt Gordon Sumner. She hadn't meant to fall in love with him, either. But she'd done both, and now she didn't know what to do. The only thing she could do was to go on as if nothing had changed, even if *everything* had changed.

At a noise behind her, she tucked the hankie beneath the hem of her sleeve and turned.

Her niece entered the store from the back. She held her little brother's hand, steadying the toddler as he walked. Fannie's crimson velvet dress featured a frilly apron. Patrick's outfit with its wide lace collar made him look like a miniature *Little Lord Fauntleroy*, the character from one of Victoria's favorite books.

Maggie put on a delighted face. She wouldn't ruin this day for the children by focusing on her misery. "Oh my, look at the two of you. You're all ready for the parade."

Patrick babbled something incomprehensible.

Fannie gaped at her. "You look just like Mrs. Claus, Aunt Maggie."

She meant the image Sum had suggested over dinner one night when he'd told the children a story about Santa and his missus. There were no pictures Maggie knew of that showed Mrs. Claus. Sum had also dictated the dress design, which had turned out beautifully. She would thank him when she saw him later this morning. She dreaded the moment as much as she longed for it.

Maggie smiled and curtseyed, holding out a berry red skirt to reveal gold and white petticoats. The sleeves and collar were trimmed with lace, as was the bonnet. "Why, I am Mrs. Claus. Who's Aunt Maggie?"

Fannie giggled.

Patrick teetered as he struck out on his own. Maggie scooped him into her arms and gave him a kiss on his pudgy cheek. He patted her hair, and powder filled the air.

"Your hair is dusty," Fannie pointed out.

"Dusty?" Maggie captured Patrick's hand before he

could ruin her coiffeur. "My hair is gray, dear. I'm not a spring chicken."

"Kee," Patrick said.

"She's not a kitty, either," Fannie replied. She seemed to have a fine grasp on Patrick's unique language, even if his logic didn't make sense. "When will Santa Claus be here?"

"Not until ten," her father replied. David passed by the potbellied stove without stopping to add fuel. Sum always made sure his store remained toasty.

"Why don't you add a bit more wood?" Maggie suggested. "Make it warmer. The air is very chilly, and I'm sure the children are cold."

David returned to the stove and adjusted the dampers. "Feels the same as it always does. No one's complained." He didn't add, *except you.*

Maggie secured Patrick's little coat, battling a surprising surge of resentment with a good dose of reason. It wasn't so cold the children would get ill. David made sure of that. He was just thrifty. Sum's extravagance with fuel could be a sign that he was wasteful. Except, he hadn't wasted a single moment of time they'd been together. He had filled every minute with wonderful memories.

She set Patrick down, not wanting the children to see her tears. "Here, Fannie. Can you take him before he pats all the powder out of my hair? It's making my eyes water."

"Yes, Aunt Maggie. I mean, Mrs. Claus."

David held out a handful of peppermint candies. "Victoria finished putting the bags of candy together. I saved some extra peppermints for you."

"You smell of peppermint...I love peppermint."

Maggie caught a sharp breath as Sum's voice slipped into her thoughts. The tears started up again. Alarmed, she spun around and made for the front door. "No, thank you.

I'd rather you save it for the children." Her voice came out wobbly, but at least she didn't break down. "I should see if Santa's sleigh has arrived yet."

Before she reached the knob, her brother's hand fell on her shoulder. "The door is still locked. It's not even eight."

She bit her lip. Shuddered. Teetered on the edge of control.

"Fannie, take Patrick with you and go find your mother." David's voice resonated in the quiet store. After a moment, he put both hands on Maggie's shoulders and gave a gentle squeeze. "The children are gone," he said softly.

She turned into his arms, fighting tears. "I'm sorry. I've been very emotional of late. I...I'm worried about collecting enough gifts for the orphans. It would be terrible if some of them were left out."

David patted her back in a big brother fashion. "They won't be. I spoke with the other merchants, and they've promised to cover any shortfall. You won't have to depend on Sumner. He's made promises he can't deliver on, I suspect."

She stiffened at her brother's critical tone. "Mr. Sumner will do his part, I'm sure."

"Maggie..." David spoke her name low and urgent. "Tell me what happened between you and Sumner the other night. That's what this is about, isn't it? What did he do to you?"

She drew back, under better control now, and met her brother's worried gaze. "If you must know, he proposed."

"He *what?*" David's angry reaction was to be expected.

"Don't get upset. I turned him down." Maggie swallowed the thickness in her throat. She couldn't let on that she was heartbroken, or give any sign of regretting her decision.

"Why did you turn Mr. Sumner down?" Victoria's question came from the back of the store.

David turned abruptly. "Why wouldn't she turn him down? He's an unprincipled rascal."

Sum wasn't a rascal, most of the time, and he had a deep core of honor, despite a few questionable practices, such as kissing her in public.

Before she could speak, Victoria replied. "I didn't ask your opinion of him, David. I want to hear what Maggie thinks. She's spent quite a lot of time with him lately."

"Only because he tricked her into being part of the parade," her husband shot back.

"From what I heard, she volunteered."

"Are you defending Sumner?"

Oh dear, David hadn't frowned like that at Victoria since she'd forgiven him for being a nincompoop and put him out of his misery by marrying him.

"I'm not defending anyone, except Maggie." Victoria planted her hands on her hips. She took that position when she was put out, or prepared to go to war.

Maggie groaned. Pitting her brother and sister-in-law against each other was exactly what she did *not* want to do. She stepped between them with a confession. "Yes, I have been spending time with Mr. Sumner, and we...we've become friends."

In spite of what she'd told Sum, she still considered him her friend. When—or if—he got around to forgiving her, he might consider her a friend as well. She hoped they could go back to being friendly acquaintances, if she could bear seeing him without bursting into tears.

"He's not a rascal. He's a very nice man. But, he's not the right man for me."

Her brother gave a satisfied nod. "There you go. She's told you what she thinks."

Victoria dropped her battle stance. "If you don't return Mr. Sumner's affections, then you did the right thing by ending it." She didn't sound as if she believed this to be the case.

"No, I can't return his affections." Spinning the truth out of joint was more difficult than Maggie expected. The truth, however, was too frightening to consider. She couldn't be in love with a man she hardly knew...even if he did make her heart race.

Victoria had entered the store trailed by the children. Fannie peered from around her back. Patrick had dropped to his knees to examine something on the floor and almost had it in his mouth when his mother scooped him up. She tugged a length of string out of his chubby fist and took him to David. "He's developed an appetite for anything that might choke him. Will you watch him while I help Maggie fix her hair?"

That was secret code for "*let's have a talk.*"

"The store opens soon. Don't be bending Maggie's ear for too long."

Apparently, David had cracked the code.

He took Patrick into his arms and ruffled his son's hair. Maggie's breath caught at the tender gesture. She couldn't help thinking about how much she'd love to have a little boy with flaming hair and crystal blue eyes.

"Fannie?" Victoria held up the string. "The cats might enjoy this."

"I'll take it to them." Fannie wound the string around her finger and pattered back to the storeroom, where the two cats prowled when they weren't curled up by the stove.

"Will you come upstairs with me for a minute?" Victoria

asked. "We won't be long. Patrick messed up your hair. I'll fix it."

Maggie knew her sister-in-law was too tactful to challenge her decision or outright tell her what she should do, something her older brother considered his prerogative. Victoria expressed her concern in a less direct manner. Nevertheless, Maggie didn't want to talk about Sum.

"My hair is fine." Maggie checked the watch pinned to her bodice. "It's almost time to go."

Victoria accepted the rebuff with a dignified nod. "Are you ready, then?"

No, she wasn't ready to face Sum. Her heart was too raw, her emotions too close to the surface. She felt like a snowflake in a blizzard, and it terrified her to think she couldn't stop what had been put into motion when she'd walked into Sumner's store to ask for his assistance.

David carried his son to the front door and unlocked it. "Let's take a peek outside and see if we spy any reindeer."

Patrick squirmed to get down. His eyes were on the shiny ornaments adorning a Christmas tree that formed the centerpiece of a window display. Rather than risk disaster, David lifted the child to his shoulders. Patrick grabbed his father's hair and rocked excitedly on his favorite perch. He yanked so hard that David took told of his hands.

"You're his favorite horse," Maggie quipped.

David bounced, giving his son a gleeful ride. "You're wise to stay away from Sumner. He's vain and self-centered. Not a man you can depend on."

Maggie's temper flared into a full-fledged blaze. She faced her brother with her hands on her hips. "Why do you feel the need to criticize him? He's done nothing worse than move in across the street and open a shop. There's no law that says he can't do that."

Her brother gaped at her as if a holly bush had suddenly sprouted from her head.

She was just getting started. She'd not allow David to make Sum out to be a scoundrel because he wasn't a scoundrel.

"Mr. Sumner runs a successful business. Even *you* have learned something from watching him." She gestured at the interior of the store, which over the past two years had been expanded, and improved with new lighting, wider aisles and prices clearly marked on merchandise. "One could say you took his best ideas and benefited from his knowledge."

"David didn't take anything." Victoria came to her husband's defense and to his side. Her expression remained polite, but her tone had a sharp edge. "Mr. Sumner doesn't own those concepts. He's doing what stores in the east have been doing for several years, which I suggested David might try."

Maggie wasn't surprised or offended by her sister-in-law's protective streak, which extended to her as well. Although David didn't really need protecting, with the possible exception of his hair.

Victoria retrieved Patrick before the toddler snatched his father bald-headed. She lovingly combed her fingers through her husband's mussed hair. "Maggie, you know your brother wouldn't steal from anyone."

David grasped Victoria's wrist, pulled her closer and pressed a quick kiss on her lips, making her blush. "Except for kisses. I steal those all the time."

Their easy affection usually made Maggie happy, but today it made her jealous.

David released his wife's arm, and when he turned to Maggie his smile fell away. "Sumner didn't just move here and open a store. He moved in, intending to take my customers and put me out of business. He'll climb over anyone and everyone to get what he wants. I'll admit he's not unique in that way, but is that the kind of man you want?"

Under attack, Maggie took a step backwards. "I didn't say I want him."

"Your eyes say it."

She shook her head, frantic to deny the truth because she knew it would hurt her brother if he thought she was in love with Gordon Sumner. "I could never marry someone who would harm you. I'm just saying he's not as bad as you think. He is competitive, yes, but he's got a big heart. He's been paying Anna Smith higher wages ever since her Pa died...and he came up with this idea for the parade as a way to collect gifts for the orphans."

Maggie tore away from her brother's accusing gaze and crossed to the front window. Snow no longer fell and people were starting to venture outside. Soon, the sleigh would arrive and she would put on a happy face and pretend to be Sum's wife. Rather, Mr. Claus's bride.

If only make-believe could be true.

She knew Sum wasn't perfect, and he wasn't right for her, but that didn't stop her from wanting him. He'd been good to her, and his flirting and teasing had been good for her. She'd forgotten what it felt like to have fun. She wrapped her arms around herself, wishing they were his arms. "I don't remember playing much as a girl. Sum teases me, and makes everything we do together fun."

David's voice came from behind. "Sis, I'm glad he can make you smile. But you know he got you into that parade for his own reasons. It'll give him fine publicity, and he managed to work it out so he doesn't have to spend much of anything to look good."

Her brother's hands came to rest on her shoulders, for the first time feeling heavy, burdensome. "Take care, *Mageen*."

Her throat tightened at the childhood term of endearment. She didn't recall her father using it, but David did. He'd been ten when their parents died in that terrible fire. Old enough to remember. All she recalled was her mother's scent—rosewater—and her father's thick Irish brogue. No photographs survived. Folks said David was the spitting image of his father. She also had their father's dark coloring and wry sense of humor. The only inheritance from her mother, as far as she could see, was the watch pinned close to her heart.

"What do you suppose Ma and Da would've advised?" she asked without turning around.

David remained silent for a moment, perhaps thinking. He wasn't spontaneous, like Sum. Her brother reflected before he spoke or acted, especially if it concerned something important.

"They would've told you to listen to your heart."

CHAPTER 8

*T*he day turned out perfect for a parade. The snow ceased early, temperatures rose to above freezing and the clouds cleared, making way for the sun. Sum didn't look up at the blue sky, else he would be reminded of what Maggie had said about the color of his eyes. Then he would start thinking he still had a chance to win her.

Dressed as St. Nick, he guided a sleigh pulled by two white horses, having to explain to children who asked that reindeer weren't native to Kansas. Santa's *sleigh* was actually a wagon with wooden panels nailed to the sides, painted to make it look like it had runners rather than wheels. An actual sleigh would've been ruined if taken over trolley tracks.

Mrs. Claus perched on the seat beside him, being generous with candy and smiles. The rich red velvet he'd selected for her dress complemented her creamy skin and dark hair, which she'd attempted to turn gray with powder. She hadn't needed to add a thing to her naturally rosy cheeks.

He'd opted for a simpler garment, a heavy green robe

cinched at the waist with rope. Fur trim would've been nice had it been more affordable. Completing the outfit, a snowy wig and a chest-length white beard secured with string hidden by a green felt cap.

Maggie looked adorable. He looked like an imposter with fake whiskers.

Sum glanced over again, unable to keep hope at bay. She might've at least smiled at him. Even a friendly look would be nice. She'd smiled and waved at everyone else. He'd done his duty with frequent *ho-ho-hos*, and refused to let on how much her disregard bothered him.

The parade wound through the main part of town, down Wall Street and along the National Cemetery Road. The festive entourage featured numerous decorated manger scenes on flatbeds, as well as children dressed up as angels and elves. Someone had gotten the idea of rounding up dogs and having them haul a cart driven by a lad dressed up as *Christmas Past*. Sum didn't remember a dog cart in the Dickens tale.

After three agonizing hours, the parade drew to an end, the last stop being the street where his store and O'Brien's were located.

"Look, Victoria is waving us over." Maggie pointed in the direction of her brother's store. "She promised me she would muster an army to help with the toy collection."

"I see Mr. O'Brien and your landlord, and Mr. O'Connor. Would that be her army, or just the generals?"

Maggie's lips inched up, a slight smile. He could do better.

He made for the hitching post, guiding the horses around a mob of children. "The troops appear to be swarming the streets. Do you think she meant to recruit dwarves?"

That should've elicited a laugh, at the very least an eye roll.

A wiser man would give up his pursuit, but he didn't know how to quit. Never had. Facing bullies as a kid, and later as a young man, he'd been beaten to a bloody pulp. Chasing his dream of having a successful store, he'd lost his shirt, his home, been threatened and forced to flee, and still he hadn't given up. Once he set his mind to something, nothing stopped him—and he'd set his mind on having Maggie.

"Do you see any toys on the sidewalk?" She sounded worried.

"No, but I left instructions with Miss Smith for all donations to be brought inside in case of bad weather. Maybe your brother did the same. We can check as soon as we get rid of the rest of this candy."

Despite their falling out, Maggie still had some measure of faith in him. He would not disappoint her. If there weren't enough gifts to go around, he would find a way to provide them, even if he had to delay repaying his debts. He could move shells around for another month, and pray no collectors showed up on his doorstep.

After all the gifts were collected, he would help her distribute them. Along the way, he could coax a genuine smile out of her, and if he was lucky, perhaps a kiss. Proposing so soon hadn't been smart. Now he'd have to start over—once he got her attention.

As the wagon rolled to a stop, the army converged, tiny soldiers screaming at the top of their lungs. "Santa! Candy!"

Sum had to scurry to prevent the frantic midgets from overrunning the wagon before he could reach the back and retrieve the candy. Hiking up the long robe, he stepped down, and then hoisted Maggie to the pavement, holding her close, lest she be knocked down.

In less than half an hour, they distributed the remainder of the candy contained in a large burlap sack. After the happy hoard raced off with their goodies, a boy dashed up and skidded to a stop in front of Sum.

The lad didn't look much past twelve, if even that. Carrot-red hair stuck out every which way and he'd been cursed with an abundance of freckles. He reminded Sum of how he'd looked growing up, when he had been dubbed *scarecrow* by his classmates.

Sum met a pair of worried blue eyes. Fortunately, he'd managed to slip a peppermint cane into his pocket in case a teary-eyed latecomer showed up. "Merry Christmas, young man. You're looking for candy, I presume?"

The boy bobbed his head, eagerly. Looked like he needed clothing more than candy. He didn't have on gloves or a hat. His pale wrists extended beyond the sleeves of a tight coat, his dungarees were patched together, and his big toes poked out of holes in his shoes. Clearly, he came from a poor family.

Sum frowned. Poor or not, he would offer his own hat and shoes before he sent his child out into the cold with his head and feet exposed.

"Felix!" A raw-boned woman in a rough woolen coat and poke bonnet stalked up behind the boy and took hold of his ear. "You don't go nowhere, lessen I say."

The child winced. "Yes ma'am."

Sum narrowed his eyes at the ill-tempered crow. How would she like it if someone twisted her ear to get her attention? "Madam, go easy on him. Boys forget themselves when they're excited. Here's a piece of candy for your son."

He held out the peppermint stick. The woman snatched it out of his hand.

"He ain't my *son*," she scoffed. "He works at our farm. Him and those lazy young'uns over there." She indicated a group of younger children, equally ill clothed and huddled in the back of a wagon with no cover. "We heard you was collectin' for orphans. Them's orphans. We come to get whatever it is you're givin' out."

Cruel *and* greedy. Her name went on the naughty list.

"A lump of coal, is that what you had in mind?" Sum inquired.

The coarse woman squinted with a look of interest. "You givin' out coal?"

Stupid hag.

Maggie came around from the back of the makeshift sleigh, looking none too happy. "Mrs. Meaney, those children are freezing. Get them out of the cold, somewhere warm."

Not even the cavalry could break through the crowd in front of O'Brien's general store. Not to mention, that place wasn't what one might call *warm*. Sum gestured across the street. "Take them over to my store. You can wait there until we sort through the gifts."

The harpy planted her hands on her ample hips and glared at him. "Jist who do you think you are, orderin' me around?"

"I'm Santa." As if he had to tell her. She didn't appear to be blind. "And this is Mrs. Claus. She's in charge of distributing the gifts. No one gets anything without going through her first."

The woman harrumphed. "Well, we better get *somethin'* after coming all the way to town."

She grabbed the boy's arm and nearly yanked it out of its

socket when she turned on her heel to leave. The bank president chose that moment to stroll over. Mrs. Meaney elbowed him aside. Looking bewildered at her rudeness, Charlie Goodlander nevertheless tipped his hat.

"Madam, Merry Christmas."

She didn't give him a moment's notice, but kept on in a beeline for her wagon.

He replaced his bowler. An amused grin pushed out the graying muttonchops on his generous jowls. "Good heavens. Who was that?"

Maggie's worried gaze followed the orphans as their guardian herded them across the street. "Agnes Meaney. She and her husband run one of the poor farms in the area. Sadly, those children are her charges."

Goodlander's amusement faded.

Sum silently vowed to make certain those youngsters received warm clothing and shoes that fit. "Why would any judge in his right mind put children with someone like her?"

"There are few places orphans can go, if no one steps up to adopt them." Maggie slipped her arm through his. Did she realize what she'd done?

Sum's heartbeat accelerated, an affliction that showed no signs of abating. Anytime she needed to hold onto him, she could. In fact, he wanted her to turn to him, and to depend on him, and—if the stars aligned just right—to fall in love with him.

She released a heavy sigh. "I wish we could take those children somewhere they could be with people who care about them."

"Poor farms aren't the best solution," he acknowledged. Sadly, he didn't have a better one.

Maggie turned her attention to the bank president.

"What about that idea you mentioned at the meeting, Mr. Goodland? For a children's home, right here in Fort Scott. Where orphans like those could come to live and get the care they need, and a proper education."

Charlie rubbed his chin thoughtfully. "You know, I have been thinking about that a great deal since you visited our committee. We'd have to find a good location, and raise enough money, and hire somebody to run it."

Sum latched onto a candidate. Convincing Maggie to move back to Fort Scott would be good for orphans like Felix. Her return would also be good for a certain shopkeeper. He didn't wait for her to volunteer. "Miss O'Brien would make an excellent headmistress. She's kind and compassionate, devoted to children, and went to a teachers' college. That job's readymade for her.

Maggie didn't leap at the opportunity as he expected. After all, it was her idea, even if she'd been smart enough to convince the bank president he'd thought of it first. Surprisingly, she appeared reluctant. "I already have a job, and I can't leave my students. Not to mention, this home we're talking about doesn't yet exist. It would be premature to hire the staff."

"I grant you, it'll take time to arrange everything, but we can get it done." Charlie folded his arms over his barrel chest. "When I came out here forty years ago, all I owned was a few carpentry tools. Started working, eventually got me a lumber mill. Lost everything in the big fire and had to rebuild. So, I built a hotel, and then started a bank. I've been poor as many times as I've been rich. Life's a struggle, Miss O'Brien. Succeeding at anything worth doing takes persistence."

"You know that, don't you," Sum said to Maggie. "And you're as hardheaded as I am."

She glanced upward and a wry smile reappeared. "Why, you flatter me, sir."

"He's right, though." Charlie grinned. "That's what it takes to make something like this happen, mule-headed do-gooders."

"Mule-headed, eh?" Sum murmured. The moniker fit. No one had ever called him a do-gooder, but there was always a first time. Besides, Maggie had enough good to make up for his bad. "You'd be a compelling spokesperson for a children's home, Miss O'Brien."

"What about you, Mr. Sumner? A sharp businessman like yourself should have some idea about how to raise the necessary funds."

He hesitated, caught off guard by her maneuver. He couldn't come up with enough money to pay his debts, much less start a children's home. "I have a feeling you're the sharper of the two of us. Are you sure I'm the right person...?"

The objection died on his lips when Maggie gave him a look that said she expected him to say as much. She saw through him enough to realize he wasn't the charitable soul he pretended to be. He couldn't expect to gain her admiration if he didn't show some courage.

"Then again, Santa ought to be able to come up with something, eh?"

Charlie slapped him on the back. "Excellent! I knew I could count on you."

Maggie's surprised gaze told him he'd been correct about her low opinion of him, which her brother, no doubt, took every opportunity to reinforce. Sum resented not being in a position to refute the slurs. In good conscience, he couldn't recommend himself to Maggie, so he ought to politely back down and honor her wishes to be left alone.

His conscience, however, had minimal influence over his desires. If he could figure out a way to win her, he would do it.

The bank president turned to Maggie with a ready smile. "And you, Miss O'Brien? What do you say? Will you assist me with this project?"

"I'd be happy to speak out in support of a local children's home."

"Not just speak out, you must consider moving back to run it."

The old gentleman's tenacity impressed Sum. Joining forces, they might just succeed in convincing Maggie to return.

"If you believe I could do a good job, I'll consider it." She fiddled with the watch pinned to her bodice, nervous about something...perhaps the idea of being in the same town with him.

"Miss O'Brien, you are capable of anything you decide to pursue," Sum stated. That included marrying her brother's competitor, but he didn't point this out. She would come around only after he proved to be a worthy suitor, which meant taking care of Maggie's orphans.

She craned her neck to peer at her brother's store. "Oh! I think David and Mr. O'Connor are collecting gifts now. I should go help them and see what we have so far.

Before releasing her arm, Sum reminded her. "You'll come by later. We can talk about our plans for fundraising. Tomorrow we'll distribute the gifts we collected."

He could break through her resistance if he could get her alone.

Maggie pulled free and shook her head. "David offered his assistance. He'll escort me, you needn't leave your store."

Sum was tired of O'Brien inserting himself between

them. Or was this Maggie's doing? She might be using her brother as a convenient excuse to avoid him. To be sure, he ought to be working in his store, making all the money he could over the next few days. But he needed time alone with Maggie. How else would he convince her to give him another chance?

"There's an extra clerk I can call in to help Miss Smith manage the store. We agreed Santa would visit the orphans. I'm Santa this year. Therefore, I'll be the one to accompany you."

CHAPTER 9

$\mathcal{M}$aggie timed her arrival to shortly after dawn, just as Sum finished loading the gifts. He drew a tarp over the items and secured the sides. Last night, she and David had brought by the items they'd collected. Sum hadn't been happy about that. She knew he'd expected her to come alone. He wouldn't be any happier today when he discovered she had invited a friend along.

What else could she do? He'd been insistent, rightfully so, that Santa must deliver the gifts. But she couldn't risk being alone with him. Plus, she had promised to help him find a suitable wife. Her friend also needed a nudge in the direction of the altar, so she'd be doing both of them a favor. If only she felt good about it.

Throughout the parade, Sum had glanced at her longingly and tried to joke with her. More than anything, she wanted to enjoy his company. Yet, she sensed he was still intent on wooing her, so she'd turned a cold shoulder—and ended up being miserable, despite smiling until her face hurt. Once he turned his charm on someone else, she would get over this regrettable fascination. She hoped.

"Three poor farms, plus the orphans at the home for the destitute." She checked her list and worriedly eyed the canvas hump. "I hope we have enough gifts. I hadn't received the names of all the children Mrs. Meaney brought to town."

Sum patted the tarp and smiled. "We've got everything they asked for, and that's after I gave Felix and the girls new clothes and shoes."

"You did?" Maggie fought the urge to hug him. That would only encourage him. Regardless, she wouldn't pretend indifference to his generosity. "Oh, Sum, I'm so glad to hear it. Those poor children were in rags."

"And I told the old witch I was good friends with the judge and would be sure to tell him how the children were faring."

"You know Judge Chambers?"

"No, but I thought if I told her I did, she'd be more inclined to take care of those kids. I do plan to check on them. If it looks like she's abusing them, I'll get to know that judge and insist he find a better place for those children."

Maggie smiled up at him, impressed. "You're so sly...in a good way"

"I'll take that as a compliment." Sum drew up her wool scarf to the bottom of her chin, as if he was afraid she might take a chill. His consideration warmed her more than the scarf.

After he assisted her into the wagon, Maggie adjusted her skirts, mulling over David's warning regarding Sum's self-serving intentions. What he'd done for those children couldn't gain him anything. He had done it out of the goodness of his heart. Although it wouldn't matter to her whether he was self-serving or not, she was glad she'd seen evidence to the contrary.

A single snowflake dropped a cold kiss on her cheek. She looked up, and a few more stragglers drifted down from the low clouds. She blinked as one caught on her eyelash. "We'd better get going, so we can deliver as many of these gifts as possible before the snow starts in earnest."

He climbed up onto the seat, adjusted his hat, tugged his gloves tighter and then took up the reins. "If we get caught in a storm, we may have to spend the night in an abandoned barn. Mr. O'Connor told me that's how he met his wife."

"He met her in an abandoned barn?" Unlikely.

"They took shelter after her buggy broke down."

"That sounds very suspicious." Maggie eyed the sturdy wheels and then looked at Sum, askance. "Your wagon appears to be in good shape. You wouldn't purposely strand us."

The devilish gleam in his eyes told her he might.

"Nancy won't like that."

Her remark wiped the smile off his face. "Nancy?"

"I invited Nancy Robinson to come along. She's expressed interest in helping with the fundraising efforts for the children's home. I thought if we brought her along it would give all of us a chance to talk about it."

Maggie fiddled with the drawstring on her purse, unable to look Sum in the eye for fear he'd see what a big fat liar she'd become. She had gone to Nancy and wheedled until she'd gotten her friend to agree to come along under the pretense of being a chaperone.

Sum's cheerfulness abated. The smiles didn't return when they stopped by Nancy's house to collect her. He assisted Nancy into the wagon. Maggie scooted over, making room next to Sum. He climbed back up and started out with nary a word. What happened to that chatty fellow who'd talked her ear off on their first outing?

Maggie made light conversation, as best she could with Nancy sniffing. "Are you ill?"

Nancy shook her head. "Just a little sniffle."

Poor thing, her nose had turned red.

Maggie worried that she might've caused her friend to feel obligated about coming along. Thankfully, Nancy had bundled up with a heavy coat, thick scarf and leather gloves. She'd gathered her pretty blond hair into a tight knot and wrapped her head in another scarf before pulling up a fur-lined hood. She looked like an Eskimo. Not ideal situation for an introduction to a potential suitor. If Sum would open his mouth, it might help.

Nancy glanced at him, appearing uncertain as to what to say to a rock. She was sweet and friendly, but not a lively conversationalist. Sum was, and Maggie had counted on him to draw her friend out.

Upon leaving town, they headed southwest along a quiet road. Snow continued to fall in fits and starts.

"What do you make of this weather, Mr. Sumner?" Nancy asked finally.

"If I were in charge of it, I'd make the sun come out."

Nancy nodded, but she didn't pick up the thread he'd dropped.

"Warm weather is so much nicer," Maggie dug behind her for another blanket and wrapped it around her friend's shoulders. "Nancy and her mother own bicycles and they like to go riding when the weather's pleasant. You like bicycles, don't you Mr. Sumner?"

"No reason to dislike them. They don't bite."

"They don't eat hay, either." Maggie enjoyed their banter, but now she had to get Nancy talking. "How nice, you and Mr. Sumner both like bicycles. Perhaps he can join you on a ride."

"Do you ride, Mr. Sumner?" Nancy asked.

"Only if my feet go on strike."

Maggie ignored Sum's attempt to make eye contact. She already knew what he thought of her scheme. Once he got to know Nancy, he would be appreciative of the introduction. "Nan, you should show Mr. Sumner some of your pieces of jewelry. Nancy weaves hair into different designs. She makes brooches and wall hangings."

"Is that so?" Sum reached up and removed his hat. "What, pray tell, could you do with this, Miss Robinson?"

Nancy eyed his bright hair thoughtfully. She reached up and fingered a strand. "Coarse hair is easier to weave. Yours is very soft, but I could probably do something. I'd need to work with it for a while before I'd know. Is there a particular piece you had in mind?

Maggie bit down on a surge of jealousy. For a split second, she entertained the thought of tossing her friend out of the wagon. She didn't want Nancy touching Sum's hair, or any other part of him for that matter. "I thought most of your jewelry was made as memorial gifts with hair from the deceased. Mr. Sumner isn't dead...yet."

Nancy gaped at her, horrified. Wasn't her fault the nasty remark had just popped out before any real thought could be put to it.

Sum held his lower lip between his teeth, appearing to fight a laugh. He returned his hat to its proper place. *Redheaded rascal.* He'd done that on purpose, knowing it would annoy her. If he imagined making her jealous would stop her from finding him a wife, he was wrong.

Maggie turned to her friend. "I'm sorry, Nancy. You're work is beautiful, and I think a piece with Mr. Sumner's hair would be lovely."

Awareness dawned on her friend's face. Her eyes

twinkled with amusement. "Oh yes, I agree, his hair would make a very striking piece. If you'd like, I'll put it in a brooch for you."

SANTA and his helpers delivered gifts to orphans on two poor farms before the weather sent them hurrying back to Fort Scott. Once the snow stopped, they would go out again —tomorrow and then the next day, and with luck, they'd have all the gifts delivered by Christmas.

Maggie's orphans would have their presents. Sum intended to ask for one, as well.

The sneaky lass had tried to set him up with her friend, before her absurd attempt backfired. Nancy had spent most of the ride home in animated conversation about all that he and Maggie had in common. He would thank Miss Robinson for her help when he went back to give her a hank of his hair and order that brooch for Maggie.

After returning the sniffling Miss Robinson home, Sum took the wagon back to his store. He hopped down and went to assist Maggie. "I'm feeling charitable. Let's celebrate our first delivery with a cup of cocoa."

She grasped his hand and stepped onto the brick pavement. Instead of accepting his arm, she backed away. "Look at all the shoppers. You'll be distracted...and I need to help David at the store."

With only a few days left before Christmas, scads of people were out, despite the snow, and both stores would be busy, but that wasn't why she wanted to dash off.

"Tonight then..." Sum brushed snow off the sleeve of his overcoat. He'd hardly noticed the cold throughout most of the trip because he'd been having too much fun making

Maggie jealous. He'd loved seeing her flush with anger when he invited Nancy to examine his hair. "I'll come by and we'll go somewhere for dinner."

This elicited a look of alarm. "No, I can't possibly. I'm busy...washing my hair."

"Be ready by seven," he said, his optimism undeterred. She'd been ready to throttle her friend for simply touching his hair.

"Sum, I'm not going out with you." As she spoke, a buggy rolled up beside them, driven by Mr. O'Connor's eldest daughter, Phoebe, an independent young woman who enjoyed spending her parents' money in stores all over town.

The tall blonde tied the reins and stepped out, adjusting her fur-trimmed coat over a fashionable cream-colored walking suit. "Merry Christmas, Miss O'Brien," she said, and then turned her bright smile on Sum. "And to you, Mr. Sumner. A very Merry Christmas."

"Merry Christmas, Miss O'Connor." He tipped his hat. "You're looking festive today. I'm glad to see you're willing to brave the snow to shop at my store."

"A little snow won't stop me. You know how I love to shop." She lifted the hem of her skirts, revealing matching leather boots, which only proved she wasn't lying about loving to shop. "My shoes may be ruined, though. I should've worn galoshes."

"Before you leave, I'll shovel the walk," he promised. "We have hot cocoa inside. Have Miss Smith pour you a cup."

"That sounds wonderful." She flashed another pearly smile. "Do join me if you have time. I need help coming up with ideas for Christmas presents for my parents."

"You might save your money. That would be a nice

present." Maggie made the remark dryly. Her face had gotten red again.

The younger woman tipped her head. To her credit, she smiled at the jab. "Yes, that would be a big surprise. Oh, and I meant to tell you, my father will stop by later to deliver presents for the orphans. We had fun picking them out. Spent too much money, I'm afraid."

After firing the sarcastic retort, she tiptoed off through the white powder.

Sum waited until the young woman entered the store, then he couldn't resist. "If you don't go to dinner with me, I could invite Miss O'Connor. She's very entertaining."

Maggie didn't blink. "Her father would shoot you. She's half your age."

"Hmm. Nineteen times two doesn't equal thirty-two. You need to work on your arithmetic, teacher."

"So, you only *look* older."

He wrapped his arms around his chest to keep from laughing. God, she was adorable. He wanted to kiss her, but if he did that out here in front of everyone, she'd never speak to him again.

This was the second round he'd won. However, Maggie wouldn't acknowledge defeat if he didn't give her a way to do so gracefully. "Come to dinner with me tonight and we can discuss more suitable sweethearts. Besides, you owe me for helping you collect all those gifts. I'll consider a night out sufficient repayment."

The tightness around her mouth eased, as did the crease between her eyebrows. He stepped closer and dusted snow off her cape and hood. Their eyes met, and his heart kicked in his chest. He hoped their children would have her gypsy eyes and midnight hair.

Where had this recent obsession with procreation come

from? He'd been with beautiful women before, but none of them had made him long to be domesticated. Never mind. He'd stopped fighting this powerful connection—love, or whatever the hell one might call it—and it was time Maggie gave in as well. Tonight, he would make her see that. After he made her his, her love for him would surpass her loyalty to David O'Brien.

He cupped his hands on her shoulders. "Dinner. Tonight. After that, you can send me back to the North Pole if you'd like."

CHAPTER 10

*A*t ten minutes until seven, Sum took a final look in the mirror, adjusted his bow tie and smoothed down the points of his collar. He'd put on a black frock coat over a snowy white shirt and tie, and spiced it up with a blue brocade vest. His father, who'd cursed him with tart-red hair, had also possessed a keen eye for complimentary clothing. That one helpful trait, however, didn't make up for the other inferior ones.

He'd also inherited his father's spontaneous nature, which had gotten him into trouble from a young age. That, coupled with a tendency to trust the wrong people, had left him in a financial bind. But if the last few days' receipts were any indication, he would soon climb out of the hole. Once he paid off his creditors, he would start saving for a proper home for his new wife.

Maggie would be his. He'd gain her promise tonight, even if he had to seduce her. Something he looked forward to. He had never set his mind on something that he'd failed, in the end, to acquire. He'd also lost most of what he'd made, but he wouldn't lose Maggie. Her love was too valuable, worth more than all his dreams put together. If she could love him, then he could believe in himself, and he would never be a failure again.

Knocking echoed from below. Had Maggie grown impatient? He could wish.

Sum trotted down the stairs and turned up the gas lever, spilling light into the store. Not seeing anyone at the door, he unlocked it and looked outside, now thinking perhaps it was a childish prank.

A man hiding into the shadows grabbed him by the throat. Putting the cold barrel of a gun to his forehead, the intruder shoved him back into the store. His attacker loomed over him, looking to be roughly the size of a bull; taller, stronger, and based on the stench rolling off him in waves, fermented in a barrel of cheap whiskey.

"Don' make a sound, or I'll hafta kill ya." The bull's foul breath wafted into Sum's face.

Sound? He couldn't speak, or swallow, caught in the man's beefy grip.

Was he a debt collector? They were generally unpleasant characters, but this one looked larger and meaner than the ones he'd encountered before. Sum tried to think over the loud hammering of his heart. Panic rarely helped. "What..." he rasped. "Do you want?"

"Your money. All of it."

So, he was a robber as well as a debt collector. Sum cursed himself for not being more vigilant. Overpowering the massive fellow wasn't a viable option. He'd fought big men, but not a behemoth that had a gun held to his head. Somehow, he had to convince the inebriated attacker to relax his guard.

"Can't...breathe," Sum choked out.

The sausage-like fingers relaxed their grip, slightly.

Sum swallowed, but was careful not to move quickly and cause alarm. The trigger-happy fool might put a bullet through his brain. "Remove the gun from my head and I'll get the money. It's in the register drawer."

He'd already put the day's earnings in the safe and there was no way in hell he would hand it over. But he kept a loaded revolver underneath the counter, and if he could get to it...

"Ain't puttin' this gun down 'til I see that money. Let's go over there so you can get it..."

Sum moved backwards, with the man advancing along with him. They inched toward the counter. "When we reach the register, you'll have to release me so I can open the drawer."

That would give him time to knock the man's gun away and retrieve his weapon—he hoped.

Dread tightened a fist around his heart. If he died tonight, he would never see Maggie again, considering they'd end up in different places. Even if she lit a thousand candles, he doubted she could pray him into heaven. Unlike her, he had never been good. Yet, he yearned to spend his life with a woman who gave him the desire to be better. He would show Maggie how much he loved her every day he was granted life.

Sum focused his attention on the flat-nosed assailant and the gun. He'd watch for his chance and get out of this, just as he'd gotten out of other tight spots.

～

MAGGIE CHECKED the watch pinned to her jacket. Ten minutes past. Not once had Sum been late. Now, after browbeating her into going to dinner with him, he made her wait.

She paced the length of her brother's store, stopping long enough to pluck a peppermint from a candy jar and pop it into her mouth. The candy would settle her stomach. It hadn't unknotted since she'd left Sum standing on the sidewalk, relishing his victory.

Arrogant Easterner. Showy as a jaybird in his fashionable suits and ties, with every strand of his gingery hair combed into place. Never mind that his smile was downright sinful, and his eyes were as blue as the Kansas sky.

Would serve him right if she went back upstairs. She could spend a pleasant evening with her niece and nephew. They would run her ragged, but that would be more relaxing than staring at Sum over a steak and a glass of wine.

The handsome charmer continued to blast away at her resistance. The terrible truth was, she actually looked forward to surrender. She'd gone mad since she'd started spending time with him, listening to his blarney. Trying to match him up with her friend, and feeling miserable about it, and then insulting Phoebe O'Connor, who was a very nice young lady, had made one thing clear—she couldn't be Sum's matchmaker. Just the thought of him being with another woman was enough to send her into a frenzy.

Crossing to the front window, Maggie squinted to peer across the street at his store. Through an open door, soft light from inside spilled across the snow. She watched for another moment, but Sum didn't come outside. Had he forgotten something and gone back for it? Or had he gotten distracted filling Miss O'Connor's order?

Devil take him. No, she didn't really mean that. She

didn't want anyone else to have him, not old Scratch, not Miss O'Connor, not even Michael the Archangel.

David was wrong about what her parents would've advised. If she listened to her selfish heart, she would accept Sum's proposal. Then where would that leave her? Pitted against her brother. Sum didn't understand how this would tear her apart because he hadn't been blessed with a close family. She longed to give him that, and more. If ever there was a man who needed her love, it was Gordon Sumner. But there could be no happiness for them if she had divided loyalties.

She squinted to read his name in shadowed letters on the large glass pane. Why couldn't he have opened a livery or a hotel, anything except a mercantile? If he'd located his store across town, at least he wouldn't be stealing her brother's customers. In spite of everything, she still longed to be Mrs. Sumner...Mrs. Maggie O'Brien Sumner.

Her stomach did a slow flip. *O'Brien. Sumner. Together.* Why hadn't she thought of it before? That made perfect sense. Apart, both men struggled, but together, as business partners, they would be unbeatable. Of course, her hardheaded brother would resist partnering with a man he distrusted. Victoria had a more open mind and might be convinced, and then she could bring David around.

The idea gathered steam. Maggie got so excited thinking about the possibilities, she couldn't wait to talk to Sum. If he agreed, they could plan for how best to approach Victoria and David. Although she'd have to give up her teaching job in Kansas City, a worthy project awaited her here, founding a children's home where orphans could be cared for and schooled.

She unlocked the front door. Hugging her cloak, she tore across the street. Gas lamps along the sidewalk illuminated snowflakes twirling in the darkness above the bricked pavement. Her heart danced with them. If she could make a way for her and Sum to be together, it would be the best Christmas ever.

Maggie thundered across the opposite sidewalk and raced through the open door. She halted, startled by a strange sight near the register. A massive, stoop-shouldered man held Sum by the throat and had a gun pointed at his head.

Terror such as she'd never felt surged through her. "No!" she screamed. "Don't shoot!"

The huge man whirled around.

She didn't think past her urgency to reach Sum. She didn't think about anything, except saving him, when she started forward.

The gun flashed fire and smoke. A loud retort reverberated. Something punched her chest.

Maggie staggered back, shocked and disbelieving, as the blood in her veins turned to ice.

I'm shot. The terrifying thought flickered through her mind, drowned out by a loud roaring in her ears, which grew louder...deafening...even over a furious shout, which she assumed came from Sum. But she couldn't see him. Darkness encroached on her vision.

Her knees buckled, and the last thing she heard was another gunshot.

CHAPTER 11

The bullet whizzed past Sum's head. A bottle on the shelves behind him crashed. He grabbed his revolver from beneath the counter and fired. The bull lumbered past Maggie's crumpled form and out the door. Smoke hung in the air and the acrid smell stung his nose.

"Maggie!" Sum rushed to her side, dropping to his knees beside her. His throat closed up like the man's fingers were still around it and fear compressed his lungs. His beloved lay sprawled on her back a few feet inside the door. Everything had happened so fast. Maggie had appeared out of nowhere, screamed and startled the robber, and the bastard had shot her.

Sum set his gun aside, cursing himself for not being fast enough. He leaned over and gently drew her hair away from her face. "Maggie? Sweetheart?"

Her eyes remained closed, her lashes forming black crescents against her pale skin. Too pale. Her lips had lost all color. His frantic gaze snapped onto a dark hole burned into her cloak, just left of center above her breast. He sucked in a sharp breath.

"God, no..." he groaned. He couldn't stop his hands from shaking as he unfastened her cloak. "Maggie...Maggie...." He chanted her name, as if saying it would vanquish the horror and she would open her eyes and smile at him and everything would be all right. His breath came in harsh, painful gasps. His heart felt like it might explode.

Her lashes fluttered and a bewildered gaze met his. "Sum?" Her voice came out small, tremulous.

Relief deflated the balloon inside his chest. If she could talk, that meant it wasn't as bad as he thought. "Be still." He smiled to reassure her. "You'll be all right. Just let me take a look."

As gently as possible, he peeled back the cloak, his gut knotted with fear. He anticipated seeing blood soaking her clothes. Her frightened gaze remained on his face as if looking at him gave her courage. For her sake, he would be strong.

The bullet had lodged in the center of the gold watch she kept pinned to her bodice.

He stared in disbelief, then released his pent-up terror in a heavy gust. "Thank God."

"How...how bad is it?" She struggled to get up on her elbows, bending her neck to look.

"You're all right, sweetheart." He gathered her in his arms, cradling her close, giddy with relief, almost laughing. The shock from being shot must've caused her to swoon. "You're not hurt. The watch stopped the bullet."

"My mother's watch?" Her anxiousness seemed to increase as she reached for the broken piece of jewelry and fumbled, trying to unpin it.

"Here, let me..." Removing the watch from the pin, he handed it to her.

She stared at the ruined timepiece, her expression

turning to disbelief. Tears trickled down her cheeks. Delayed reaction, perhaps. Gratitude. God knows he wanted to kiss the thing, preserve it as a relic, a miracle.

He fished a fresh handkerchief from his vest pocket.

She shook her head when he tried to give it to her. "I already have one of yours, thank you."

"Do you have it with you?"

She sniffed. "No."

"Then take this one and you'll have two." He dried the tears from her cheeks and tucked the handkerchief into her hand.

She reached for her bonnet, which had been knocked askew when she fell. He helped her straighten it. Their eyes met and he saw his unspeakable fear reflected in her gaze. She turned into him and put her arms around his neck, clinging to him. "You-you're all right?"

"I'm fine—" The words backed up in his throat. He hugged her close, vowing he would never again let anyone hurt her. He'd make sure she stayed safe, even if it killed him.

Gunshots came from outside in rapid succession.

Sum tightened his hold instinctively and reached for his revolver. The gunfire wasn't too distant, just down the street. The bull hadn't gone far. Now he was causing further mayhem. No one could rest easy until the animal had been put down.

"Come on, let's get you somewhere safe." He tucked the gun into his waistband, and then pulled Maggie into a sitting position and helped her to her feet. She still looked dazed.

He pressed a kiss to her forehead. "Upstairs. You'll be safe there while I check things out. Lock the door behind me."

Thundering steps sounded outside on the walkway.

Alarmed, Sum thrust Maggie behind him and drew his gun.

Her brother burst into the store.

"Don't shoot!" Maggie cried. Before Sum could lower his gun, she stepped between them. His heart slammed to a stop, at the same time her brother jerked to a halt, eyes wide with surprise.

Releasing a furious breath, Sum lowered the gun and reached for her. "Damn it, Maggie! Stop putting yourself in harm's way."

Her brother's gaze moved between them, confused. "Did you hear the gunshots? Mr. O'Connor came by, and some idiot dragged him off his horse and tried to kill him. I've never seen O'Connor use that gun...He wears all the time. By God, he's a crack shot. Hit the madman right between the eyes when he charged..." O'Brien's voice trailed off as he approached his sister. "Maggie, what's wrong? Why are you crying?"

"The man O'Connor killed is the same one who tried to rob me, I suspect," Sum hoped the bastard roasted in hell. "He shot Maggie. Her watch saved her."

"Shot? Watch?" Her brother honed in on the hole torn in her cloak. Not surprisingly, he paled with horror. "My God, Maggie. Are you all right?"

Lifting her hand, she opened her palm, showing him the ruined jewelry. "I'm sorry, Davy. The bullet, it...it broke Ma's watch. That's all we had left, and I...I..." The tears began to flow again. So, her initial reaction hadn't been one of gratitude.

Sum couldn't grasp her despair over the ruined heirloom. He'd never treasured anything as much as he treasured Maggie, and would give up any object, no matter how precious, to keep her safe.

O'Brien grasped his sister's arm and pulled her into a tight embrace. His quick action jostled the ruined watch and it fell out of her hand, landing with a clunk on the floor. "Don't cry," he murmured, stroking her back as she clung to him, weeping. "Here now, Ma would be glad of it. She saved you, *Mageen*."

His dark gaze shifted. When his eyes met Sum's there was murder in them. "Why didn't you stop him?"

A question Sum had asked himself over and over. He had no answer. No excuse. He bent down and picked up the watch. "Her mother did a better job of it, I'll admit."

Maggie pulled back with a frown on her tear-streaked face. "David, don't get angry with Sum. He didn't have time to do anything. That horrid man had a gun on him when I came in—"

Sum refused to let her defend him. "I should've reacted faster. Had this watch not stopped the bullet, you'd be dead."

With a dark look, O'Brien curled his arm around his sister's shoulders. "Come Maggie, we're going home."

She didn't resist when he guided her to the door. Sum remained where he stood. She twisted around with longing in her eyes, as if she expected him to object to her leaving, or maybe she thought he'd follow.

He couldn't do either because she didn't belong to him. Moreover, he shouldn't have put her into danger. His life was a disaster waiting to happen. Even if he could ensure her safety, he shouldn't have reached so high. Maggie was an angel. He didn't deserve an angel.

"Mr. O'Connor went for the sheriff. I imagine he'll want a statement from you," O'Brien said as they neared the threshold. His tone remained accusing, though his condemnation couldn't hold a candle to the curses Sum piled on his own head.

Maggie tore away from her brother's protective hold. "It was a robbery, David. Not Mr. Sumner's fault."

She thought so well of him, he hated to disappoint her. He wasn't the man she thought he was, the honorable man he pretended to be. Feeling exposed, Sum folded his arms across his chest, but then he forced them to drop. Confession didn't come easy for someone who'd avoided it for so long, but it was time he came clean.

"No, Maggie, your brother's right to be worried. It's my fault that man was here. I owe money to a creditor back east. He's not a very patient man, nor is he a nice one. He's sent his thugs after me before. I thought if I paid him part of the money, he'd give me time to come up with the rest. Looks like he's tired of waiting. You need to stay away from me. It's not safe."

Disbelief flickered across her face, then sadness, and finally, disappointment.

Her eyes had been opened, and now she saw the selfish creature she'd allowed to crawl into her heart. Hopefully, she would expel him quickly and get on with her life.

AFTER MAGGIE'S brother took her home, Sum went to find the sheriff and provided his account of the shooting. The dead man had nothing to say for himself. Mr. O'Connor reported that he didn't have much choice but to the kill the bastard when the other man stole his horse, took a shot at him and tried to run him over. Any jury would agree on self-defense, so the sheriff didn't bother to bring charges. The lawman did question Sum at length after learning the unidentified man might be a debt collector.

Two hours later, Sum returned to his store, numb with fatigue, He wasn't so numb that he couldn't feel the heavy press of emotion. He'd slipped Maggie's ruined watch into his pocket, after showing it to the sheriff, who'd shaken his head in disbelief.

Sum retrieved the watch to look at it again. Broke his heart to know she mourned the heirloom. He didn't think it could be fixed, but he would ask the jeweler. If not, he would order one that looked just like it. Somehow, he'd pay for it, even if he had to sell his own watch. It was the least he could do. Although nothing would make up for what had been taken from her.

He removed his coat, rolled up his sleeves and went to work to keep his mind off Maggie. During the exchange of gunfire, two bottles of Dr. Bradfield's Female Remedy had been shattered. He picked glass shards off the countertop and the floor, and then wiped up the sticky syrup. His shot at the misbegotten cur had sent a bullet into the doorframe. He pried the slug out of the wood and vowed to practice his aim so he wouldn't miss the next time.

After putting things back in order, he went upstairs. His apartment seemed emptier than usual, even though none of the furniture appeared to be missing. The regulator clock on the wall carried on with a rhythmic tick-tock. With nothing to occupy his mind, guilt rushed in.

Maggie had come within a hair's breadth of being killed. He couldn't have lived with that. Had she died, he would've turned his gun on himself. As it was, he might consider suicide as an option. Death would be preferable to living the rest of his life knowing he'd ruined hers.

For some reason, she'd come across the street looking

for him. The anguish in her eyes as she left with her brother told him he had finally succeeded in tearing down her defenses. She cared for him, possibly loved him. Or had, before he enlightened her to his true nature.

He'd wounded a beautiful soul. He might as well have pulled the trigger on the gun that nearly killed her.

Sinking onto the sofa, he braced his elbows on his knees and put his head in his hands. His throat ached, his eyes stung, and still, he couldn't cry, even if it might help release pent-up grief, not to mention self-loathing. He pressed his fingers against his eyes and rubbed. Pity wouldn't help. If he harmed himself, Maggie would feel worse. The best thing would be to sell everything, repay his creditor and go somewhere far away. She'd be hurt, but eventually she would get over it and be better off without him hanging around, making her worry about him putting her brother out of business. More likely, the clever Irishman would put him out of business.

O'Brien had adjusted well to competition. He was a survivor. So was Maggie, even if she didn't see it. She viewed her brother as responsible for what she'd accomplished. O'Brien might've footed the bill, but she had worked hard to reach her dreams. She'd been orphaned at a young age and might've remained dependent on her older brother, but she'd gone on to become a teacher. Not only that, she'd taken up a cause and would see it through. Maggie let nothing stand in her way.

Sum sat back. He stared at his fingers, surprised by the moisture. *Tears?* That was something new. He couldn't recall the last time he'd cried. It might've been when he was four, the day his father informed him that his two older brothers had perished at Gettysburg. Far as he could recall, he hadn't wept since then.

A noise came from downstairs, sounding like something had fallen.

Sum came to his feet, heart pounding. He reached for the gun he'd set on the side table. He had locked every door and checked twice, as was his habit. That meant someone had broken in, possibly through the back by the sound of it.

Could be the bull hadn't been working alone and this was his partner or another collector. That made the most sense because being robbed twice in one night was about as likely as lightning striking repeatedly in the same place.

Taking care to remain quiet, Sum crept down the stairs leading to the storage area with the revolver cocked. He strained to see in the darkness. If someone was down there, he didn't want to turn up the lights and make himself an easy target. Plus, he had the advantage of knowing where he'd put everything. As he placed his foot on the next riser and shifted his weight, the wood creaked.

Sum froze.

Scurrying sounds, like the fast movement of feet, came from the back.

A window had been pried open, though it didn't look like the space was large enough to allow a man to crawl through, unless he was a small man. Whoever the intruder happened to be, it sounded like he was on the other side of that stack of boxes. He'd be expecting someone at the base of the stairs.

Sum leapt over the railing and landed on the floor with a thud, then shoved the boxes on top of the cockroach crouched behind them.

"Ow!"

The voice sounded young. Whoever it was, he was buried beneath shoeboxes.

Sum slid the gas lever upwards. Light glowed from a

lamp mounted to the crossbeams above his head. He leveled the revolver, aiming where the intruder was likely hiding. "Come out of there. Keep your hands where I can see them. I've got a gun, and I won't hesitate to shoot your sorry ass."

The boxes shifted, a narrow hand appeared, and then another...a shock of bright red hair.

"Sonofa...," Sum muttered. He eased the hammer down and stuck the gun in the back of his waistband before he latched onto the skinny wrist and hauled the intruder to his feet.

"Stupid kid, what the hell are you doing? I almost shot you."

Felix trembled so hard Sum could feel the vibrations quivering up his arm. The boy might've wet his oversized dungarees. Smelled bad enough. A wonder the stink hadn't reached the apartment before the sounds.

Sum released the child's bony wrist. No point frightening him to death. He already looked like death warmed over, with no coat, no gloves, no hat, and...someone else's boots, at least two sizes too large. A miracle he hadn't made more much noise tromping around.

"Where are the shoes I gave you," Sum demanded.

Felix wrapped his arms around his chest and hung his head. Maybe that's why he'd broken in, to steal more shoes. Possibly, someone had stolen his.

Sum modulated his voice to a calmer level. "Did you lose them?"

The boy shook his head.

"What then?"

"Gave 'em away."

Well, hell... Sum heaved a frustrated sigh. "I'm not really Santa, you now. I don't have a workshop, and don't know of any elves that make shoes. Which means I can't afford to keep giving them away."

Felix raised his head with a challenging look. "Boxer needs shoes more than me. I know you ain't Santa, but you still got lotsa shoes."

"Who the hell is Boxer?"

"My little brother. His real name's Harold, but we call him Boxer because he likes to climb into boxes and hide."

Sum tried to ignore the tug on his heart. For all he knew, the kid was making this up. "And what about the clothes? You give those to Boxer, too?"

"Gave him the coat. Gave the shirt and trousers to Elsie, so she can wear them under her dress and keep warm."

Sum rolled down his sleeves, chagrined by what he was hearing. "How did we miss Boxer and Elsie the other day?"

"Mrs. Meaney knows if she brings Elsie and Boxer and me into town together, I'll take them and run away. She keeps them locked up in the house most of the time. I sleep in the barn." Felix scratched underneath his arm.

Sum eyed the raggedy child. Dark circles looked like bruises under his eyes and his cheeks were gaunt, as if he hadn't eaten in a while. "How did you get back to town?"

"Waited until Mr. Meaney left and then crawled into the back of the wagon. He's deaf in one ear, so he don't hear so well. He can't see real good, either."

"The four girls I met, are they related to you?"

"No, they're from other families."

"How many children are out there on the farm?"

"Eight of us, if you count the baby." Felix reached behind his neck, going for another itch.

"Someone gave that old witch a baby?" Sum declared, astonished. "That's worse than giving *me* an infant."

A reluctant smile pulled at the boy's lips. "Tommy's Ma

was an Indian and nobody else wanted him. One of the older girls takes care of him. Mrs. Meaney will put him to work soon as he can walk. She says white folks can make slaves outta Indians. It ain't against the law."

"The hell it ain't." Sum clamped his teeth shut. He was starting to sound like Felix. "I'll talk to the judge about this. He'll take you and the other children away from the Meaneys."

Felix pawed at his chest. "No room on the other poor farms, that's what I hear; and you can't make us go to that destitute house. That's worse than puttin' up with mean old Mrs. Meaney." He looked around and scratched his head. Possibly he had lice. He didn't look, or smell as if he bathed regularly. "Could we live here? I'd work for you, and Elsie can cook. Boxer's only seven, but he can help out with odd jobs."

Sum shook his head. The very idea of taking on three children was absurd. He wasn't even married, not to mention he had terrible parenting skills, having learned from two of the worst. "That isn't possible. I won't be around much longer."

Felix looked surprised. "Where you going?"

"Haven't decided."

"Is Mrs. Claus going with you?"

The dull pain centered in Sum's chest began to throb. If only he could take her with him. Once he paid off his debt, they wouldn't have to worry about his creditor sending thugs after them. *Wishful thinking.* He would never ask Maggie to leave her family behind, knowing how important they were to her. "No, she won't be going."

Felix scratched behind his ear. His scratching was making Sum itch.

"How long since you've had a bath?"

The boy shrugged, making it clear bathing was unimportant to him.

"How about since you've eaten?"

His eyes lit up at the mention of food. "I could eat somethin', if you're offering."

Sum couldn't throw the kid out. Maybe a month ago he would have, but not after meeting Maggie and learning about the plight of orphans. He also couldn't turn his back on the situation the children faced on that poor farm. With Christmas two days away, it was unlikely a new home could be located, although he would talk to His Honor first thing in the morning.

He would ask the judge to put the three siblings with him until their case could be heard. He had an extra bedroom for the girl and could make a pallet in his room for the two boys. It would only be for a few weeks at most, until someone else took them. In the meantime, he'd start looking for potential buyers for his inventory. Maybe O'Brien.

Sum motioned to Felix. "Come on, then. But you have to take a bath if you expect to sleep upstairs. Don't want the place infested with...with whatever it is you're scratching."

CHAPTER 12

*T*he doctor ordered Maggie to remain in bed after what he called a *terrible shock* to her system. He pronounced she could succumb to illness if she didn't rest and remain quiet. A bruise above her left breast appeared to be the only injury, as far as she could tell. She still got nauseous when she thought about how close she'd come to dying, but she wasn't so weak she needed to remain abed through Christmas Eve, especially given Sum's surprising revelation.

He had some nerve telling her to stay away from him. After hounding her for weeks and finally wearing her down, he thought he could send her away with the snap of his fingers? It would take more than an unprincipled creditor to frighten her off.

She selected her favorite striped suit, which reminded her of candy canes, and paired it with a white shirtwaist fastened with tiny buttons. The collar had a nice bow. She sat down at the dressing table in Fannie's room and took extra care arranging her hair. It took over an hour to pin up the heavy tresses and make the style appear casual. A figured bonnet completed the look.

Gazing at her reflection in the mirror, she touched the spot on her chest where the gold watch would've been pinned and tears gathered in her eyes. That watch was all she had left of her mother. Perhaps the works could be rebuilt, or if not, she would still wear it. The imbedded bullet would serve to remind her that her mother had a hand in saving her life, not once but twice. Ma had been the one to tell Da to put her and David out on the porch roof to get them away from the smoke while their parents tried to find another way out.

Maggie crossed to her suitcase and took out the jacket she'd been wearing, and then recalled she'd removed the watch. Only the pin remained. Perhaps she'd given the ruined watch to David.

Making her way downstairs, she heard the children before she saw them. Fannie and Patrick were playing near the back of the store at a small table David had set up, which had toys they were allowed to touch.

Victoria, wearing a white apron over a festive green dress, was assisting an elderly man in selecting a nightgown for his wife. She must've insisted on David wearing that plaid waistcoat. He wouldn't have picked it out. He waited on another customer while four others stood in line, their arms filled with last minute shopping.

The potbellied stove in the center of the store radiated warmth and the air smelled wonderful: baked goods, fermented cider, chocolate, pickles, leather and tobacco. She and David used to guess which new items their parents stocked going by smell alone. Funny, how she remembered that, but couldn't call her Ma's face to mind.

When the elderly gentleman joined the others waiting

to pay, Victoria headed in Maggie's direction. Her frown made it clear she wasn't pleased to see her sister-in-law up and dressed. "What are you doing out of bed?"

"Coming to see my family." Maggie smiled sweetly. She was just as stubborn as her brother's wife. "I wanted to know if you had any luck convincing David to partner with Sum. It makes so much sense."

"For Mr. Sumner, I imagine it does."

Victoria's droll tone grated on Maggie's nerves. "You don't agree it's a good idea? How can you not? We've always known both stores can't continue to thrive across the street from each other, carrying the same goods. David nearly went under two years ago, before you came along and showed him that he was resisting progress for no good reason. He's good at operations and finances, but Sum is a natural salesman. He could sell tea to a Chinaman. Can you not see how well they could work together?"

Victoria laid a hand on Maggie's shoulder, speaking low. "I'm not saying it's a bad idea."

David had heard her outburst, if that frown was any indication. She would get nowhere by airing their disagreement in public. "Then why do you say it's only beneficial to Mr. Sumner?" she whispered. "I believe David would benefit from Sum's expertise."

"If he's such an expert, how did he get into debt?"

"I'll be asking him that, but it doesn't mean David shouldn't consider a partnership, or at least be open to talking about it. You'll help me convince him, won't you?"

"Mama!" Patrick tugged on Victoria's skirt. "Kee!"

Victoria lifted the toddler onto her hip. He'd soon be too big for his mother to lug around. "We'll go see the kitty in a moment, sweetie. Let me finish talking to Aunt Maggie. You go play with the train Dada gave you."

She set him down and he toddled off in the direction of a table stacked with glassware. Fannie intercepted him and guided him back to their toys.

"She's good with him," Maggie observed.

"Oh, yes. Without Fannie's attentiveness, we'd have a lot more broken dishes."

"Fannie adores her little brother, and she adores you, too."

Victoria's eyes grew bright. She withdrew a handkerchief from her apron pocket. "Now you...look, you've made me cry."

The former Boston socialite, who'd come to town with no housekeeping skills and little knowledge about children, had turned out to be a wonderful mother. She loved her stepdaughter as deeply as if she'd borne the child. Fannie hadn't spoken for two years after her mother had abandoned her and her father. Then Victoria had come along, and had taught her sign language so she could communicate without words, and eventually won Fannie's trust. When Fannie had started talking again, it had been Victoria she'd spoken to first.

For being so petite, Victoria had a huge heart. Maggie was counting on it.

She hugged her sister-in-law. "You know I love you as much as if we'd always been sisters."

Victoria returned the hug, and then dabbed at her eyes. "I'll help you convince David without you buttering me up."

"I'm not buttering you up." Maggie smiled. "Well, maybe just a wee bit."

Victoria kissed Maggie's cheek and leaned forward to whisper in her ear. "I'm willing to help you because I know you're in love with Mr. Sumner...and he loves you."

Maggie drew back, now she was the one tearing up. "How do you know?"

"Oh, Maggie. Everyone who knows the two of you is aware of it. Even Nancy mentioned to me that she's anxious to see you and Mr. Sumner wed."

"Nancy?" Maggie's cheeks grew warm. "I tried matching them up."

"Oh, yes, she told me all about it. I wish I could've been there."

Victoria's expression turned from amused to serious. "Mr. Sumner has been by to check on you, but David wouldn't let him upstairs, said it wasn't proper, and Mr. Sumner seemed reluctant to push it. I'll talk to David again about considering a partnership, but you may have to wheedle a proposal out of Mr. Sumner first. Then it'll be harder for your brother to say no."

Or David would get pigheaded about it. The chances were fifty-fifty. But those odds were better than the odds with no proposal. That is, if Sum's offer was still good.

Maggie squared her shoulders. Now that she'd accepted the idea that she was in love with the annoying, charming, pretend Santa, she wasn't letting his guilt or fear stand in the way of their future together. "I'll take care of the proposal. You work on David. He's difficult to turn once he's got the bit in his mouth."

"Put that down!" Sum raced over to where the seven-year-old stood on tiptoe at the edge of the counter, reaching for a bottle of Dr. Bradfield's Regulator.

Startled, the boy twisted, and his heel slipped.

Sum caught Boxer as he fell, and set him on his feet. His

clerk had been with another customer, and he hadn't been paying enough attention. The little imp could've broken his neck, or pulled the shelves down and been crushed beneath them. The wave of fear receded into anger. "What were you doing up there?"

"I asked the child to fetch my medicine." Widow Dobbs barely topped the counter, yet she managed to look down her nose.

Boxer set the bottle on the counter. He looked up accusingly through a long fringe of white-blond hair, and then darted around Sum's right side, heading straight for the storeroom. He'd hide in one of the umpteen boxes back there, and it would take hours to find him.

All right, so the boy had been helping a customer. Earlier, he'd been helping himself to the fresh doughnuts. Sum heaved a frustrated sigh. He'd been out of his mind when he agreed to take on three children, even for a couple weeks.

The judge hadn't hesitated when he'd asked for them—temporarily. He had assumed some kindly matron who'd raised a pack of her own would be eager to take in three children...until he'd gotten to know them better.

He'd caught Felix sneaking pastries after devouring a huge breakfast. The eleven-year-old had to have two stomachs, like a cow. The boy never stopped eating. Hopefully, Felix wouldn't eat the groceries he was supposed to be delivering. And his nine-year-old sister Elsie knew how to cook all right. Oatmeal. She could make gobs and gobs of oatmeal. Right now, she had her sticky hands all over a shiny glass display top, peering eagerly at bejeweled hair ornaments.

Sum finished filling his customer's order—always medicine, sometimes a black handkerchief or shawl to go with her gloomy wardrobe. She'd become a professional mourner after twenty years of practice. He smiled, ruefully. "Sorry, Mrs. Dobbs. I'm not used to having children underfoot."

"That's obvious," the widow drawled. "You ask me, young man, I think you better get yourself a wife before you start taking in young 'uns." With that, she picked up her sack of medicines and tottered away.

The old lady was no sooner out the door than in waltzed Maggie O'Brien, wearing a candy-striped suit and looking delicious. Sum's heart slipped faster than Boxer's heel. Sadly, there was no one around to catch it.

He straightened his coat and smoothed his hands over the wool fabric. Nervous. Elated. Despairing. He had no choice but to send her away.

She approached the counter with a smile that tied his insides into knots. "Merry Christmas, Mr. Sumner."

He fought the urge to drag her over the counter and kiss her silly. Not only would that be ill advised in a store filled with customers, he had sworn to keep his hands off her. It took all his willpower to return nothing more than a polite greeting. "And to you, Miss O'Brien. I trust you're feeling better?"

"I thought I would be." Her smile lost some of its luster. She appeared dangerously close to tears. He couldn't keep up this pretense. He cared too much for her. If he explained why he had to leave, she might not like it, but she would understand and be able to deal with it. Maggie had a deep well of strength. His had about dried up.

"Would you like some cocoa?" He came around from behind the counter and ushered her to the rear of the store, nodding gratefully at his clerk as she moved to take over at the register. "I just made a fresh pot...if the children haven't finished it."

She glanced at him with surprise. "Children?"

He motioned with his head toward Elsie, who'd taken a seat and was trying on a pair of ladies' boots while a young woman looked on. He'd asked the girl to assist customers if they needed help. Perhaps she thought that meant trying on clothes for them.

"The Erickson children, all three of them. That's Elsie. She's nine and knows how to cook oatmeal. Her seven-year-old brother Harold, they call him Boxer, is hiding somewhere in the back. He's upset because I yelled at him. He tried to help a customer and almost pulled a shelf down on top of him. Felix, you'll remember meeting him after the parade, is out making deliveries. I've got custody of them until another family can be found. The judge is also looking for a home for three other girls and an infant, so if you know of anyone—"

Maggie placed her fingers over his mouth. Then she lifted up on her toes and replaced her fingers with her lips.

His breathing ceased, his thoughts stalled. *For the love of Pete...* He wrapped his hand around the back of her head, threading his fingers through the heavy curls. Oh God, she tasted wonderful, and he'd been starved for her.

She broke off the kiss much too soon, and slipped onto a stool at the back counter as if nothing had happened, like she hadn't noticed the world tilting on its axis. Patting the stool next to her, she smiled. "You are a dear man, Sum, but you aren't making any sense. Sit here beside me and tell me how you ended up with three children."

He sat. She couldn't have been thinking clearly, to kiss him in full view of everyone in the store. Now, he wasn't thinking clearly, because he couldn't think about anything except kissing her. But that wasn't why he'd brought her back here. He had to explain why they couldn't be together, after answering her question.

"The Meaneys aren't taking care of the children who were placed in their charge," he explained. "Felix ran away. I caught him the other night trying to steal shoes. He'd given his new clothes to his brother and sister. Didn't look like he'd eaten for days. For a fact, he hadn't bathed in a month. The judge said he would look into the situation. In the meantime, he put the Erickson children with me. It's only for a few days. I'm selling out."

She'd been leaning on the counter, her chin propped on her hand, gazing at him with a look of amusement, until he uttered the last sentence, and then she jerked up straight. "Selling out? What do you mean selling out?"

"If I sell the inventory, I'll have enough to repay my creditor in full, so he won't send more of his goons after me."

"But...you said business had been good this month."

"It has been, but I haven't earned enough to pay off my debt and keep my doors open."

"Why did you borrow so much money from that awful man?" Her chagrin acted like acid on his soul.

Sum rubbed his fingers on the counter, reluctant to tell her how stupid he'd been, but that was already obvious. She'd damn near been killed because of his stupidity. He turned on the stool and straddled the fall of her skirts in order to face her while he told her the bitter truth.

"My father, I told you about him, he was always chasing the next big idea. He'd make money and then lose it, invest and go broke. I wasn't going to be like him, so I put my money into a store and went into business with a partner. We did very well...so well my partner up and vamoosed with all our money. No bank was willing to loan me enough to start over."

Her eyes rounded and sympathy welled in the fathomless depths. "Oh, Sum. That's awful, a man you trusted..."

Sum released a dark laugh. "Yeah, he also happens to be my cousin. I don't have a large family, but the one I do have is worthless. I should've known better."

She grasped his forearm and gave him a reproachful look. "Of course you'd trust your family. I would. That doesn't reflect poorly on you."

"Sure it does." He slid his arm back until he could take her hand, brushed his thumb over her smooth, warm skin. So weak, he couldn't resist. Nor could he stop thinking about trailing his fingers over her bare body. "I wasn't careful enough, didn't have money put aside. Just like my father, I invested it all in the business. Couldn't pay my employees, and I burned bridges with suppliers when I didn't pay my bills. I left Philadelphia when the collectors came after me, and I moved onto this corner because I thought it'd be easy pickings."

She gazed at him sadly. Now she knew he was opportunistic, selfish and deceitful. That ought to be enough to warn her away from him.

He let go her hand and plowed his fingers through his hair. He had no business touching her. Only a cad would compromise a lady. "I can't risk staying here and exposing you to danger. Even if I get the loan paid off, there are other people out there who'd take a piece of my hide if they could get it."

Maggie drummed her fingers on the counter. "So, that's why you're treating me like I have poison ivy."

He smiled at her tart reprisal. "Aw, now, it's only been a

couple days, and you've been holed up at home. I did come by."

"That's what Victoria told me. The doctor doesn't think I have a strong constitution. He wanted me to stay in bed until tomorrow. That's ridiculous. The only thing bothering me is not seeing you."

Her sweet sentiment soothed his aching heart, although he didn't deserve her care and concern. He took her hand, stroking her slender fingers because he couldn't help himself. "Maggie, sweet Maggie. Don't tempt me. I'm trying to be a gentleman."

She leaned in, her eyes twinkling with mischief. "I don't want you to be a gentleman, Sum. I want you to ask me to marry you and give me another kiss."

Thank God she kept her voice low. He, on the other hand, almost fell off his seat and had to brace his feet on the floor. Ironic, how just two days ago, he'd been plotting to make her fall in love with him, and now that she wanted him, he had to push her away. No, not ironic, it was a miserable shame, and even more so because he'd wooed her, knowing he wasn't worthy of her.

"I shouldn't have gotten involved with you. Your brother is right. You need to stay away from me."

She blinked, looking astonished. "Do I have wax in my ears, or did you just say my brother is right? You've been telling me all along, he has nothing to do with us."

"Yes, well..." He had said that, and still thought her brother had no right to dictate who she married. "The point is, you ought to go back to Kansas City. Teach children. Fall in love with a good man."

"Faith. The fairies must've taken my Sum and left a mewling changeling in his place."

"Mewling changeling?" He would've smiled at her

colorful choice of words if he weren't so miserable. "For Pete's sake, Maggie. I'm trying to do the right thing for a change. Something unselfish."

She gripped his coat sleeve. "If I wanted someone selfless, I'd marry a priest."

His lips twitched. Lord, how he loved her. She somehow managed to inject humor into even a heated exchange. "Priests can't marry," he pointed out.

Maggie sat back, releasing his arm. She flicked her finger at imaginary lint on her skirt. "Yes, of course I know that, and it's a good thing, too. What with their vows of chastity and all."

Sum swallowed a laugh. "Why are we talking about priests?"

"I don't know. We should be talking about the children."

"The children?"

Maggie cocked her head and gave him a look that said his mind had become slow. "As I've told you before, there aren't many places orphans can go if they aren't taken in by a family. I suspect the only way to find families for the Erickson children will be to split them up."

He didn't like her point, nor did he agree with it. "They can't be split up. You, of all people, ought to know that. They're siblings. All they've got left is each other."

She gave him a pleased smile. "Yes, you're right. That's why you need a wife."

Sum crossed his arms over his chest. She might think she could trip him up by talking in circles, but he was wise to her methods. "A wife? Now, why would I need a wife, when I'll be leaving...without the children."

"You can't ensure they won't be split up," she insisted.

"What about your brother? He could take them."

"They don't have room for five children...and Victoria is expecting."

There went that idea. "I'm sure someone has room."

Maggie folded her arms in obvious mockery. "If so, why hasn't someone taken the children by now? They were orphaned two years ago, and no one stepped up to adopt them. They don't want to be separated, so the judge let them go to the poor farm together."

Sum frowned at her logic. "There's no point arguing. The judge will deal with it."

"He put them with you. I think he knew what he was doing."

"He only put them with me because I *offered* to take them, temporarily. He's aware of that."

Maggie lowered her arms and her expression softened into something approaching pity. "You know what I think? I think you wouldn't mind if it was more than temporary."

Darned if that didn't feel like a stab to the heart. To be honest, which he wasn't, he had been thinking about settling down and having a family...with Maggie. He hadn't thought they might start out with three children. Wait, they weren't starting out at all.

He huffed, hoping he sounded convincingly disdainful. "The other Sum might not mind, but this one isn't interested in being a daddy."

A loud wail drew his attention.

Sum glanced at the front. Elsie had put the boots away and it appeared she had taken a doll from the shelf over to a little girl, who looked to be about four. The mother glared at Elsie, not appreciating the kind gesture, probably because her spoiled child clutched the doll, crying, and wouldn't be appeased unless it was purchased for her.

"Take that doll away," insisted the frazzled mother. "You shouldn't have brought it over here in the first place."

The woman's churlish tone got under Sum's skin.

Elsie's fair complexion bloomed bright red as she stammered an apology. She tried to take the doll away from the little child, who clung to it and screamed to high heaven.

"Excuse me," Sum said to Maggie. "I'll be back in a moment."

He strode down the aisle between the display cases. When he reached Elsie, he put his arm around her thin shoulders and gave her a reassuring hug. "Thank you for helping out. Why don't you see if Miss Smith might need some assistance?"

The girl's grateful smile turned a key in his heart. He didn't want to admit Maggie was right, because the very idea of taking on three children scared him to death. He would talk to the judge. There had to be a good family out there, somewhere.

The irate mother finally succeeded at wrenching the doll away from her little angel. She hoisted the weeping child into her arms, and turned to him. "Mr. Sumner, you really shouldn't let your children run wild in the store. It's very disruptive."

"Elsie was spreading Christmas cheer. I'm sorry if you find that disruptive."

The woman harrumphed, whirled on her heel and marched out the door. The crying faded, and the store became blessedly quiet.

Maggie came up from behind and put her hand on his shoulder. "Just think, we could give the Erickson children so much more than presents for Christmas. We could give them a home. You are a fine man, Sum, and you'll be a very good father."

He reached across his chest and laced their fingers together. Letting go of Maggie and the future he'd dreamed of having with her hurt worse than he'd imagined. He spoke low, so only she could hear him. "Maggie, even if it would be safe for you to be with me, and I'm not convinced it would be, after I pay off what I owe, I won't be able to support a wife or children."

She pressed her cheek against his arm. "I know. That's why you and my brother have to go into business together."

CHAPTER 13

Christmas Eve had always been Maggie's favorite time of year. She and her brother would go to Mass together, then they would come home and open gifts. Even though they knew what was in the boxes, they still pretended to be surprised. When David had expanded his family, the tradition continued, with the addition of songs and games, thanks to Victoria.

Tonight, however, promised to be the worst Christmas Eve ever, because the two men Maggie loved were behaving worse than fractious boys in a schoolyard. David refused to partner with Sum, declaring him to be a financial risk. Sum —stubborn man—refused to consider a partnership because he'd lost everything to a thieving cousin and had vowed never to trust anyone again. Maggie wanted to put them both in separate corners until they agreed to sort out their differences.

Sitting on the sofa, she watched Patrick tear into a box and chortle with glee at the newspaper stuffed inside. He completely missed the toy.

Fannie sat next to her, holding her favorite doll, the one

Victoria had given her shortly after arriving in Fort Scott. The exquisite *Jumeau* doll had been Victoria's salvation because Fannie immediately became attached to it and David was forced to open his eyes and see that all women weren't like his faithless first wife. He still needed better vision when it came to Sum.

"Aunt Maggie, open your last gift." Fannie set her doll aside to retrieve a beribboned hatbox from beneath the Christmas tree—another compromise David had made for his wife. He hadn't wanted trees, or anything that could catch fire, upstairs. Not after a fire had burned the old store to the ground, killing their parents. Victoria had talked him into putting up a tree two years ago. They didn't light candles, but the branches were covered in decorations, including painted Santa ornaments that David had ordered from New York. Maggie had read about the new electrical lights invented by Mr. Edison, but that wasn't something they could afford.

Fannie plopped the hatbox in Maggie's lap. "It's from me and Patrick."

Patrick didn't move from where he sat tearing up newspaper.

"Oh, I wonder what this could be?" Maggie shook the box near her ear. She didn't expect anything breakable because Victoria had asked her what the children might give her, and being practical, she'd suggested warmer gloves.

She opened the package, removing a nice pair of leather gloves tucked inside, along with a folded piece of paper. When she opened it, Fannie's smile broadened.

"You've drawn me a picture!" Maggie turned the paper to the side. On it, her niece had sketched a crude house complete with pointed roof and odd-shaped windows. Out front were a few large flowers and half a dozen little stick figures, some with dresses, others with trousers. "What is this Fannie? Is this supposed to be the store?'

"No." Fannie frowned with disapproval. "It's the children's home you told me about. The one you said would be built for the orphans. See them?" She pointed to the stick figures. "They're smiling. They have a place to live."

"Oh, yes, I see now." Maggie's throat thickened. Much as she wished she could help make the home a reality, she couldn't stay without a job, or more importantly, without a husband who could support and help her. Sum had told her he was leaving, and once he was gone, she knew she would never see him again. He was breaking her heart.

Near tears, she hugged Fannie. "Thank you, dearest. I love my gloves and my picture."

David stood and scooped Patrick into his arms. "Time for bed, little man."

Her sister-in-law turned from where she sat at the piano. They'd been singing carols earlier, and Victoria played better than anyone. "I'll take him and change him. Fannie, come along. You need to get to bed, too. Santa won't arrive if you're awake."

Fannie gave Maggie one last hug, and then ran for her room.

David moved to sit beside her. He remained quiet for a moment, perhaps thinking about how to explain, again, his reasons for refusing to consider being in a partnership with Sum; not that it mattered, Sum wouldn't accept a partner.

If neither man budged, she could do nothing except return to Kansas City to the classroom. Teaching had been enough for her before she'd recruited Gordon Sumner's help with collecting gifts and he'd showed her the kind of life they could have together. Now he'd taken the dream away. She sighed, slipping deeper into melancholy.

"Will you walk to church with me to light candles?" David asked finally.

This was something they did each holiday, light votive candles and say a prayer for their parents. She had no doubt her folks were in heaven. The prayers were more beneficial to those left behind. She nodded. "Of course. We could've stayed after Mass."

"The children were restless."

True enough. No right-thinking person would allow Patrick near lit candles.

"I'll get my cloak..." She reached for the hatbox. "And wear my new gloves."

David checked his watch as they left the building. Out of habit, she reached inside the cloak for the watch pinned to her bodice, and started. "Did I give you Ma's watch?"

"No. I thought you kept it."

She frowned, trying to remember. "I can't imagine where I would've put it. If Sum had found it, he would've returned it." Even if the watch had been ruined, she didn't want to lose it. She would scour the bedroom and her bags after they returned.

Although it was cold outside, it hadn't started snowing, so the walk wasn't unpleasant. She reminisced about walking with Sum to be fitted for their costumes, when he'd kissed her beneath the mistletoe, and afterwards dragged her down a hill and made snow angels. He could annoy her so thoroughly, and at the same time make her laugh and feel young as a girl. She hadn't wanted to start loving him, and now she didn't know how to stop.

She followed her brother inside the church and over to one of the small side altars, where statues of the saints stood watch over rows of flickering candles with pieces of paper slipped in between. Petitions from congregants and passersby, anyone who longed for answers, or miracles, or both.

David dropped coins into a donation box and then withdrew a match from his pocket and used a candle that was about to go out to set his match ablaze. She couldn't recall why he did that, but he always did, and then he prayed for that person's intentions as well.

He touched the match to the wicks of two unlit candles. "One for Ma and one for Da, to remember them. We'll pray as they taught us."

Maggie couldn't recall her parents' instruction. David had taught her how to pray, among other things. He'd been more than her big brother. He had been a surrogate father. Her anchor.

David had worked hard, he'd scrimped and sacrificed so she could have an education and a better life. Asking him to make Sum his partner fulfilled her dream, not his. She had no right to expect him to share ownership in a business he'd worked hard to build. Then to make him feel guilty for refusing only demonstrated her selfishness. She'd been praying for God to change David's mind, when she ought to be praying for a change of heart.

She pressed her hands together in front of her and bowed her head. It was so hard to trust. God might decide she and Sum shouldn't be together. If so, she had to accept it, and bear the pain. "O, blessed Lord and blessed Mother Mary," she prayed in a low voice. "Accept these burning candles as a sign of our faith and our love for Thee. Please hear our prayers, and also include the intentions of the one whose candle burns low. If it is Your Will, grant our petitions. But above all, cleanse my heart of selfishness and make me loyal and faithful to you, no matter the circumstances or the outcome. Amen."

"Sacred Heart of Jesus, have mercy on us," David added.

After a few minutes of silent reflection, he escorted her outside into the dark.

The wind picked up loose snow from the ground and whirled it around their legs. Streetlights lit their way, the moon hid behind low clouds.

"It's getting colder. The air smells like snow," she observed.

"What does snow smell like, *Mageen*?"

She hugged her brother's arm. "It smells clean and bright, Davy. Everybody knows that."

He sniffed the air. "Wood smoke. That's what I smell."

"A cozy fire, and hot cocoa."

"You can smell cocoa?"

"No, but I can almost taste it. Let's hurry back and make some."

As they neared the store, she recognized the man in a long overcoat crossing the street. He held onto the brim of a bowler hat, presumably to keep the wind from taking it away.

Sum halted in front of the steps leading up the outside of the building to the rooms upstairs. He tipped his hat. "Merry Christmas, O'Brien. Maggie."

"Merry Christmas, Sumner," David said politely.

Maggie had no idea where Sum might be headed, but she didn't fool herself into believing he'd come over to tell her that he'd decided to stay. He had been firm about his decision.

She fought a wave of anguish and then straightened her shoulders. This must be a test. God wanted to see if she was willing to trust Him. She smiled warmly at the man she loved with all her heart, determined to be thankful for what he meant to her, no matter what happened. "Merry Christmas."

Sum rubbed his arms. "Cold night for a walk."

"We've just been to light candles," David informed him. "Are you on your way to church?"

Sum claimed membership at St. Andrew's Episcopal Church, although he wasn't particularly faithful—two strikes against him in David's book.

"I went to an earlier service this evening." He withdrew something from the outside pocket of his coat. "No need to keep you standing out here in the cold. I just wanted to bring something by. For you, Maggie."

She took the small box, wrapped in pretty paper with a silk ribbon tied in a bow. Her heart fluttered in anticipation. What had he gotten her? Not a ring. "Oh, I didn't expect... I have a gift for you inside. I thought to bring it over tomorrow, along with my gifts for the children."

"They'll be happy to have them," Sum glanced over his shoulder before he replied. "Though I've told them if anything is out of place upon my return, Santa won't be stopping by."

Maggie found his attempts at parenting endearing, if ineffective. "Don't threaten consequences unless you intend to follow through. That's the first thing I learned about dealing with children."

Sum smoothed his mustache, which he sometimes did to hide a smile. "I'd appreciate any wisdom you can spare. Now, I should get back."

No, she didn't want him to leave. Not yet. A miracle could still happen. After all, it was Christmas Eve. "If you can trust them a while longer, you could join us for a cup of cocoa."

She looked up at David, who nodded.

"Yes, come inside," he said brusquely. "Let's get out of this cold."

Sum threw another glance over his shoulder, and when he looked at her, his lips twisted in mock chagrin. "All right. I'll give them a half-hour to wreak havoc."

CHAPTER 14

*S*um followed Maggie upstairs to her brother's apartment. "There's something I need to show you," he whispered near her ear. "The advertisement, I think it's about perfect. I hope you'll agree."

She cast a worried look over her shoulder. "The personal advertisement? Why do you—?"

"Later, I'll explain. First, I need to talk to your brother." He had carefully planned how he would approach her. That is, if O'Brien agreed to his proposition.

He had tried—he really had—to let go of his dream. But giving up wasn't in his nature. He wanted Maggie, and he wanted her more than he wanted anything. Wealth, success, none of it mattered if he couldn't share it with her. But he'd about ruined everything by sending her away and refusing the solution she'd offered. He still couldn't do what she wanted, but he hoped his compromise might earn him another chance.

After taking care of everyone's coats and hats, David O'Brien disappeared into the kitchen with his wife. Those wonderful baked smells filled the air and Sum's nose took notice.

Maggie retrieved a box from beneath the Christmas tree, took a seat on the sofa and patted the cushion. "Sit here, by me."

Her inviting smile did things to him he didn't dare confess.

Sum sank onto the sofa, draped his arm over the back and crossed his leg over his knee. The comfortable furniture, which had been nice at one time, looked worn. Then again, O'Brien didn't have to sell out to pay his debts. Tightfisted, perhaps, but he managed his business well. So well, in fact, he'd expanded. But O'Brien could do even better—with Sum's help.

Maggie handed him a flat, decorated box. She placed her gift in her lap, fingering the bow, but didn't untie it. "You want to go first?"

"Open your gift. You can't wait." In fact, neither could he. He hoped she'd be pleased.

"No, I can wait. I want you to go first."

"As you wish." He ran his hand over the top of the box. "You decorated this?"

"Yes, Christmas cards with snow scenes." She flashed him a mischievous look through her lashes. "I know how much you enjoy the snow."

Sum bit back a laugh. He loved her tart humor, and the fact that she had enjoyed rolling around in the snow as much as he had. "That's true," he murmured. Lifting the box lid revealed a knitted scarf woven with brilliant shades of blue.

"I used woolen thread that matches the color of your eyes," she pointed out.

"Thank goodness you didn't try to match my hair." A

lump rose in his throat as he lifted the scarf out of the box. He couldn't recall getting a gift someone had made to draw attention to his features, to remind them of something about him they found attractive and compelling, and yet, it was so...Maggie.

"It's beautiful. I'll wear it with pride." More than pride, every time he looked at it, or touched the soft weave, he'd be reminded of how much he loved her.

He wrapped the scarf around his neck and gave her a proper kiss on the cheek, which brought on an adorable blush. "Now it's your turn."

She whipped off the ribbon and tore away the paper, eager as a child. That was another thing he loved about her, her childlike sense of wonder and her love for adventure. Maggie appreciated beauty in all its many forms, and she had a flair for creativity, just look at the pains she'd taken to make a box special. He held his breath as she withdrew the drawstring bag and opened it, and released a relieved sigh when she cried out with pleasure.

"Oh, Sum...my mother's watch!" With a delighted smile, Maggie held it up by a gold chain, the fob that had recently held his watch. He'd buy her a new chain when he had more money.

"The jeweler put new works in it, but he was able to salvage the case." He twirled the watch around. "See? Almost as good as new, just a few scratches."

She clasped the watch tight and threw her arms around his neck, planted a kiss on his cheek, but sat back before he had a chance to embrace her. "You are a dear man, Mr. Sumner. Don't let anyone tell you different."

"That's what I hoped you'd think. My plan must be working."

"What plan is that?" Maggie turned the watch in her

hands, lovingly examining it. Her joy with the gift sent his heart soaring.

He would do anything for her, give up everything, that's what he wanted to say—but he had to make sure he was in the position to ask for another chance. "I'll tell you, but first I have to speak with your brother."

"What is it you want to talk about?" O'Brien returned from the kitchen. He carried a tray of china cups filled with hot cocoa and his wife followed with a dish of cookies. He set the tray on the low table in front of the sofa. "Have some cocoa."

Somehow, he made it sound like an order rather than an offer.

Sum tamped down a surge of doubt. This plan would work, if he could keep his pride in check. He would swallow it whole, if it meant he could spend the rest of his life with Maggie. "I'll pass for now."

He leaned forward, picked up a cup and gave it to Maggie. "Here, you were eager for cocoa, as I recall."

"Yes, thank you." She slipped a slender finger through the delicate handle, rested the cup in her other hand, and took a careful sip. Her gaze searched his and a flicker of anxiety returned.

O'Brien took a cup and found a seat on a cushioned chair. He kept his eye on Sum.

The Irishman didn't trust him, which didn't bode well.

Mrs. O'Brien put the cookies in front of him. He'd swear the smile she gave him was meant to be encouraging. She stood, primly folding her hands in front of her. "I think I'd better go check on the children."

She was making herself scarce. Maybe that smile hadn't meant anything.

Sum knew better than to ask Maggie's brother to take

him on as a partner. Hell, *he* wouldn't take him on as a partner, if he were in O'Brien's shoes. No, he had to present a palatable alternative, even if he didn't like the taste of it. "You may have heard I'm selling out."

O'Brien gave a solemn nod. "That's what Maggie told me."

No false sympathy from this one. At least he didn't appear to be gloating.

Sum sat straighter and adjusted his coat. "There's a proposition I'd like to make. I'll offer you my inventory at a discount if you'll buy all of it, so I can clear my debts."

O'Brien dipped his chin. "Agreed. On the condition I see what you've got and deem the price fair."

"It will be." Sum knew the value and O'Brien would be getting a deal. "Another thing..." This would be a tougher sell. "I'd like to offer my services."

"Your services?" O'Brien set his cup down, his expression solemn. "What you mean is, you want me to make you a partner."

That had been Maggie's idea, and much more than he deserved. "No, I wouldn't ask you to give me part of your business. I'm offering to work for you. My preference would be to start out as a head clerk, but I'll do whatever job you need done."

Beside him, Maggie gasped. He couldn't interpret whether it was a gasp of surprise or dismay. She might not wish to wed a clerk. That was something he'd thought about, but he couldn't come up with any other reasonable plan for remaining in Fort Scott. He could work for another mercantile, but O'Brien had the most successful store in town and would be able to afford a head clerk because the business would double in size. Sum knew how to sell things, he just wasn't very adept at holding onto them.

The lease on the building across the street had been paid through the first six months of the year, which would give him and Maggie, and the children, a place to live until he could make enough to rent rooms elsewhere.

O'Brien rubbed his chin, appearing deep in thought. He held Sum's gaze for another uncomfortable moment. "Why would you do this? Why not take out a loan from the bank and pay off the creditor, keep your doors open."

Sum had already told Maggie why that wouldn't work, but it appeared she hadn't shared his shameful past with her brother. Considerate and trustworthy, two more qualities he loved about her. He'd add those to the list in his pocket. When they'd worked together on the personal advertisement, she'd assigned a number of good traits to him, although her perspective might've changed now that she knew him better. Her brother already thought poorly of him, and he would be adding more to what were too many reasons already. If he managed to pull this off and win Maggie, it would be a miracle.

Sum folded his arms over his chest, for fear his hands would shake. "No self-respecting financier will loan me money once they find out I defaulted on a bank loan in Philadelphia and left without paying my suppliers."

O'Brien's expression remained unreadable as a rock. This confession wouldn't help his cause, Sum knew that already, but he wouldn't enter into an agreement without putting all his proverbial cards on the table. Honesty and trust had to be the basis of any relationship or it wouldn't work.

"I found a creditor willing to give me enough to open a store out here. He was willing to take the risk in return for a high interest rate for the use of his money. He's the one I thought sent that thug. As it turns out, the bull who tried to rob me was a wanted criminal. He must've thought my store looked like an easy mark. But, Mr. Sikes has sent collectors after me before. I've no doubt he'll do it again, which is why I need to repay him as soon as possible."

Taking a deep breath, Sum rested his hands on either side of him, trying to appear calm but unable to keep from curling his fingers into the sofa cushion. Maggie gripped his hand. He tightened his fingers, holding onto her.

If she let him, he would hold on for the rest of his life. The kind of stable, secure love she offered was something he hadn't experienced and wouldn't have believed in if he hadn't met her. He prayed she wouldn't retreat now that she realized how poor they'd be. If O'Brien turned him down, he would have to rethink his options. Which were, admittedly, few.

MAGGIE CLUNG TO Sum's hand. He appeared calm, his lips in a customary half-smile, but his tight grip on her hand said otherwise. Her heart constricted in sympathy. He had to be dying inside, waiting for David's answer. Sum was a proud man. Yet, he'd set aside his pride and come to his chief competitor with his hat in his hand, begging for a job.

Why?

He loved her. There could be no other reason he'd go to such lengths, save to keep the children. Maybe that was part of it, too. He'd thought about what she told him about the possibility they'd be split up and had decided he couldn't entrust their future to someone else. She didn't think it possible to love him more, but she did. Entirely. Completely.

She continued to hold Sum's hand, despite her brother's questioning gaze, letting David know that she could not, would not, let go. Sum needed her and she needed him, and they would find a way to be together, even if David refused to hire the man who would soon be his brother-in-law.

David leaned back and threaded his fingers through his wavy, black hair. A sign he found the decision difficult. Why couldn't he just say, *yes?* Sum had agreed to do whatever job David assigned him. He couldn't bow any lower.

The prayer she'd recited earlier nudged her conscience. She'd asked forgiveness for being selfish, but was it selfish to love someone? The Blessed Lord had given everything out of love. Sum had given up his pride and his dreams to be with her. Now she knew why he wanted to share that letter.

"May I see the advertisement you worked on?"

He appeared uncertain, and she thought he might not give it to her. Then, with a wry smile, he reached into the small pocket in his waistcoat and withdrew a folded paper. "I took the opportunity to tweak it."

The edges were a bit ragged, as if he'd been carrying it around. He'd never posted it, and now he wouldn't have to because she would see to it that he got the bride he wanted.

She plucked the paper out of his hand and spoke to her brother. "Sum agreed to let me help him craft an advertisement for a mail-order bride, as he found himself in a need of a wife. You'll remember how well I did with yours. Oh, and by the way, you've never thanked me for Victoria."

David pulled his arms around his chest and arched an eyebrow at her. It appeared he wouldn't be offering his gratitude tonight, either.

Maggie unfolded the paper and smoothed it on her lap. Sum's bold handwriting appeared, above her small, neat script. Indeed, he had altered it, and added a few things. "Let me read you what Sum and I came up with."

"Unattached shopkeeper," she started, and then looked at him with surprise. "You removed successful."

Sum shrugged. Modesty didn't become him. She missed the cock-sure man who'd pursued his dreams and her with supreme confidence. He'd be back, just as soon as he got his feet under him again.

"You are successful, you know. Successful in the ways that count."

She started over with her original version. *"Successful shopkeeper in fast-growing Western community seeks educated, attractive young woman with exemplary reputation for purposes of marriage. Applicant must be kind and cheerful, willing to work long days, and will need patience..."* She slid a glance at Sum and smiled, remembering his initial reaction when she'd read it the first time.

His expression remained neutral but his eyes gleamed with amusement. *"Will need patience with children...three to start with."*

Just as she'd thought, he meant to keep them, dear man.

"Glossy black hair and gypsy eyes preferred; playful and good-tempered, keen on riding sleds and making snow angels." She swallowed a laugh. *"Will provide a comfortable, safe home and be a loving husband and father; am occasionally humorous, engaging, affectionate and generous. Signed, Santa Claus."*

"Describes you perfectly," she told him, and then turned to David, who had a tight smile on his face from struggling to not laugh out loud. "I believe I meet this gentleman's requirements. I'm going to respond...and I hope he'll answer."

Sum gazed at her with love shining in his eyes, as well as a hint of mischief. Her life with him would never be dull. He put his arm around her. "No need to wait. I'll answer right now. Will you be my Mrs. Claus?"

"Gladly." She leaned in for a kiss and he obliged her. His lips were firm, smooth and warm, and his mustache tickled. She didn't mind the soft hair above his lip but was glad he didn't have a full, flowing beard.

"I love you," he murmured in between kissing.

"I love you, too." She threaded her fingers through his thick, burnished hair, and melted against the lush pressure of his lips. His hands moved up her back, sending delicious tremors through her.

"Are you two done yet?" David's pointed remark burst their amorous bubble.

Sum drew back with a half-smile on his lips. "We're just getting started."

"Not here in my parlor."

Maggie knew she had a stupid grin on her face, but she couldn't stop smiling. Sum had proposed. They would be married—although they might not be able to stay in Fort Scott if Sum didn't have a job. That would be all right, they could come back for visits. "If David doesn't hire you, we can live in Kansas City and I'll continue teaching. We'll adopt the children and take them with us."

"Slow down, Maggie." David shifted forward in his chair. He rested his arms on his knees and clasped his hands together. He wasn't smiling, but he wasn't frowning, either. "Give me a chance to say something."

She gripped Sum's hand tighter. "Yes?"

David didn't address her. Instead, he spoke directly to Sum. "Hiring you as a clerk isn't the best option."

Sum took the news without flinching, and didn't even act angry. "Very well, I'll look elsewhere."

David held up his hand. "Hear me out before you do that. I'm of the mind that you should continue to run the Five Cent Store, concentrate on what you do best. Frankly,

I'd prefer to focus on hardware and expand the bicycle shop. We can split up the business that way—two stores offering different merchandise under a combined name—and still be responsible for our own operations. We'll take a share of each other's profits. Insofar as your debt is concerned, sell off any excess inventory to whoever will give you the best price, and I'll make up whatever difference remains."

For once, Sum didn't speak right away. Actually, he appeared stunned.

Overjoyed, Maggie leapt up and ran to hug her brother's neck. "Oh, David, thank you. Thank you." He returned her embrace without comment or fanfare, in keeping with his nature, which was to downplay his generosity.

She turned to Sum, smiling. "It's a good idea, don't you think?"

"It's a generous offer." His russet brows drew together. "But I can't take it."

Maggie gaped at him. "You can't take it? What do you mean, you can't take it?"

"I'll not accept charity. If, after I sell my inventory, there's enough money left to do as David suggests, then I'd be happy to go into business with him."

There might not be enough, but she wouldn't embarrass her fiancé by saying so, and she understood his reluctance, yet... "I've invested a little money in Mr. Ford's new company. I'll sell my shares."

Sum's eyebrows jumped. "No. Keep your investment, I hear there's a fortune to be made in Ford's horseless carriages."

David harrumphed. "Those wind-up machines won't replace horses."

"What wind-up machines?" Victoria returned to the parlor from her extended departure. Maggie knew her sister-in-law had left to give them privacy to discuss sensitive matters, and she also suspected Victoria had put some ideas into David's head. He was a smart man, but his wife was every bit as clever.

"The horseless carriage," Maggie explained. "I've invested a small amount of money, but Sum and I will be married, and we may need the extra cash."

"Married?" Victoria's eyes grew wide. She rushed over and threw her arms around Maggie's neck. "Congratulations, darling. I'm so happy for you! I knew you two would work things out."

"They've worked out their marriage. Now Mr. Sumner needs to decide whether he'll go into business with me," David said.

Sum stood and moved next to Maggie, slipped his arm around her waist. The possessive gesture produced a thrill. "Call me Sum," he said to David. "All my friends do, and seeing as you'll be my brother-in-law—"

"And your partner," Maggie reminded him. "Sum and David are going into business together," she announced to Victoria.

"That's splendid news." Victoria sailed to her husband's side and gave him a quick kiss. He smiled and wrapped his arm around her. She reached up and stroked his hair, lavish in her affection, another endearing quality. "You should announce the new partnership in the newspaper."

Maggie went along with Victoria's gentle prodding. "I think that's a marvelous idea."

"First, let's see if I can cover the costs," Sum warned. He hugged her, though, and so reassured her that he wouldn't be backing out on his proposal, even if they ended up having to leave town.

Victoria turned in her husband's arms with a thoughtful

expression. "My father recently sent me a small sum of money to invest after I wrote to him about the business opportunities out here. I'd like to invest in your Five Cent Store, Mr. Sumner."

Sum didn't look a bit fooled by her attempt to bankroll him. "If we go into business together, we'll share the profits."

"That's between you and my husband. I'm talking about a separate agreement. My father has never trusted me in business matters before now. You won't let me down, will you?"

Maggie circled her arm around her fiancé's lean waist. "He'll double your money, I'm sure of it."

"Maggie, you can't promise her that," Sum muttered next to her ear.

"You can."

He shook his head, utterly serious. "I'm done with risking so much. My family deserves a more prudent provider."

David, for once, spoke first. "Sum, your risks would've paid off if your partner had been honest. As Victoria will tell you, I'm a stick-in-the-mud. I need someone who will push me to take more risks. We'll balance each other out. And I happen to think my wife is right, you'll double her father's investment."

David walked over and put out his hand. "Let's shake on our new venture. *O'Brien and Sumner.*

If Maggie hadn't been watching Sum's face carefully, she might've missed the flash of emotion David's remarks elicited before the familiar wry smile reappeared. Her beloved hesitated only a moment and then shook David's hand.

"*Sumner and O'Brien* has a better ring, don't you think?"

EPILOGUE

December 23, 1901
Goodlander Home for Children, Fort Scott, Kansas

"$\mathcal{F}$ ear not! We bring good tidings of great joy..." A freckled lad standing in front of the small-fry choir shouted the verse loud enough to pierce every eardrum in the parlor.

The band of angels that broke into song wouldn't have frightened shepherds. They were cute as all get out. Their smiling director and teacher, Mrs. Sumner, waved her arms and kept them singing. More importantly, she gave them a reason to sing about miracles. Under her tutelage, the *Goodlander Home for Children* prospered.

Charlie Goodlander leaned back in the folding chair, one of a dozen set up in the front parlor of his father-in-law's former home for the purposes of a Christmas concert. He shifted his substantial weight to relieve a cramp in his back and rested his arms across his chest, grinning at a little girl in a white dress with a pair of wings off-kilter. His knees didn't like sitting this long, but he'd put up with the aches and pains to see the smiles on these kids' faces and to know he'd played a small, but important role in putting them there.

The children's home had opened its doors earlier this year, moving into what had been the old fort's officers' quarters and later the home of pioneer settler Horatio T. Wilson.

Charlie squeezed his Lizzie's soft hand. His wife thought it a wonderful idea to turn her family's former residence into a safe, loving home for orphans. She'd declared she would consider the children who lived here to be their children, as they hadn't been blessed with any of their own. He was glad he could give her a family, at last.

"Hark the herald angels sing, glory to the newborn King," the children sang. They sounded pretty good. Not heavenly, but close.

It had taken darn near ten years to get this dream off the ground, starting with talking Mr. and Mrs. Sumner into being on the board and then convincing them to run the place. They'd moved in earlier this year with their brood: Elsie, a blond beauty of eighteen, Davy, a rambunctious eight-year-old who looked just like his namesake, and six-year-old twins Annabelle and Francis, blue-eyed cherubs with hair red enough to catch fire. Felix Sumner, the oldest adopted boy, now a strapping young man of twenty-one, and his tow-headed sixteen-year-old brother, Harold, had remained in the apartment above their father's store where they worked.

Also living at The Goodlander Home were twelve orphans, all under the age of ten. Soon, that number would swell. Mrs. Sumner had a hard time turning children away.

As the last verse came to a close, Charlie clapped loudly along with the others. Board members mostly, and the Sumner's large and extended family, which included David and Victoria O'Brien and their clan of six children and one on the way.

"Bravo!" Charlie hefted his heavy frame out of the squeaky chair. Sounded like it might not hold out. Better to stand. He'd hate to end up on the floor on his big ass.

He clapped his good friend, Buck O'Connor, on the back. O'Connor, being a tall fellow, wasn't as fat, but he had whiter hair. "Those kids better be in this year's parade, Mr. Mayor."

"They will be," Buck assured him, with a smiling nod at his wife, who'd gone over to congratulate Mrs. Sumner. "Amy and the girls helped with the costumes."

His daughters were grown with families of their own, but he still called them *girls*.

The big man leaned down and cupped his hand to his mouth, whispering in Charlie's ear. "You better tell her they look nice. I mentioned an irregularity with the wings and about got my head taken off."

Charlie chuckled. "'Course you did, because you had to open your big mouth. I swear Buck, you and Amy enjoy a good dispute better than any married couple I know."

"It's not the dispute we enjoy so much," O'Connor drawled. "It's the making up afterwards."

Charlie couldn't contain a bellow.

"What's got you laughing this time, Mr. Goodlander?" Gordon Sumner's wry smile said he'd like to be in on the joke, whatever it was. He had a sharp sense of humor, as dry as O'Connor's. The two made good drinking buddies.

"Oh, nothing in particular, just O'Connor here. He has a funny-looking face."

Sumner smoothed his hand over a fake white beard, which he'd donned for the event, along with a green robe and a long cap. Didn't seem to bother him to look ridiculous. He eyed the Mayor. "Hmm, maybe." Then Sumner turned to Charlie. "Have you checked in the mirror lately?

Charlie gripped the smart ass by the shoulder. "No, Santa, I don't look into mirrors. Reminds me why Lizzie turned me down three times."

"Attention everyone!" Mrs. Sumner said loud enough to be heard over the conversation. "We'll be serving cookies and cocoa in the dining room."

The parlor cleared of children in a matter of seconds, with their excited voices trailing behind.

Mrs. Sumner sallied over, all dolled up in a pretty red dress with a white lace cap. She still had to put powder in her hair to make it look gray. Her dark gaze roved each man in turn, suspicious, but still smiling. "What are you three conspiring about over here?"

"What makes Charlie's face so funny," her husband answered smoothly.

"Methinks it's the muttonchops," O'Connor said, with a deadpan expression.

"When they lay me out, will you make sure not to invite these two?" Charlie begged her.

She hugged his neck. "Your face isn't a bit funny-looking, just jolly. In fact, I was telling Sum the other day that you should play Santa in next year's parade."

Charlie's heart darn near gave out. He wouldn't have to don a white beard or wig, already being well grizzled, nor would he need any padding around the middle. But he wasn't about to put on that bathrobe and cap and ride around town in a fake sleigh. He'd never live it down.

"Oh, now, you don't want to sit next to an old man like me."

"I'd be honored." She said it with nary a smile.

He wouldn't do it for anybody else, save maybe Lizzie, who wouldn't have asked him in the first place. But this was Maggie Sumner, the woman who had helped him achieve his dream of leaving a legacy. He couldn't disappoint her. "Why, that's mighty nice of you to ask, Mrs. Sumner. I reckon if I could play Santa in the parade next year, I'd die a happy man."

He'd speak to Lizzie later. She'd help him find some way out of it before next Christmas.

AUTHOR'S NOTE

Both *Victoria, Bride of Kansas* and *Santa's Mail-Order Bride* are set in the historic town of Fort Scott, Kansas. I fell in love with this town when I first visited Lyons Twin Mansions, a Victorian B&B. After I toured the Fort Scott National Historic Site, part of the U.S. National Park Service, I became interested in Fort Scott's past and knew I wanted to write historical romances set in this fascinating town.

Her Bodyguard, my debut novel, takes place in Fort Scott and the surrounding counties, circa 1870, during the early railroad boom. In that book, Buck O'Connor is the primary protagonist. He is featured as a key secondary character in the two novellas, *Victoria, Bride of Kansas*, and *Santa's Mail-Order Bride*, which are set in the early 1890s.

All three books feature historic locations, events, and colorful local pioneers. One of these early residents was Charles W. Goodlander. His fictionalized character makes an appearance in *Her Bodyguard* and *Santa's Mail-Order Bride*. I'll admit, he is one of my favorite "real" characters because he was *such* a character!

Charlie, as he liked to be called, was a leading citizen

and generous philanthropist. He arrived in Fort Scott as a young man in 1858, the first passenger on the first stagecoach from Kansas City. (He'd later declare he needed his "medicinal" flask for the wild, bumpy ride.) He took up contracting and building, and over the years expanded into other ventures, including a lumber mill, a brickyard, a furniture store and hotels. He made and lost several fortunes, his mill being destroyed by fire and rebuilt twice. He helped organize the Citizens' National Bank as its president and served a few terms as mayor of Fort Scott, but largely steered clear of politics. His career was that of a successful businessman, marked by ability, honesty, integrity and fair dealings with his fellow man. His never-give-up approach to life exemplified the spirit of the men (and women) who settled this town.

In 1901, Goodlander bought from the heirs of Col. H. T. Wilson, his father-in-law, the old Wilson home, previously officers' quarters within the old fort, and converted the large structure into *The Goodlander Home for Children*. The orphans' home served over 800 children from Fort Scott and the surrounding vicinity until it closed in the early 1960s.

On Dec. 17, 1872, Mr. Goodlander wed Elizabeth Clay, daughter of Col. H. T. Wilson. They had no children. Mr. Goodlander passed from this life on May 22, 1902. To my knowledge, he never played Santa Claus.

THE CHRISTMAS WISH

E.E. BURKE

The Belmont House, Parsons, Kansas,
Christmas Day, 1873

The tart-sweet smell wafting through the lobby made Billy Frye's mouth water. His nose led him to the cozy kitchen in the back of the Belmont House, a hotel serving railroad travelers passing through Parsons. With today being Christmas, no trains were running so there few guests, which meant more food for him.

Billy crept closer to a worktable where the source of the wonderful aroma sat cooling, keeping a wary eye on the woman at the sink peeling potatoes. Despite the fact she didn't stand but a few inches taller, Mrs. Daines was a force to be reckoned with—and she didn't tolerate stealing. Not even if Billy's stomach insisted it was starving.

When he'd first come to live here, he would've hooked that pie without a second thought. Then, when she threw him out, he'd declare he didn't care. He'd rather be on his own than stuck with another family that didn't want him.

But Mrs. Daines had turned out to be different from other folks he'd lived with.

For one, she was a sight easier on the eyes. Her warm brown eyes danced with laughter more often than not, and her skin had few lines, except for between her brows when she was thinking hard.

Billy liked to imagine that his temporary guardian looked like his real Ma. Although he didn't remember much about the woman who'd birthed him, other than her leaving him at a stranger's home when he was four and telling him to be good. After that, he hadn't wanted to be good. Matter of fact, he was bad every chance he got. Why should he mind someone who didn't care about what happened to him?

Over the past eight years, he'd bounced around from home to home, and if he didn't have a home, he slept in an abandoned railcar. One day, the Katy Railroad's former general manager caught him *trespassing*. (That was another word he knew; wasn't one of the good ones.) He told Mr. Stevens he wanted to go to work for the railroad. The chief said he was too young and brought him to live with the Daines and ordered him to behave, holding out the promise of a job later in life if he did.

Mrs. Daines didn't demand constant good behavior, which was a relief because being good all the time would've worn him out. Oh, she scolded him when he went astray, but she was just as quick to praise. After he'd settled in and realized she intended to feed him regular and not whip him too often, he'd grown grew less inclined to break her rules.

He might could get away with pinching off a small piece of crust. She hadn't made tasting a crime—yet.

"Keep away from the pie," she warned.

Billy jerked to a halt, his finger and thumb a mere inch away from the golden brown crust. She hadn't even turned around to look. Must have eyes in the back of her head. He peered suspiciously at the thick roll of brown hair confined in a net. No extra eyes that he could see. She had good ears, though, if she'd heard him sneaking up. After years of practice, he'd learned to move around quieter than a mouse.

Not about to confess to wrongdoing, he tucked his hands beneath his arms. "Ain't touchin', just sniffin'."

"You aren't..." She turned with a partially peeled potato in one hand and used a paring knife to gesture. "You *aren't* touching."

He got her point without the knife. "No ma'am. I told you, I ain't touched it."

"Ain't isn't a word."

Billy puzzled over this revelation. "Then what is it?"

"Poor grammar. You have better words to use to express yourself."

He huffed in disbelief. "Not if you keep taking 'em away."

She set the potato and knife aside and wiped her hands on her apron. "Tell you what, I'll give you new words to replace the old ones."

Billy was dead certain the new words wouldn't be as good as the old. However, he'd try them out, if for no other reason than to please the kind woman who'd taken him. Temporarily. He didn't stay nowhere for long. Most like a stray cat. A body might feed him and keep him around for a while, so long as he was helpful, but they didn't care if he eventually ran away.

What if Mrs. Daines decided she wanted to be rid of him today?

The knot in his stomach tightened. He could try to be better. Only, being good wasn't in his nature. How to be lovable wasn't something he knew much about either, which was why he didn't have a family. At least, that was what everybody told him. Except for Mrs. Daines. She used words like *smart* and *likeable* and *fine young man* to describe him. Those were good words, and didn't sound like someone who'd grown tired of him.

Yesterday, she'd spun a fantastic yarn about a fellow named Saint Nick who loved all children and rode around in a sleigh hitched to reindeer, dropping off presents. Good children got gifts like toys, bad ones got a piece of coal, but at least they got something. Mrs. Daines suggested Billy write St. Nick a letter and list the things he wanted. He felt pretty sure he wouldn't be getting gifts, and he wasn't that interested in coal.

She went over to the stove and picked up a tin plate sitting on top and held it out. Bits and pieces of baked crust sprinkled with sugar and cinnamon. "Here, I baked the extra dough. You may have some. We'll save the pie for later."

Billy sampled a flaky piece. His heart sang. So did his stomach. Rather than waiting for another invitation, he scooped up the remaining pieces and crammed them into his mouth. "'S'good," he mumbled.

When Mrs. Daines cocked up her eyebrow, Billy swallowed before he spoke again. Talking while chewing food wasn't polite in front of a lady. Men weren't so particular.

"You sure are a good cook."

Women also liked it when they got compliments, or so she'd told him.

"Thank you for saying so." She reached out to straighten

his collar. Something she did even when it didn't need straightening. "I'm very glad you're here to enjoy my cooking."

"You are?" Billy couldn't recall anybody being glad to have him around, much less being happy about feeding him. Mrs. Daines didn't lie though, so she must mean it. Maybe she just liked feeding folks. She and Mrs. Kelly cooked for everyone who stayed at the hotel.

He started to wipe his sticky fingers on his shirt, but then stopped when he recalled it was a mean habit. He licked them instead.

She shook her head and handed him a checkered napkin retrieved from a shelf stacked with table linens. The folded napkin looked fancy, much nicer than his shirtsleeve, but if she wanted him to use it instead, he would.

"Have you decided what you want for Christmas?" she asked.

He peered around her shoulder, sniffing. "A cherry pie?"

"Is that all? You don't have another wish?"

Wish? Sure, he had a wish. Didn't matter, though. He'd never get it. He'd even prayed about it until the preacher told him that God didn't grant selfish wishes. He shrugged.

Sadness tugged her lips downward, but then she brightened up. "Well, I have a wish...and it's about to come true."

"That's nice." Billy didn't know what else to say. He was glad she could get something she wanted. Being such a sweet lady, she deserved it.

"I have a surprise for you."

What this had to do with her wish, Billy wasn't sure, but maybe she'd moved onto something else. He cut a quick look at the cooling pie. "Is it something I can eat?"

Amusement flashed in her brown eyes. "It's better than pie."

"Nothing's better than your cherry pie." He was quite certain about that.

"What about being adopted? Do you think that might be better?"

Billy's heart jumped into his throat. Then it wouldn't budge no matter how many times he swallowed. *Adopted.* He knew *that* word. "You...you want to keep me?"

The smile she gave him was ever so soft, the kind of smile that made him willing to do extra chores, even the ones he hated like changing bed sheets or dumping chamber pots.

"More than that, Billy. We'd like for you to be our son."

"Your son," he echoed, thinking he might've heard wrong. Or maybe he was imagining things. For as long as he could remember, he'd longed to have a family. Only, he'd never expected to get one. Everyone he'd lived with had eventually thrown him out. None of them had wanted him to stay, much less adopt him.

Her smile faltered. "Don't you want to be adopted?"

Confusing emotions bounced around inside his chest. He was real fond of Mrs. Daines, and he liked living at the hotel—for the most part.

Billy rolled his eyes to the ceiling. Just above were the family's private quarters. Her husband hibernated up there, nursing what she called *war wounds*. He looked well enough, and had all his limbs. Billy wondered whether he was just lazy. When he ventured out of his rooms, which was rarely, he was grouchier than a grizzly bear with a sore paw. His surly moods reminded Billy of the man from his dreams.

The nightmare always started out the same. Billy hid in

the dark under a bed, his stomach cramped with fear that he might be found. Mud-caked shoes. That was all he ever saw of the man who tromped back and forth, cursing and raging. A woman was in the room, too, but he couldn't see her. He could hear her voice, though. The two were arguing about killing him. Then, he'd feel strong fingers lock around his ankle. He'd wake up, sweating, his heart pounding.

Sometimes at night, noises came from the room next to his: Mr. Daines' booming voice, Mrs. Daines pleading with him. Billy had put his ear to the wall a couple times. They were never talking about him. In fact, what the man said made no sense. Maybe he walloped his wife like some men did. She never said anything about it, but in the mornings she looked wore out, like she hadn't shut her eyes all night.

She reached out and brushed something off Billy's shoulder. He generally shied away at being touched, but he put up with her fussing 'cause she didn't overdo it. "If you're worried about Mr. Daines, you needn't be. I can assure you, he's amenable to the idea."

"A-mean..." Billy searched his memory. That was a word she hadn't given him yet.

"He's agreed."

"Agreed to adopt me?"

"Yes."

Billy's heart fluttered down to its usual perch. Still flapped like a durn bird. He couldn't imagine Mr. Daines had any use for him. Then again, her man might not care if his wife wanted to adopt herself a son so he could help her around the hotel. After all, Mrs. Daines expected him to pitch in, though she didn't work him like a hired hand or treat him like a slave. After his lessons, she let him go to the train station and run errands for the workers. One day, he'd go to work for the railroad. In the meantime, he'd have a home and a mother who treated him kindly.

"I hope you'll agree." She sounded as nervous as he felt. "Adopting you would be best gift I ever received."

He'd been called lots of things, but *gift* wasn't one of them. If he weren't so choked up, he might find it amusing, the idea of being wrapped up with a bow. After swallowing a couple times, he found his voice. "Well...I don't mind being a gift. But I'd rather take you up on that offer to be adopted."

"Oh, Billy, I'm so glad..." Mrs. Daines threw her arms around him and hugged him tight.

That might be overdoing it. Still, he returned her warm embrace because he didn't want to hurt her feelings. At first, it felt awkward. After a moment, the strangeness faded and the hug got real comfortable.

He'd got his Christmas wish...being part of a family. Belonging somewhere. Being somebody. His heart swelled so big it filled up his chest. He hadn't thought he would ever be good enough to get what he wished for, and now that he'd got it, he didn't know what to say.

She stroked his hair, a motherly gesture he'd seen countless women use with their sons.

His eyes started to sting, and he blinked hard so he wouldn't shame himself. Babies cried. Not twelve-year-old boys.

As she drew back, still holding his arms, tears ran down her cheeks. Women were allowed to be weepy. "Merry Christmas, Billy."

He cleared his throat. "Merry Christmas—Ma."

Ma. That was a good word. The best.

Billy drew a wobbly breath. He caught another whiff of that heavenly smell.

Didn't mothers bake treats for their boys?

The biggest grin spread across his face. "I do got another wish. I wish we could eat a piece of that pie!"

The End

You can read more about Billy Frye and his adventures in my series, *Steam! Romance and Rails.*

ALSO BY E.E. BURKE

SERIES AND BOOKS

The New Adventures

Tom Sawyer Returns

Taming Huck Finn

Steam! Romance and Rails

Her Bodyguard

Redbird

A Dangerous Passion

Fugitive Hearts

The Bride Train

Valentine's Rose

Patrick's Charm

Tempting Prudence

Seducing Susannah

American Mail-Order Brides

Victoria Bride of Kansas

Santa's Mail-Order Bride

The Brides of Noelle

Twelve Days of Christmas Mail-Order Brides

Jolie, A Valentine's Day Bride

The Drum (Twelve Days of Christmas Mail-Order Brides)

ABOUT THE AUTHOR

E.E. Burke is a bestselling author of historical romances that combine her unique blend of wit and warmth. Her books have been nominated for numerous national and regional awards, including Booksellers' Best, National Readers' Choice and Kindle Best Book. She was also a finalist in the RWA's prestigious Golden Heart® contest. Over the years, she's been a disc jockey, a journalist and an advertising executive, before finally getting around to living the dream--writing stories readers can get lost in.

Find out more about her books at her website: www.eeburke.com.